S. VENKATESH

KAALKOOT

THE LOST HIMALAYAN SECRET

TreeShade Books

Published by TreeShade Books (VB Performance LLP) in 2018

KAALKOOT

THE LOST HIMALAYAN SECRET

ISBN : 9788193642450

Published by
TreeShade Books (VB Performance LLP)
Ansal Corporate Park, Sector142, Noida, Uttar Pradesh - 201305, India
Email - publish@TreeShadeBooks.com
www.TreeShadeBooks.com

Printed and Bound in India by
Thomson Press (India) Limited, 18/35 Delhi Mathura Road,
Faridabad – 121007, Haryana, India

Cover Design by
Munisha Nanda

S. VENKATESH

KAALKOOT

THE LOST HIMALAYAN SECRET

TreeShade Books

www.treeshadebooks.com

To my parents,
my wife Nithya and
my daughter Arundati.

PROLOGUE

January 1944

Near Kausani, Kumaon Division, United Provinces (current Uttarakhand), India

Manohar Rai winced as a dart of pain shot through his wounds. The steep uphill climb had left him gasping for breath, and the suddenness of the departure from the previous hideout made him feel quite disoriented.

But none of this concerned him in the least, consumed as he was by a rapidly rising panic.

The fate of millions rested on his tired shoulders, and he was feeling hopelessly inadequate to the task.

His mood was in stark contrast to the surroundings. The dimly lit hut stood on a hill facing a picturesque valley. The meandering streams and snow-capped Himalayan peaks epitomised tranquility, as did the villages dotting the landscape. At this hour of the night, the vista was dreamlike, almost magical, as distant lights from the valley complemented the glow of village lanterns.

But all this was lost on Manohar.

A million deaths, maybe more, on his conscience. It was just not fair.

He had scrupulously followed orders all his life, never stopping to question his leaders, not even when the orders had involved braving police bayonets or enduring weeks in prison.

But having to decide for millions of people was not a burden that he had signed up for. Yet here he was, thrust by history into this role in the seventh decade of his life.

There was a loud bang in the background, echoing across the hills, jolting Manohar from his ruminations.

He shuddered. It was a grenade explosion, probably at their previous hideout. Had his compatriots made it out in time?

This was not the time to worry. He had to decide. Fast.

He swallowed hard as he hobbled nervously around the hut. It was indeed a dark hour. The World War was dragging on, the Japanese knocking menacingly at India's door. Within India, the freedom movement was in shambles; 'Quit India' in disarray. It had now been over a year since Gandhi-ji had been incarcerated in Poona, his communication with the outside world restricted. An entire generation of freedom fighters was behind bars: Sardar Patel, Pandit Nehru, Jayaprakash Narayan, everybody.

Manohar wondered whether Bapu would approve of the secrecy. But with so much at stake, perhaps he would understand?

A burst of gunfire sounded from a distance, sending a shiver down Manohar's spine.

He turned to look, almost as if seeking reassurance, at the only other person in the hut—a young man of just over twenty. He was six feet tall, with broad shoulders, a firm gait and a steady gaze. For all of Manohar's anxiety, the young man had not displayed any sign of nervousness. In fact, he had not moved an inch in the entire time that Manohar had shuffled around the hut.

For the first time in the last hour, Manohar permitted himself a sigh of satisfaction. Wherever else he might be going wrong, he was confident that he had not erred in his choice of person for the task.

Manohar opened his mouth to speak, but his voice failed him. Millions of lives at stake. Who was he to decide? He wished to somehow reach the leaders in jail and pass on the responsibility to them. Or, by some magical toss of fate, come face-to-face with Ram Manohar Lohia, who was broadcasting over underground radio from an unknown, hiding place.

But then his memory took him to the village that the young man and he had visited recently. The sunken eyes, the shrivelled bodies, the sheer horror of everything, and he knew that he had to act.

With supreme effort, he summoned up some energy and croaked, 'Beta, the time has come.'

The collective weight of history had just been transferred to the young man's shoulders. However, he did not even bat an eyelid. That, in fact, was precisely why he had been chosen.

'And Beta,' Manohar added as an afterthought, 'remember, you need to wait till the last of them is gone. Till the danger is no more.'

The young man merely nodded and bowed as he left the hut in two swift steps.

***

The young man walked through the undulating terrain in brisk yet measured strides. Despite the urgency and immensity of the task, he had an air of imperturbability about him. He walked half-a-mile downhill, not breaking a single step until he reached a jeep parked behind a clump of bushes.

As he opened the door, he took a quick look at the rear to make sure that the contents had not been disturbed. His eyes skimmed through the numerous small packages, all intricately encased. He paused as his gaze fell on a small package no more than two feet long.

Despite the time pressure, he could not resist opening it. As the casing came off, he took a long, deep breath as he took in the sight—a bronze figurine of a king, dating back to the Indus Valley civilisation—one of the oldest and best preserved historical treasures of all time.

The figurine of a queen, the king's consort, was already with him, tucked away in a place in the Himalayas that was meant to be hidden even from time.

He could not help feeling a small flicker of satisfaction; he had done well so far.

He permitted himself no more than a flicker, though. The job was far from over. And what he was doing now was far more important than all his previous expeditions put together. Far more important than any statues or figurines.

He started the jeep with a renewed sense of purpose. He would have to hurry.

***

Manohar, partly out of habit and partly out of a desire to recover his composure, spent the next hour writing his diary, as he had done every day for the last thirty years.

The young man was already out of Kausani by then.

***

Two hours later, the police, headed by a British officer from the Imperial Police, discovered the cluster of huts near Kausani where Manohar, along with his family and friends, was holed up. They shot dead every person they could find, including women and children. Manohar's last actions before a bullet went through his head were to burn his diary and to try, in vain, to usher the children to safety.

***

More than three years later, a very old nation underwent a dramatic rebirth as India broke the shackles of imperialism.

Over the next seventy years, thousands of books and papers would be written about India's freedom struggle. Myriad seminars, academic forums and panel discussions would dissect the plots and sub-plots leading up to the final moment when India won Independence. Manohar Rai's 'peripheral role', too, would find mention in a couple of them.

But nowhere would there be any mention of the matter that occupied Manohar in his final days. Nor of the young man who left Kausani that evening.

PART I: THE IMPERIAL GUARD

BANI AND DAMINI

CHAPTER 1

June 2018

Colaba, South Mumbai, Sunday, 8 p.m.

The unruly monsoon winds lashed against the thick stone walls of the Victorian era buildings near Regal Cinema in Colaba.

Every year there would be a couple of days and nights when Mumbai would grind to a halt, as the city bowed to the fury of the south-westerly monsoons.

This night was one of those.

Next to Regal Cinema stood a string of cafes and bars, all tightly shut. Outside the only café that was open, a cab sputtered and coughed as it plodded through the water and wheezed to a halt.

A lean, tall and very wet man with a backpack stepped out of the cab. He walked into Café Mondegar with firm, athletic steps as a lanky waiter motioned him in.

After spending four months trekking through the remotest corners of the Himalayas, Steve Watson had just reached a momentous decision, and he wanted to have a quick drink before he left the country.

He could not wait to get back home. The drink would have to be a *really* quick one.

***

Steve sighed as he looked at the water oozing out of his climbing boots. The past three weeks, with only a yak for company, had been particularly tough.

Not that Steve was a stranger to rough situations. He had, in his various avatars as mercenary, mountaineer and bounty hunter, seen more than his share of those.

What was more exhausting was the feeling of having been on a wild goose chase.

Steve trusted his instinct more than anything, or anyone, else. It had, more than once, prevented him from being shot in the head, and, in one instance in Afghanistan, from being blown to pieces by a bazooka. It had kept him alive in the grasslands of Uganda when faced with a choice between being trampled by charging elephants and beheaded by blood-thirsty poachers.

Steve smiled. He had chosen to take his chances with the poachers. If there is one sure way to die, it is to place yourself in front of a charging herd of elephants.

Yet, this time, it seemed his instinct had deserted him.

Maybe Professor Bani Bhattacharya was crazy, after all. Maybe he should not have wasted four months looking for a clue based on the professor's nonsensical riddle. Maybe he should have just stayed home to enjoy the English summer.

Anyway, better late than never, Steve thought. His decision was made now.

Somewhere in his subconscious mind, he knew that the quest would draw him back to India some day . . . to the country and the mountains that he loved so dearly. But for the time being, he had had enough of sleeping bags, stale bread and foot callouses.

He longed to be back in his house in Richmond, off London; maybe hook up with his on-and-off girlfriend, Angie; have a cup of hot coffee beside the fireplace and retire to his bed.

Steve stretched his legs and arms as he sank deeper into the chair. The first thing he would do after getting out of Café Mondegar would be to head to a cybercafé and book tickets to London.

***

Steve had barely taken a sip of his drink when the realisation hit him.

Maybe it was the memory of his Richmond home and the fireplace. Or maybe it was the cartoons on the walls of Café Mondegar.

Whatever the reason, Steve realised, to his amazement, that the truth had been right in front of him all this while, staring him in the face.

There was no mistaking it. Doubtless, there was still work to be done, but he now had the key to it all.

There was no time to waste. Steve yanked out a five-hundred-rupee-note from his wallet and handed it to the open-mouthed waiter as he jogged out the door.

Thankfully, the convenience store down the street was open. Steve forgot his English manners for a moment as he interrupted a middle-aged gentleman talking to the counter clerk.

Two minutes later, he emerged with a recharged SIM and a new battery for his mobile phone. He inserted the battery into the phone and dialled a Kolkata number.

He hoped Professor Bani Bhattacharya was home.

***

Sunday, 8.10 p.m.

As soon as Steve switched on his mobile phone and dialled the Kolkata number, a computer beeped many miles away in a room in a hitherto abandoned warehouse.

The 'Mansion', as the warehouse was known to its occupants, was located in a nondescript industrial complex near Mumbai, and was, by design, completely below the radar of the authorities.

The room resembled an airline cockpit, complete with control panels and computer consoles, yet the tastefulness of the interiors would have done a maharaja's palace proud. Rajasthani carpets with intricate designs covered the floor. The exquisite drapes had been woven by artisans from a remote *gali* in Lucknow. Even the computer monitors were ensconced in ornate rosewood casings.

As soon as the beeping started, a tall, heavy-set man sitting on a chair gave a slight exclamation, picked up a pair of earphones and started to listen in on the conversation.

As he pressed a button on his keyboard, a map came up on his screen and progressively converged on to a narrow area.

Colaba. Somewhere near Café Mondegar.

The heavy-set man smirked.

Steve Watson had finally shown up. It was time for some action.

***

South Kolkata, Sunday, 8.15 p.m.

Professor Bhattacharya's hands trembled as he picked up his notepad and stared at the ten stanzas of verse.

The room was largely dark, with just one lamp lighting a table cluttered with books. In the background, a shelf lined with more books cast an eerie shadow. This was the room where Bani, as Professor Bhabani Bhattacharya was known, spent most of the day poring over ancient texts, taking copious notes with his Sheaffer pen and pondering over matters from another era. The other two rooms in his quaint, independent house in Alipore were dark. Bani could not be bothered with trivialities like switching on lights around the house.

He was still reeling from the impact of the phone call. The rather oblique clues Steve gave him over the phone did seem to add up. This might be the real thing.

It had to be in person, not on the phone. Steve Watson had been pretty clear about that.

Bani's teeth almost chattered in anticipation as a shiver ran up his spine.

Not that Bani was a man of nervous disposition. He still retained his passionate yet determined demeanor from the time he earned the nickname Pele as a teenage footballer in his *para* in south Kolkata, and he looked somewhat younger than his sixty-two years. While in his thirties and forties, Bani never sought the safety of a podium as he delivered lectures on Indian history and anthropology all over the world in his booming baritone. He would stand, proud and confident, looking taller than his 5'10", perched right at the centre of the dais, making eye contact even with those hidden in far corners of the room.

Never mind that his heyday was past, the speaking engagements and felicitations long gone, replaced by murmurs of a brilliant mind in decay, of a senile old man and his crazy theories and obsessions. And then the murmurs had grown stronger and had reached a crescendo, until one day they had died down abruptly, almost as if he had never existed—the ultimate sign of the world having written him off.

None of this had changed Bani much. To him, the world that he inhabited in his inner mind was more real than the world outside.

And yet, that evening, after Steve's call, Bani was having an attack of the nerves. He picked up his notepad with quivering hands and stared at one of the translated verses.

The Worthy Heir shall reach the sanctum

Only after enduring the four Great Agonies

Through faith, fearlessness, stillness and silence

Shall the Worthy Heir conquer the Agonies.

He wiped off beads of cold sweat from his forehead as his shadow on the wall formed an ominous backdrop to the cramped room.

CHAPTER 2

Two hours later. . .
Mumbai, Sunday, 10.30 p.m.

The room was spinning around Steve. He retched lightly as he desperately tried to hold up his head.

The men had left him to recoup, but he had no doubt that they would be back in a few minutes for the next round of questioning.

He had revealed nothing, but he was not sure he would be able to hold out much longer. From his time as a mercenary soldier, Steve knew that everybody eventually buckled under torture.

He had to escape. Now.

And then there was this thing that he had overheard.

KaalKoot. The Demo. The stuff of his worst nightmares.

He hoped that he had heard wrong. But he knew he hadn't.

Less than three days to stop it. He had to get word out. Somehow.

He tried twisting and turning his hands, but the knot seemed tight.

Or did it, really?

Steve's eyes regained some colour as he sensed an opening.

After a few minutes' struggle, he managed to free his hands. And then his legs.

That was exactly when the door opened.

***

Both the men had knives. Even through the pain, the dizziness and the nausea, Steve knew he had to play this carefully.

He made his first move when one of the men came close enough. Steve kicked him hard in the stomach, and snatched his knife as the man was reeling, just in time as the second man threw himself at him.

Steve had managed to step sideways, but the second man's knife nevertheless slashed his left shoulder, drawing blood. The man swiftly turned around and lunged at the Englishman again, but Steve, his reflexes honed through years of roughing it out, was faster, wooziness notwithstanding.

Steve's knife got the man right in the stomach, and he slumped, never to wake up again.

The Englishman did not even glance at him as he tried to wobble out of the room. This was no time for softer emotions.

The first man, meanwhile, had regained his footing. He executed a jump and landed right on Steve, throwing him down to the floor. The Englishman's head hit the floor with a loud bang, but not before his knife went right through the man's chest.

Steve summoned up his last reserves of strength as he extricated himself and stumbled out of the room.

***

He missed a step and almost tumbled down the staircase. The entire stairwell was spinning around him wildly as his head throbbed. He could barely keep his eyes open, even as he could see blood oozing from his wounds.

He had to find a phone and get through to Bani. *Fast.*

Before *they* got to him.

CHAPTER 3

Shillim (near Mumbai, off Lonavla), Sunday, 9 p.m.

The rain fell in long, dreary drops on the imposing hills of Shillim in what promised to be a long and dark night. When a black Toyota Camry made its crooked way up the steep road that led to Kanchenjunga Kutir, all that was visible from up the hill was the intermittent feeble gleam of the headlights, like two serpents playing with each others' tails.

The Camry entered the sprawling compound of the farmhouse after an iris scan of the occupants.

Despite being only a two-hour drive from Mumbai, and a shorter drive from Lonavla, a popular weekend getaway, security systems of any sort were still a rarity in Shillim.

But then Kanchenjunga Kutir was no ordinary farmhouse. It was protected by one of the most sophisticated surveillance systems in Asia; its fences were made of crash-proof material and it housed a bank of servers which could access satellite feeds for every square mile of Indian soil.

In one of the rooms inside the farmhouse building, a tall, imposing man was engrossed in reading by the table lamp, a cup of hot masala tea by his side.

Sunil Gaur's name was always taken in hushed whispers in the rarified echelons of the international intelligence community. But to the employees at the Anti-Conspiracy Group, ACG for short, he was simply the 'Chief'. When the Indian government had formed this undercover group in the aftermath of the 2008 terror attacks, the Chief had chosen this picturesque farmhouse as its operational command centre.

Sunil Gaur had earned his nickname many times over, not least after a particularly dramatic operation in the Himalayas where he had taken on ten heavily armed enemy agents single-handedly with just a few dry twigs for defense. That operation was still taught to new recruits as a case study on how to start a fire and set up a distraction in the shortest possible time.

But today, the Chief was a worried man. All the signs pointed to something big brewing. He needed answers, and he needed them quickly. He hoped that Damini Thakur would not disappoint him.

***

Inside the Camry, a tall, athletic woman of around twenty-nine, wearing a set of tracks, was frowning over a series of photographs on her smartphone. She knew that the photographs would automatically erase themselves in another minute, thanks to a self-destruct app that the ACG used.

It was not in Damini's character to be stumped very often, but this was clearly one of those times. The men in the photographs seemed to have nothing in common other than the fact that their photographs had been clicked in Mumbai, and that they seemed to be up to no good.

She sighed, again uncharacteristic of her. As the Camry came to a halt, she paused for a second, took a deep breath and collected herself.

***

Back to her usual assured self, Damini looked every inch of her very fit 5'8" frame as she stepped out of the Camry.

Monu, the housekeeper at Kanchenjunga Kutir, was waiting in the courtyard. As she lightly patted him on his cheek as she passed through, his face turned pale.

Damini chuckled. Back in his village, Monu was unused to dealing with women in tight track-suits, much less them touching him in any way.

She walked past into the room where the Chief was sitting.

She crossed her hands and looked the Chief straight in the eye. 'This better be good,' she said. 'Your man interrupted me in the middle of my yoga class. I didn't even get time to change.'

Monu gulped at this show of irreverence. Almost everybody at the ACG, and many outside it, trembled at the mere mention of the Chief's name.

The Chief had a hint of a smile on his lips. 'Don't worry about the change of clothes,' he said. 'Monu has arranged for that. And I know better than to disturb one of my best agents during her rest and rehab.'

The Chief was openly smiling now. He would not tolerate insubordination from lesser mortals. But Damini was different. He still remembered the results from her psychological aptitude test. 'A hawk-like awareness of her surroundings, a heightened sense of justice and an insatiable curiosity', it had said. The test report also went on to mention that she had 'a dangerous disregard for authority and a fascination for recklessness, which, if channelised properly, could work to the ACG's advantage, but if left unbridled, could result in disaster.' The Chief had read the last bit with mild amusement.

'Change and be back within five minutes,' he said, the smile fading as he heard the clock ticking.

***

Stepping out of the shower, Damini paused in front of the mirror as she slipped on her clothes.

Dragged without notice to a farmhouse a hundred kilometres away from her home. Five minutes to shower and change into clothes that did not belong to her. All in a normal day's work.

Damini smiled. She had chosen this life. And the ACG had chosen her.

Despite the late nights at her job, the irregular meal times and the ubiquitous stress, she had managed to maintain her figure. A ruthless exercise regimen, complemented with yoga, had taken care of that. As she traced the outline of her toned legs all the way up her body, a tingle went up her spine.

She hadn't seen much action on the personal front in a while. Her job, to put it mildly, was not very compatible with any extra-curricular activities.

The only person she had dated over the last year was the guy from Pali Hill that she had met in yoga class. Their first date had been on a Saturday, and the guy had attempted to make light conversation. But Damini had spent the previous night hiding in a trash dump in a seedy part of town, engaged in a gunfight with three spies. The only image in her mind during the date was of blood gushing out of the dead spy's head as he had shot himself.

She had ended it after that.

Then there had been that short-lived tryst with a US agent she had met while on joint anti-terrorism exercises two years ago. But two undercover agents working for different countries was not exactly a recipe for a stable relationship. And that was it.

She hastily regained her bearings as a knock on the door told her that she needed to hurry up.

***

There were two people in the meeting room besides the Chief and Damini. Kunal, at thirty-five, was Damini's peer at the ACG despite being six years older, a fact that troubled him immensely. Then there was Mini, a systems and data mining expert who could navigate the world of computer networks, surveillance cameras and satellite feeds with the ease of a knife cutting through butter.

The large LCD screen displayed an image of a man with Oriental features. 'Recognise this man?' the Chief asked.

Almost immediately, Kunal held up his hand. 'Yes, Chief. Ji-hoon Kim. North Korean agent. Their point man for striking deals for arms purchases, nuclear technology and the like.'

'Bingo,' the Chief said.

Kunal beamed with pride as he flashed an insincere smile at Damini.

Damini rolled her eyes. Some people never grew up.

The Chief scrolled down to a series of photographs, the same ones which had been forwarded to Damini's smartphone. 'These are photographs of people from groups as diverse as the Cali drug cartel of Colombia, the Slav gang in eastern Europe, ISIS and African dictatorships visiting India. All of these have been clicked in Mumbai over the last month.'

'Why didn't we do anything over the last month?' Damini asked, bewildered.

'The vagaries of international cooperation,' the Chief said. 'We obtained the photos from different sources: one from the US Drug Enforcement Authority, DEA; one from Interpol; and one from MI6. The international agencies tossed the information to us only after they got nowhere with their investigations. Only Ji-hoon was captured directly by our cameras today.'

He continued: 'We need to find out what these deviants have been hatching in Mumbai. Fast. Before anything big blows up on us.'

The Chief took a sip of water. 'Damini, you will be the lead agent on the field. Kunal and Mini will man the control room and assist you with data feeds, satellites and surveillance.'

Kunal groaned. He wanted to be in on the actual action on the field, not manning a desk. He glared at Damini and was just starting to speak when the Chief sharply said, 'No arguments,' looking directly at him.

The Chief continued, somewhat conspiratorially. 'This could be a pretty delicate assignment. The US DEA and Interpol will be watching us closely, and maybe the CIA, too. But the control should not slip from our hands. At any cost. If you encounter any foreign agents, you have permission to deactivate them if needed.'

Damini's eyes widened slightly. She knew what 'deactivation' could mean.

'Damini, you are to report any findings directly to me, and to me only.'

Damini understood. Certain elements in the government had

a vested interest in undermining the ACG's influence, and the Chief wanted to avoid the glare of harsh scrutiny by keeping a tight lid on information flow out of the ACG.

Damini cleared her throat. 'Any active clues on what these guys were up to here?'

'Zilch. On Ji-hoon Kim, though, we may have gotten lucky. This photo of him coming out of Shree Motel near Metro Inox multiplex was taken this evening. Ji-hoon Kim went back into the motel at 8.30 p.m. after dinner, and hasn't come out since. Our field operative is stationed outside the motel. Damini, you can relieve him and take over tonight.'

Damini permitted herself a half-smile. The fun was just beginning. She knew what that meant—late nights, inadequate sleep, pounding veins, split-second decisions and near-death experiences. She was ready. And she knew it would be worth every minute.

There was no other job in the world that she'd rather be doing.

CHAPTER 4

Shillim, Sunday, 11 p.m.

The gushing rain had slowed down to a drizzle. As the Toyota Camry pulled out of Kanchenjunga Kutir, Damini found herself reminiscing as she admired the view of Lake Pavana glistening in the moonlight.

Six years ago, she would never have dreamt of this life. After two years in an advertising agency and as a yoga instructor, becoming a secret agent was not exactly a natural career progression.

But she had always had a vigilante streak. It had reared its head right from her schooldays, for instance, when she had found out that her brother, Sushant, was being bullied. Nobody else got to know what transpired that evening, but the bullies started avoiding Sushant by a mile, and one of them had his hand in a cast for the next three months.

Damini chuckled. She had always had a mind of her own. When her classmates and cousins in the small town of Mirzapur had hit the marriage 'market' at twenty-one, she decided that she did not give a damn, and took up a job at an advertising firm in Lucknow.

Her parents did give a damn, though, and moved around with crestfallen faces for years after that, repeatedly trying to get her hooked up with potential NRI marriage prospects.

Meanwhile, she moved to Delhi and spent a year working as a yoga instructor, until a woman in her forties from her yoga class asked if she might be interested in interviewing for a 'challenging' job.

The interview had required her to climb twenty obstacles, dodge trapdoors, outrun mock bullets, figure out how to calm an aggressive pit bull, run thirty kilometres without shoes and swim through turbulent waters, all in quick succession.

That was how Damini had ended up with the ACG six years ago.

That had been the proverbial nail in the coffin as far as her parents' attempts to get her married were concerned.

***

Damini's smartphone beeped as Mini sent her a briefing memo on Ji-hoon Kim.

The memo started with a brief history lesson. It chronicled North Korea's nuclear tests, and the hostility with South Korea, the US and Japan. After years of belligerence and threats to use nuclear weapons, the current ruler, Kim Jong-un, dramatically changed track in 2018. He met the South Korean leadership, and agreed to halt tests and work towards denuclearisation. The turnaround surprised most observers, with some attributing it to economic reasons, some to pressure from North Korea's long-time friend China, and some to the tactics of the US President. Some others were skeptical and felt that the turnaround was just a charade.

The memo detailed Ji-hoon's role as the North Korean regime's 'weapons' dealmaker' and a member of Kim Jong-un's coveted inner circle of advisors. He was rumoured to have struck deals for designs for centrifuges, one of the key components of the nuclear weapons' programme.

Ji-hoon Kim had mysteriously vanished from the radar since Kim Jong-un's peace overtures in 2018. Earlier, there would be the occasional meeting with an African dictator, or a hushed rendezvous aboard a ship with a militant group; but there was absolutely no sighting recorded since December 2017.

One rumour was that he had been 'neutralised' by Kim Jong-un since he was no longer relevant in a denuclearised North Korea. Another theory was that he had been sent underground by Kim Jong-un to develop a covert weapons' programme—a 'Plan B'—in case the peace overtures backfired.

The theories made his sudden appearance in a seedy motel near Metro Cinema in South Mumbai all the more intriguing. Damini could not wait to get there and take up position outside the motel.

***

Five hours later. . .

Metro Inox, South Mumbai, Monday, 4 a.m.

Metro Inox is a remodelled multiplex version of the iconic Metro Cinema in South Mumbai. Damini had parked herself in an alcove in one of the old, rather shabby buildings located in the vicinity.

The ramshackle building was deserted at that hour, though Damini had to dodge a couple of rats that seemed to want to share her alcove. The heavy rains had eased off, giving Damini a clear line of sight to Ji-hoon Kim's room.

His choice of motel left no doubt that he was up to no good. Shree Motel was decidedly down-market, even by the earthiest of standards. Certainly not the kind of place in which Ji-hoon Kim would stay if what he was doing was above board.

He was clearly sleeping. There had been no movement from the room for the last three hours. Nevertheless, Damini had not once taken her eyes off the room's window.

Her body longed for a quick walk and stretch. She wondered if she should attempt it, given the risk of blowing her cover. But then she looked around—at the deserted road, and the silent and dark interiors of Ji-hoon's room—and decided that she would go for it.

She had barely stepped out onto the street when she realised that the move was a big mistake.

***

A speeding Fortuner came to a screeching halt right next to Damini.

She cursed silently and snatched a look at Ji-hoon Kim's window. No movement. She heaved a tentative sigh of relief.

There were four men in the SUV. All in their twenties. All drunk, all leering at her.

'Get in, baby, we'll show you a good time,' one of them said. Another stepped out of the front seat of the SUV and tried to take what he thought was a menacing position. 'Get into the vehicle,' he said, his breath heavy with alcohol.

Frustrated young men with no direction, spurred on by a milieu where everybody felt entitled and nobody felt accountable. Damini could dispatch them then and there, but it would create a commotion and might wake Ji-hoon Kim up. She could not afford that.

Hopefully, the backup ACG van stationed in the lane next to Metro Inox would not lose Ji-hoon Kim's trail.

So she would play along with the idiots from the SUV. For now.

***

Near Metro Inox, Mumbai

Two minutes and half-a-kilometre away, a safe enough distance from Shree Motel, the SUV screeched to a halt again. The setting was quite different this time.

Two of the men, including the one who had tried to tower menacingly in front of Damini, had suffered concussions after trauma to the head. They were unlikely to wake up for another hour.

The third guy in the rear seat lunged at Damini, only to be unceremoniously silenced by no more than a light tap to his temple.

Damini had learnt in the first month of training at the ACG that the human body offered enough opportunities to flatten somebody out without resorting to theatrics. This one would not wake up for a couple of hours.

The fourth man, who was driving the SUV, had panicked and brought it to a halt by the roadside. He had desperately reached for his mobile phone, only to have it hit the dashboard along with his palm, and had begged for mercy as the pain seared through his broken fingers.

He had just begun crying when he, too, was flattened by a light blow to the side of his head.

As Damini started walking back to the building opposite Shree Motel, she let a small smirk escape her face. The police constable who had been informed by Damini would have a nice laugh.

This wasn't subtle. But then subtlety wasn't Damini's style, and she was proud of that. A subtle person would not last a day in her line of work.

'Bloody distraction,' she said to herself as she rushed back, hoping that Ji-hoon Kim had not woken up and given her the slip.

CHAPTER 5

South Kolkata, Sunday, 8.30 p.m.

The table lamp shook as Bani got up with a start.

The rustling sound felt unnervingly close this time. Maybe right outside the window of the study.

He darted across and peered out of the window in a sudden, swift motion, hoping to take anyone lurking outside by surprise.

There was a slight nip in the air, signalling the impending arrival of the monsoon, rather early this time. But there was nobody in sight.

Bani sighed. This was not the first time. He had been hearing strange noises of late, and more than once, had had the feeling of being followed.

Had the endless hours of solitary work begun to get to him?

Bani quickly shunned the thought. He was not somebody who succumbed to fear or self-doubt.

Even through all the ostracisation from the academic community, he had never allowed himself to feel despondent. The only night he had permitted the vulnerability to seep through had been when Muneera had finally left him, taking Tutul with her, having had enough of his erratic work hours and mood swings. He had sat that night by the record player they had lovingly bought together for their first wedding anniversary, listened to his favourite Kishore Kumar hits, and had bawled like a baby.

But the following morning, he had gone back to the quest that had consumed him all these years. And the previous evening had been filed deep in the alcoves of his memory, far away from his conscious mind.

As Bani walked back from the window to his study table, he brushed away his fears about being followed. After all, nobody would care to stalk a cranky, old professor with some obscure theories.

At least not till he made his discovery public.

***

South Kolkata, 9.00 p.m.

Bani got up from his table again as he heard a rustling sound from the porch. His instinct proved right this time, except that it was no intruder who had caused it.

It was Mukhshuddi Pal, Bani's long-time friend. Mukhshuddi Babu, as his neighbours called him, walked with a slight shuffle, and had dreamy eyes that colluded with his signature dull grey shawl to give him a permanent melancholic look. Souvik-da, their common friend, joked that Mukhshuddi seemed straight out of a Satyajit Ray movie.

Bani and he had been friends from the time they used to play *kancha*, or marbles, together as kids. He had stuck with him ever since, through thick and thin. Bani, on his part, felt grateful and also enjoyed the fact that Mukhshuddi Babu's earthy humour would take him away, albeit temporarily, from his preoccupations.

***

Mukhshuddi had a cup of warm chai in his hand. He loved *adda*, or conversation over chai.

He looked, fascinated, as Bani moved aside a bunch of hardbound books from his table.

'Bani-da, I've been meaning to ask you for a while,' Mukhshuddi said, adjusting his shawl. 'What is this thing that you work on with such enthusiasm that it consumes all your days and nights?'

'Hmmm…' Bani hesitated. Mukhshuddi Babu did not exactly constitute a marquee audience. But he could never say 'no' to an audience. Besides, his last guest lecture, over a year ago, had been with the 'Society for Discussion on Aliens, UFOs, Elvis, the Loch Ness Monster and other Mysteries'. Not exactly Harvard.

'Okay, Mukhshuddi,' Bani said, settling into his chair and picking up his chai. 'I'll tell you.'

'I'm all ears, Bani-da.'

'The story dates back to the turbulent 1930s. The western world was wilting under the Great Depression, and Britain was no exception. It was a period of collapsing industry, spiralling unemployment and hunger marches. Against that backdrop, a difference in opinion started developing in Britain as to what was to be done with India, the jewel in the crown of the British Empire.'

Mukhshuddi slurped while drinking his chai, smiling sheepishly as he realised that the sound was rather pronounced.

Bani continued: 'Some elements in British society, including some in the Labour Party, felt that Britain's policy should gradually move towards self-governance by Indians. This march towards

Indian self-determination gained impetus with the somewhat conciliatory Gandhi-Irwin Pact of 1931, and also with the British parliament recognising the autonomy of Indian provinces in 1935.'

Mukhshuddi nodded, though the references to the Labour Party and Irwin seemed only vaguely familiar.

'There were sections—powerful sections—in Britain that felt otherwise, and were alarmed by this growing phenomenon of what they perceived as "rats gnawing at the foundations of the British Empire". They were firm believers in the notion of racial superiority of the British, the "White Man's Burden", as Kipling called it.'

Bani noted that this had piqued Mukhshuddi's interest. 'This was when some of the more extreme elements among these sections came together and set up a clandestine organisation.'

As Mukhshuddi leaned forward attentively, Bani continued: 'These extreme elements comprised certain influential members of the British political class, the civil services and the armed forces. They called this secret organisation the "Imperial Guard". Until twelve years ago, the existence of this organisation was unknown to the world, but thanks to the efforts of a certain professor from Kolkata, that is no longer the case.'

Mukhshuddi stared blankly at Bani for a few seconds, then suddenly lit up as realisation dawned on him. 'Bani-da, you!?'

Bani could not suppress a satisfied smile.

'Wah, Bani-da, I never knew,' Mukhshuddi beamed. 'How did you uncover the existence of this organisation?'

'I went through tens of thousands of pages of correspondence, speeches, letters, meeting minutes and file notings by British bureaucrats, politicians and other government officials, before I discerned a coordinated pattern of lobbying. The Imperial Guard had covered their tracks well, which made my job quite challenging. Finally, twelve years ago, I was able to decisively prove to the international academic community that the invisible hand of the Imperial Guard had influenced many of the British government's decisions of that era.'

'What sort of decisions were these?'

'To begin with, these were subtle pushes to the British government's decisions, such as stalling tactics on self-governance.'

Bani continued: 'But then, in 1941, the tide turned sharply, and the Imperial Guard got more desperate. Hitler had invaded Russia, and the Japanese had attacked Pearl Harbour. Meanwhile, pressure was mounting on Britain from its allies—the US and China—to favourably consider Indian demands for self-governance. Churchill, the diehard imperialist, was forced to send Stafford Cripps to India with a conciliatory proposal.'

'Was Churchill a member of the Imperial Guard?' Mukhshuddi asked.

'Tantalising thought,' Bani said. 'Churchill is reported to have said "I hate Indians" and described us as a "beastly people". And he did more than his share of damage, ruthlessly dismissing requests for help during the Bengal Famine, instead reportedly asking, "Why hasn't Gandhi died yet?" But we really don't know if Churchill was a member of the Imperial Guard.'

Mukhshuddi grimaced. 'I never did like the British.'

Bani stopped himself just as he began to reply. As with most things, the truth about British rule was more nuanced than that, but he was not sure he would be able to communicate that to Mukhshuddi.

'Anyway, back to the story,' he continued. 'The war, meanwhile, had lurched in dangerous directions. Japanese forces took control of Philippines, Malaya and Hong Kong, and within a few months Singapore and Burma had fallen from British hands into the Japanese.'

Mukhshuddi nodded.

'Then the Quit India Movement was announced in August 1942, and that was the last straw for the Imperial Guard. Coming in the middle of the war, they viewed this as an act of audacity by the Indian subjects. And yet, the Imperial Guard realised that the tide was irreversibly turning towards Indian independence. And thus, what was hitherto a loose agglomeration of like-minded people turned into something more sinister.'

Mukhshuddi's hand, holding the cup, froze in mid-air as he intently waited for Bani's next words.

'The Imperial Guard got their idea from something that the British did in the coastal districts of India in anticipation of the Japanese invasion in 1942. They destroyed thousands of houses, crops, wells, bridges, boats, bicycles and the like, so that none of these would be of any use to the Japanese in case they attacked India. In war, this is known as the "scorched earth" policy.'

Bani picked up the kettle to refill Mukhshuddi's cup.

'From then on, the policy of the Imperial Guard was one of destruction. If they could not continue ruling India, they wanted to make sure it was reduced to rubble. Their invisible hand was at play in matters of policy, except this time it had a more destructive sweep. All major Indian leaders were imprisoned in the wake of the announcement of the Quit India Movement, and the movement itself was put down with ruthless force. Arthur Hope, the Madras Governor, asked for Gandhi to be deported to Mauritius or Kenya and reportedly wrote, "If he fasts, let it not be known. If he dies, announce it six months later."'

Mukhshuddi sighed.

'And yet that was not the last straw. It is now widely accepted that the extent of damage caused by the Bengal Famine of 1943 and 1944 was largely the result of Britain's faulty policies at the time. The diversion of food grain for Britain's military needs, the refusal to send wheat to India and redirection of ships which could have been used to import foodgrain, all came together in a deadly cocktail, culminating in over three million deaths. And behind many of these policies and decisions was the same hand of the Imperial Guard.'

A shocked Mukhshuddi said nothing. He had heard stories from this father of the horrors of that time.

'Let's take a break,' Bani said abruptly, always emotionally overwhelmed when the topic of the Bengal Famine came up.

***

South Kolkata, Sunday, 9.40 p.m.

'So, you uncovered the existence of this Imperial Guard twelve years ago,' Mukhshuddi was saying. 'What have you been working on since then?'

Bani paused. That was the point where his departure from the international academic circuit had begun. 'Something I came across during my work on the Imperial Guard caught my attention.'

Mukhshuddi perked up.

'In the hills of what is known as Uttarakhand today, there lived a man named Manohar Rai. He was an ardent follower of Gandhi, and he coordinated activities in the region as part of the freedom struggle. He seems to have led an unremarkable life, largely following orders and organising protests. Yet, between 1942 and 1944, something interesting happened to this man, who was then already in his seventies.'

Bani noticed that Mukhshuddi was listening intently.

'In August 1942, during the Quit India Movement, thousands of freedom fighters were arrested, including all the luminaries, many of whom were not permitted access to the outside world. Overnight, the freedom struggle lost all its leaders, and it was left to second and third rung leaders to carry on the struggle on their own. Many of them went underground to carry on the struggle from secret hideouts.'

'Wow'.

'Indeed,' Bani said. 'There are many stories of intrigue and courage from those times. For example, Usha Mehta, a woman from Bombay, set up a secret radio station which broadcast speeches from the likes of Ram Manohar Lohia. With the British hunting desperately for them, she and her compatriots had to move locations every day.'

'Very interesting,' Mukhshuddi said.

Bani continued. 'Anyway, coming back to the story, Manohar Rai, too, went underground. He functioned from a hideout in what is now Uttarakhand. That was when he came upon a secret which altered everything for him.'

'What was this secret?'

'He got to know of a plan by the Imperial Guard to "wreck India before the Empire leaves". We do not know how Manohar got this information, but what we do know is that this plan of the Imperial Guard involved two legs.'

Bani bit his lips as soon as he said this. He ought not to reveal too much, even to his childhood friend.

He continued quickly, 'The Imperial Guard's plan was to destroy or desecrate iconic signs of Indian civilisation, including artefacts, manuscripts, sculptures and paintings of profound historical significance. The objective was to undermine India's cultural roots so that they would strike at the heart of Indian civilisation. They wanted to seek out and destroy every single such sign, so that, in their words, "The beastly natives could realise the triviality of their culture and bow forever before the splendour and grandeur of western civilisation."'

'Wow, Bani-da,' Mukhshuddi exclaimed. 'Quite sweeping.'

'The academic community didn't think so. They dismissed Manohar as a person of no consequence in history, and this plot as being a figment of his imagination.'

Bani could still remember the numerous guest lectures and conferences to which he had been invited post the Imperial Guard discovery. He had been detached from the accolades and felicitations, choosing instead to be fascinated with Manohar's secret discovery. The fascination had soon turned into an obsession, and that was when the guest lecture invitations had started dropping.

'Manohar wrote about this plot in a letter to a fellow revolutionary, intending that in case he was captured, the knowledge of this plot should not die with him. This letter, unfortunately, never reached the intended recipient, who had died in a gunfight. I found the envelope unopened during the course of combing numerous records during my researches.'

'Bani-da, now you are reminding me of Feluda,' Mukhshuddi quipped, referring to the popular detective in Satyajit Ray's series. 'Anyway, what was the second leg of the Imperial Guard's plot?'

Bani's heart skipped a beat. Mukhshuddi, his slowness notwithstanding, had not overlooked the slip.

'Uhh...,' he stammered, his mind quickly conjuring up an explanation. 'Just that this plot to destroy the iconic signs of Indian civilisation was to be implemented in two stages.'

Bani continued. 'The letter mentions a few more interesting things. With all the senior leaders in jail, Manohar had to take matters into his own hands. He spent most of 1943 travelling the length and breadth of the country, visiting museums and private collections, painstakingly collecting rare manuscripts and artefacts. These artefacts went right back to the Indus Valley and Vedic times to the Mauryan period, the Gupta regime and the Mughal reign. In other words, an uninterrupted series of manuscripts, artefacts and paintings dating back over four thousand years, a veritable treasure trove for a historian.'

'That's why you have been smitten by this,' Mukhshuddi nodded, slowly comprehending.

Bani smiled sheepishly. He had been smitten by history ever since Professor Mitra had, many years ago, taken him through the portals of the Asiatic Society of Bengal.

'How did Manohar manage to do all this alone?' Mukhshuddi asked. 'You said he had lived a pretty unremarkable life.'

Bani looked up, startled. Mukhshuddi was not just listening, he was thinking, too.

'That, Mukhshuddi, is the most interesting part.'

CHAPTER 6

South Kolkata, Sunday, 10 p.m.

'Continue, Bani-da,' Mukhshuddi said. 'What was the magic wand that enabled the unremarkable Manohar to accomplish this mammoth task?'

Mukhshuddi was sitting on the edge of his seat. Bani could not escape a smug smile as he continued: 'I spent many years following up on every conceivable lead on any freedom fighters who, in the 1940s, had ever been to what constitutes Uttarakhand, Uttar Pradesh and Himachal Pradesh today. I sifted through personal belongings, museums, government archives, post office records, private correspondences, diaries and interviewed hundreds of family members. Some interesting things emerged—a pattern of awed whispers.'

'What whispers?' Mukhshuddi asked, himself involuntarily speaking in a hushed tone.

'About a young man of extraordinary capabilities, who was probably just around twenty years old at the time.'

Mukhshuddi looked up at Bani quizzically.

Bani continued. 'Various accounts exist. One account, in the diaries of a village sarpanch, describes how a heroic young man single-handedly defended the village from a campaign of rape and destruction unleashed by the colonial police; that he "seamlessly alternated between the stillness of a lake and the intensity of lightning", completely throwing off the opponents. Another account mentions a man who was adept at mechanical devices—from rigging makeshift alarms to wiring an entire village to ward off intruders. Yet another revolutionary describes how this man had probably read "every book of consequence since the dawn of Indian civilisation." He was supposedly equally well-versed in the Upanishads, the Buddhist treatises, the chronicles of Chinese travellers and the famous European plays.'

'Wow,' Mukhshuddi exclaimed. 'This person seems like a cross between Superman, Thomas Edison and Gurudev Tagore!'

'There's more. Another account, written by a revolutionary from jail, describes a youth who emerged from six weeks' solitary confinement in a six-feet-by-six-feet cell totally calm and actually looking somewhat healthier and refreshed. When asked what he did all day for those six weeks, he replied that he was meditating all the while. This young man was supposedly well-versed not just in English, French and half-a-dozen modern Indian languages, but also in Sanskrit and Pali. It took me some time to piece together these accounts and realise that they all referred to the same person.'

'Ah, so he was a bit like Swami Vivekananda, too,' Mukhshuddi said, revelling in his uncharacteristic burst of mental activity. 'What was this man's name? Where did he come from?'

Bani stole a glance at Mukhshuddi, happy that the story was keeping him spellbound. 'Nobody knows. All that was known was that he learnt yoga, meditation and languages in his teenage years under a guru in the Himalayas, and then proceeded to master both the ancient eastern treatises and the western works on science, art and history. One aging revolutionary wrote that this man represented the "best of Indian civilisation". In the revolutionary circles of those days, this young man was simply referred to in hushed whispers as *Yogyaveer,* meaning the Worthy, Brave One, in Sanskrit.'

'Wah,' Mukhshuddi said.

'And then, sometime in early 1944, these stories abruptly ceased, almost as if this man vanished from the face of the earth.'

'Hold on; what does this story have to do with Manohar Rai and the Imperial Guard?' Mukhshuddi asked.

'In the unopened letter to his friend, Manohar wrote that he had enlisted the help of a remarkable young man of extraordinary capabilities, a man who "could rival the ancient king Vikramaditya in prowess". With this man's phenomenal appreciation of Indian history, Manohar put together this treasure trove of artefacts, manuscripts and sculptures that represented the best of Indian civilisation dating back from the Vedic times. This young man was to go into hiding and preserve this for posterity, just in case the Imperial Guard's plan to destroy iconic symbols of Indian civilisation came to fruition.'

'Where was this young man to hide?'

'This man—I will simply call him the Yogyaveer—was to hide in "a place no human could penetrate, till the last of the sympathisers of the Imperial Guard were known to be no more". Manohar referred to this place as the *Gupt-Kandara*; in the Sanskrit language, this means the Hidden Cave. Manohar was aware that this task demanded enormous inner strength, patience and integrity, and he could think of no better person for the job.'

Mukhshuddi nodded, slowly comprehending. 'So, Bani-da, for

the last twelve years, you have been trying to trace the hiding place—this Hidden Cave—hoping to find this treasure of priceless artefacts.'

Bani nodded. 'Most academics think I am insane.'

***

'So, are these manuscripts and artefacts likely to be worth a lot?' Mukhshuddi asked.

'Priceless to someone like me. But universities, museums or private collectors would pay maybe a few hundred million dollars for it. Maybe even a billion.'

'Really? Do people pay that kind of money for ancient books?'

'Well, a single painting from the 'The Card Players' series, by Paul Cezanne, sold for two hundred fifty million dollars in 2011. Another painting, 'Salvator Mundi', by Leonardo da Vinci, sold for four hundred fifty million dollars in 2017. In 2010, a sculpture by Alberto Giacometti was auctioned for over a hundred million dollars. And here, we are talking about an entire collection. Easily a few hundred million dollars, if not a billion.'

'A billion dollars,' Mukhshuddi nodded in comprehension. 'That's a lot.'

'That's not the point, Mukhshuddi. I don't give a damn about the money. For me, being able to lay my hands on a continuous chronicling of Indian history, dating back all the way from four thousand years ago, would be an "Alice in Wonderland" feeling.'

Mukhshuddi glanced at the books on Bani's table as he got up to leave. There was one book titled *The Black Death and the Transformation of the West*, another titled *The Journey to Mount Kailash*, and a notepad with the words 'KaalKoot' prominently scribbled on it.

'Your work seems very interesting, Bani-da,' Mukhshuddi said, impressed. 'Now I know why you have been excited all these years.'

He adjusted his shawl as he began to walk to the door. 'But I still think none of this was worth leaving Muneera for.'

'I didn't leave,' Bani said tersely, 'She did.'

CHAPTER 7

Kolkata, Sunday, 10.30 p.m.

Bani spent an uneasy half hour bent over his desk, poring over some old notes.

At 10.30 p.m., by the dim glow of the lamp, he saw something that made him jump up in alarm. It was the silhouette of a face outside his study window.

***

Bani still retained some of the reflexes from his early soccer days. He got over the shock and dove up to the window within a couple of seconds. But the silhouette was not visible anymore.

His hands were shaking a little bit as he fumbled with the light switch. When the lights finally came on, he stepped outside the house and took a look.

No sign of anybody.

He shook his head, cursed and headed back to his study. He found it difficult to do any work after that.

Could it be one of his rivals, Bani wondered; somebody who wanted to claim the credit for himself? But then, historians weren't exactly known for stalking people and taking up positions outside their windows.

Could it be an antique thief who wanted to sell the treasure trove of artefacts and make some money? But a thief would probably busy himself with something that offered more tangible and instant gratification, such as robbing a bank. Or becoming a politician, Bani chuckled.

There was a third, and more sinister, possibility. A possibility that made Bani nervous. Very nervous. A possibility that centred around the contents of a scroll hidden in Bani's bank locker.

A possibility that revolved around KaalKoot.

***

Bani had discovered the scroll four months ago in Nepal.

Before hiding the scroll in, of all places, a bank locker, Bani had translated and copied the contents—ten verses in Sanskrit—in his notepad.

There were only two people he had shared the contents of the scroll with: Steve and Shrikant.

Shrikant was an expert on Himalayan plant and animal life. He was one of the few eminent researchers who didn't laugh at Bani on the face. Bani and he had known each other—as close friends and collaborators—for over twenty-five years. With their shared fondness for soccer, Bani and Shrikant called each other Pele and Zico respectively, after their favourite Brazilian stars of the yesteryears.

Shrikant had come back just the previous week with a very intriguing insight. An insight that opened up the possibility that Bani might be followed, by a bunch more sinister than just historians trying to claim credit or thieves trying to get to the artefacts.

Bani quivered a little as he picked up the notepad in which he had jotted down the verses. His eyes darted to the fourth verse.

The secret shall be revealed only to the Worthy Heir

That person alone, of supreme faith, courage, stillness and compassion

Shall be able to conquer the Agonies

And prevent KaalKoot from striking again.

Bani's heart beat faster. He had struggled to find the master key that would enable him to interpret the verses correctly. Something that Steve would hopefully shed light on tomorrow.

Bani couldn't bear the wait. He walked up to the telephone and dialled Steve's mobile phone number.

It was switched off.

***

Sunday, 11.30 p.m.

After having unsuccessfully tried Steve's number a few more times, Bani was worriedly pacing up and down the room when the phone rang.

Bani dived towards the phone. 'Ha! I can still do a mean football tackle,' he thought for a split second.

'Who's this?' slurred a seemingly intoxicated voice on the phone.

'Prof. Bani Bhattacharya. Who's on the line?'

'Look . . . erre . . .' the voice continued, 'I got a laddie 'ere who is muttering your number.'

It was not an Indian accent. Probably British, though Bani could barely make out the words underneath the wheezing and slurring.

'Who is he?'

'Says name's Steve. 'as given your number.' The man coughed and sputtered violently. Bani could practically feel the man's phlegm through the phone lines.

Bani registered that this was not a man who was high on alcohol. Or even marijuana. He was probably on stronger stuff.

But Bani didn't care about that. He just wanted to make sure the guy did not hang up the phone.

'Can I talk to Steve?' he asked. 'Please,' he added as an afterthought.

For a second, the line seemed to have gone dead. Bani's heart skipped a beat. 'Hello?' he asked apprehensively.

'I don't want no trouble. Here I was, good old Jeff, peacefully smoking me joints and doing my mantra chants, and now this bloke got me all messed up. He seems like a decent bloke, so I'm doin' it for him. But I don't want no trouble.'

Bani sighed. At least he had a name now. 'Jeff, I'm just a professor. Can I talk to Steve?'

'Him?' the man slurred. 'He's knocked cold. Badly bruised all over. My buddy, he's with the Red Cross, he's fixed him up for now, but Steve ain't gonna talk for some time. Just wheezed out your number before he conked out.'

Oh gosh! So Steve was hurt. Badly. 'Tell me where you are and I'll see you,' Bani was desperate.

'I'm heading to Goa now. With him. If you bring any cops, I'm gonna vanish as sure as the sun sets every day.'

'Don't worry; I, too, hate cops.'

'Goa. The rave party at Lotus Café. See me 'morrow at 10 after sundown.'

'How do I identify you?'

'I'm not gonna tell ya. I've had enough trouble already. I will find ya. I can spot a guy who duhn't belong in the rave the way y'all can spot a white bloke in a bazaar.'

'Where in Goa is Lotus Café?' Bani asked, his anxiety rising to a shrill pitch. 'Is Steve hurt? Is he even fit to travel from Mumbai to Goa?'

But the slurring man had hung up the phone.

***

The Mansion, Sunday, 11.35 p.m.

The tall, heavy-set man at the ebony desk at the Mansion dialled a phone number as soon as he finished listening in on Bani's phone conversation. He had been instructed to call this number only in exceptional circumstances, and this one qualified.

A deep voice emerged from the other end of the phone. It had a mildly echoing quality to it, and it sounded somewhat sinister, as if it had emerged from the depths of darkness itself.

'Tell me.'

The tall, heavy-set man at the desk was a hardened thug who had seen, and inflicted, more than his fair share of horrors. Yet, every time he heard that voice, it sent an involuntary shudder down his spine.

'Sir, Steve seems to be with some doped-out hippy who has made contact with the Professor. They are going to meet in Goa tomorrow evening.'

'Coordinates?' The man at the other end liked to keep things brief.

'It seemed like a public phone booth. My guess is that he's taking a train from Mumbai to Goa. We'll try to intercept all possible train combinations. But our best bet is the rendezvous point in Goa tomorrow.'

There was a pause as the man at the other end contemplated this for a moment. When he finally spoke, his voice exuded an eerie chill.

'We have had one goof-up already with Steve's escape. Tail the Professor, and move to Plan B. This time, Bruce, you handle it.'

'What about Andy, Doc?' Bruce blurted out, then bit his lip. He should have kept his trap shut.

'Andy is out of play,' the person at the other end, whom Bruce called the Doc, said calmly.

Bruce's heart fluttered mildly as he realised what that meant. Andy had goofed up with Steve, and he was now history.

Just as Bruce would be if he goofed up with Plan B. Especially now that KaalKoot was imminent.

'I will handle things in Goa tomorrow, sir,' Bruce said, somewhat tamely.

But the man at the other end had already hung up.

***

Alipore, Kolkata, 11.35 p.m.

Bani's heart was beating so fast it felt like a sledgehammer. The image of the face silhouetted outside his study window, the memory of his last conversation with Shrikant, and the thought of a badly injured Steve were all coming together to form an unholy potpourri in his head.

The only thing Bani was clear about was that he needed to head to Goa at the earliest. Everything else was a muddle.

He needed to clear his mind. Fast. Maybe over a walk. Or else he, too, might end up like Steve.

Bani loved walks. Every morning, he would head to the Kolkata Maidan, taking in the sights and sounds of the city. For a person who didn't watch TV, didn't carry a mobile phone and spent most of his day absorbed in books, this was one way of staying sane.

But it was almost midnight, and the Maidan was no place to go to in the dark.

Bani decided, on a whim, to head to Park Street. At least the party-hopping crowd would lend the place a cheerful vibe at this time of the night.

Before leaving for Park Street, he called his friend Shrikant's office phone number in Mumbai. As with Bani, Shrikant didn't carry a mobile phone, and he did not even have a phone at his residence.

It went to his voice mail. Bani left him a message with the nicknames that they used for each other.

'Hey, Zico, Pele here. Drop everything and meet me in Goa. 8.30 p.m. tomorrow, Monday. In front of the band at Ephesus Hotel. And watch out for people following you. This is getting dangerous. Very dangerous.'

***

Park Street, Kolkata, 11.55 p.m.

Bani had got off his cab on Park Street, a few steps from the iconic hotel 'The Park', when he spotted them.

There were two of them, in a nondescript grey Honda City which had been maintaining a dubiously close-yet-not-too-close distance from his cab.

No sooner had Bani spotted them than the Honda City accelerated towards his cab. Bani involuntarily quickened his steps, until he realised that he needed to break into a run. This was a do-or-die situation.

Bani's mind moved in a hundred different directions as he ran. He did not know whether his pursuers were armed. Staying out in open view at Park Street was not a good idea.

It would be better to get to a place where he could mingle with the crowd.

An idea flashed through Bani's mind.

Tantra, the booming nightclub at The Park, opposite the main hotel entrance, was the partygoers' paradise, and the hub of Kolkata's nightlife. It would be shutting down at midnight, and the crowds would be streaming out.

There was no time to waste. Bani ran towards Tantra, his footballer's muscles swinging back to life, even as he secretly thanked his brisk morning walks for keeping him agile and fit.

The Honda City had screeched to a halt at the place where Bani had disembarked from the cab moments ago. The two men got off and started running towards him, the distance between them and Bani only around thirty metres. One of them had taken out a revolver.

***

Bani rushed headlong into the swarm of people streaming out of Tantra. The crowd was spread out in haphazard ways, slowing Bani's progress. He ploughed his way right into the sprawling nightclub, fervently hoping that he was not committing a blunder by entering an enclosed space.

He could hear the spontaneous howls of protest from outside the nightclub, probably his pursuers running into the crowd or maybe brandishing the revolver. The sounds grew louder and nearer, and Bani knew they were steadily gaining on him.

He panicked. Should he run back out of Tantra and try to enter the main hotel? Maybe his pursuers would hesitate to shoot in a hotel lobby?

But he knew he could not bank on that.

The yelps from near the Tantra entrance were much louder now.

There was only one way to go. Bani ran towards the kitchen, hoping that it would lead on to the rear exit.

***

Something drew him to a small door to his right.

Bani could not resist a second glance at it. It was an inconspicuous door that was hidden in the shadows.

Bani rushed closer and peered in, his heart still pounding.

Inside, there were empty crates of drinks, a mop, and a table with a few chairs piled on top. Towards the leftmost corner of the room, there were stacks of old newspapers, along with boxes of provisions.

A storage room.

That was when he saw it.

There was a small loft in the leftmost corner, hidden in the shadows, built into the upper wall, with a few small boxes of cardboard on it, but otherwise ripe to accommodate any person who was foolish—or desperate—enough to squeeze into it.

Would this loft escape the attention of prying eyes? Bani did not know, but there was no time to think. He moved a chair to use as a base to hoist himself up into the loft.

This was a desperate gamble from a desperate man. If they did find him, they would smoke him out like a rat from a hole.

***

After climbing up the loft, Bani used a mop he had taken up with him to move the chair away from his position. The chair made a creaking sound as he prodded it away.

For a second, Bani froze, afraid the creaking noise may have given him away.

Nothing moved. Bani eased up slightly, desperately stifling a sneeze as the dust from the cardboard boxes enveloped him, as did the darkness and the fear.

He could hear some noises in the distance, probably his tormentors entering the kitchen.

Bani did not exactly believe in God, but that instant, he prayed that none of the chefs and waiters in the kitchen should have noticed him entering the storage room.

Bani's rumination was disturbed by the sound of heavy footsteps and the noise of a couple of voices harshly questioning somebody. The voices sounded like they were right outside the storage room.

The loft was dark, and uncomfortable, and Bani's knee was throbbing. But even more distressing was having to desperately avoid a sneeze. Bani could hear every sinew in his body beating in rhythm with his heart, and it seemed like this beat was audible a good ten metres away, within earshot of those that hunted him, like wolves sniffing out a prey.

***

The footsteps seemed to come closer, and then the door to the storage room opened.

There was the sound of one pair of footsteps entering the room. To Bani, the sound seemed deafening as thunder, as did the sound of his heartbeat and his breathing. He almost wished there was a way he could stop breathing altogether.

The footsteps grew louder. The man was probably coming closer. There was some noise as the man kicked around a few of the cardboard boxes below. This was followed by a loud cacophony of clanging noises and glass hitting the floor.

The man had probably stumbled on a crate of drinks.

Bani could hear him swearing.

The footsteps paused for a few seconds, then receded and finally died away.

Bani waited in the loft another twenty minutes before jumping down and then gingerly venturing out of the storage room. His pursuers were nowhere to be seen.

He closed his eyes and heaved a sigh of relief. But his relief was short-lived as he realised that his pursuers would have probably stationed themselves at the front entrance and rear exit of Tantra.

The only way he could avoid falling into their hands would be to stay locked up inside all night, hoping that they would give up their watch posts after seeing the last of the staff troop out.

***

Three hours later. . .

Kolkata, Monday, 3 a.m.

The night dragged on slowly. Bani had slumped into one of the chairs in the storage room, his feet on another chair, hoping to get some shut-eye, but his agitated mind and hypersensitive reflexes did not allow him to sleep a wink.

The chefs, waiters and the partygoers were all long gone, the pitter-patter replaced by an eerie silence and all-encompassing darkness, the revelry of three hours before now a distant memory.

Bani got up, startled, as he heard a sound from the opposite corner of the storage room. He walked up the place and realised that there was nothing there. Was his imagination playing tricks on him?

He tried to distract himself from the tension of the moment by replaying the verses from the scroll in his mind.

He clearly recalled one of the verses:

He who is still in the face of the most intense motion

He who observes the flow of the universe with equanimity

For that person, the waters shall not pose a danger

He shall reach his destination without much effort.

Steve had probably found some clues to crack the verses, and now he was injured, maybe even dying.

Did a similar fate await him?

***

Kolkata, Monday, 6 a.m.

After the longest six hours of his life, Bani was quite on the edge as he heard the sounds of a key turning in the lock, accompanied by the sound of footsteps.

Through the slightly ajar door, he noticed that the cleaners had come in through the rear door to clean the club.

All clear so far.

Bani gingerly made his way towards the rear exit when nobody was looking, hoping that he was not walking straight into a trap.

***

Park Street was just about beginning to wake up. The shops and restaurants were still closed, but a few walkers were purposefully striding away. The cries of birds and panting of stray dogs provided a familiar backdrop to the morning.

Bani permitted himself a mild sigh of relief only when he found himself a few hundred metres away from The Park.

There was no way he could head home now. He would be walking straight into a trap. He would just have to head to Goa directly.

He remembered the message he had left for his friend Shrikant.

'Hey, Zico, Pele here. Drop everything and meet me in Goa. 8.30 p.m. tomorrow, Monday. In front of the band at Ephesus Hotel. And watch out for people following you. This is getting dangerous. Very dangerous.'

He hoped that Shrikant had heard the message. Bani knew that he would be walking straight into a storm in Goa, and he could use an ally.

Bani located a pay-phone and called his neighbourhood travel agent, Souvik Das.

'Souvik-da, I need a ticket to Goa. Urgently. Don't send the ticket to my home; keep it with you and I will pick it up.'

Souvik-da spat the paan he was chewing and spoke into the phone, 'What, Bani-da . . . Goa, and that too a one-way ticket? Have you found a *mishti* woman for yourself there?'

CHAPTER 8

Shree Motel, near Metro Inox, Mumbai, Monday, 8.15 a.m.

Ji-hoon Kim started his day with the zeal of a man on a mission. He showered, shaved, changed and checked out of his hotel room, all in the span of twenty minutes.

Damini surveyed him enviously from her spot in the alcove. After the overnight vigil, she, too, could do with a shower.

She was dressed like a college student, complete with faded jeans, a T-shirt and a rucksack. The cover of a college student allowed her to blend in with the scenery. St Xavier's college was not far from Metro Inox, and the area attracted its fair share of students anyway.

Even though she was twenty-nine, she could easily pass off as a student. At least as a Masters' student, she muttered to herself.

Her cover had not been blown despite the unsavoury incident with the idiots in the SUV. That was fortuitous; the Chief would have skinned her alive if she had lost their only lead.

Unfortunately, her relief was short-lived. Ji-hoon Kim settled the bill at the hotel reception, crossed the road and headed straight for the alcove where Damini was hiding.

***

Damini heaved a sigh of relief. Ji-hoon Kim had headed straight not for her but for Kyani, the iconic Irani bakery in the adjacent building.

Damini settled a few tables away from Ji-hoon and ordered Kyani's famous bun-maska with tea. She was ravenous. It was not every day that you got to eat at Kyani's while on an ACG surveillance mission.

She had radioed the ACG control room, manned by Mini and a very jealous Kunal, to inform them that she was hot on Ji-hoon Kim's trail. The backup van, manned by two ACG operatives, was on high alert and had moved position to the main road. Damini's motorcycle, her vehicle of choice for its ability to manoeuvre traffic snarls, was parked in the lot right next to Kyani's.

As Ji-hoon Kim sipped on his coffee and buried his head in a newspaper, the pendant that Damini was wearing, which had a small high-resolution camera on it, was beaming images that the ACG control room was dissecting in real time.

Damini's earphones were plugged into her smartphone as she sipped on her chai.

'Identification confirmed.' That was Mini on Damini's earphones.

Damini turned casually around so that the camera could capture the other patrons at Kyani's. There was the old man behind the counter, a couple of old ladies two tables away from Damini, a man with deep eyes at the corner table, a couple of college students sharing a samosa and a guy who looked like a bodybuilder eager to gain viewership for his biceps.

'No matches found for any customers yet.' Mini again.

Damini whispered. 'There are still a couple of customers I need to point the camera towards.'

Her antennae suddenly went up as Ji-hoon walked up to the counter and asked for the bill. As he was waiting, he reached for his mobile phone to check a message.

Damini acted quickly. She got up and walked towards the counter, pausing for just a split second at an angle where her pendant camera could capture an image, even if somewhat imperfect, of Ji-hoon Kim's smartphone screen.

'Wait, getting that,' Mini was saying.

'Fast,' Damini said.

Damini was just about reaching the counter as Ji-hoon, with lightning speed, bounded out of Kyani's onto the main road and was promptly picked up by a Honda Civic that had stopped right outside.

'Dammit, he's getting away,' Damini shouted as she slammed a hundred-rupee-note on the counter and ran to her bike, mentally noting the license plate number of the Civic. She barked on the microphone, 'Mini, I need speed. What did the damn message on Ji-hoon's phone say?'

It was Kunal on the line. 'Not good. We caught only one word, and that was "tail". Most likely somebody messaging him that he had a tail. Your cover is probably blown.'

***

'Damn,' Damini barked as she got onto her bike and accelerated toward the Civic, which was now far ahead on the road. 'There must've been somebody else watching. Backup van, where are you?'

'We are right behind you.' This was Najeeb, the ACG operative in the backup van.

'Ok, wait for my instructions,' Damini said, as she narrowed down the distance between her bike and the Civic. The crowded road gave her an advantage as her bike snaked through the traffic.

Damini braked as the Civic took a sharp turn into a lane on the left. This was a narrow lane just before the main road.

Damini's sixth sense, honed by hundreds of hours of fieldwork, told her that something was not right.

'He knows he has a tail, and yet he has avoided the main road and has just turned into a small lane with only one exit. He's going to try something.'

'What?' Kunal asked.

'I don't know yet, genius. I'm still figuring it out,' Damini barked.

'Damn you,' Kunal cursed.

Damini turned into the narrow lane behind the Civic.

'Najeeb, don't follow me. Get on to the main road and await my instructions,' Damini said.

'Ok,' was Najeeb's terse reply as he manoeuvred the backup van in the traffic.

Sure enough, the Civic screeched to a sudden halt in the lane outside what looked like the rear of a shop.

'Near Parsi Dairy,' Damini barked into the microphone, referring to Mumbai's iconic dairy that was located on the main road. 'He's getting in from the rear end of one of the shops next to it, and is probably going to come out of the other end on the main road. Najeeb, I need you in position there.'

Ji-hoon Kim had jumped off the Civic and had disappeared inside the shop near Parsi Dairy.

Damini jumped off the bike and followed, and was immediately accosted by a maze of provisions and supplies in the shop.

She ignored the baffled stares of the employees as she ran after Ji-hoon Kim right through to the shop's front entrance.

Her hunch was right. In a practiced series of steps, Ji-hoon bounded out of the front door of the shop and into the waiting open doors of a Ford Endeavour SUV.

'This guy's a goddamn pro,' she radioed to the control room as she ran out of the shop around forty seconds after Ji-hoon Kim had jumped into the Ford Endeavour.

'Of course, he is,' Kunal retorted. 'He just helped North Korea build a nuclear arsenal.'

Damini ignored Kunal's jibe as she spotted Najeeb's van. She hopped into the van just as Najeeb stepped on the accelerator pedal.

***

The road outside Parsi Dairy leads on to a flyover that is crowded even at the best of times. At 9 a.m. on a weekday morning, it resembled chaos itself. Blaring horns merged with the sounds of a million footsteps as Mumbai's morning madness played itself out on the streets.

As luck would have it, a big, ugly bus that was belching smoke through its rear was positioned right in front of Najeeb's van, blocking any possible view of the Ford Endeavour.

'Can we have satellite imaging on the Ford Endeavour, please?'

Damini asked.

Kunal replied. 'The Endeavour is at the far end of the flyover, and it looks like it is heading for Marine Drive.'

'Far end already?' Damini exclaimed, puzzled. 'That seems a little too quick, considering the traffic.'

Kunal snorted. 'So you've started to disbelieve satellite images in favour of your own imagination, huh?'

Again, Damini ignored the jibe.

Out of the corner of her eye, she sensed a motion which made her jump up.

Ji-hoon was jumping over the railing on the opposite side of the flyover.

***

Damini jumped out of the van and rushed towards the railing.

The Ford Endeavour was still clearly on the first half of the flyover. Why the hell was Kunal's satellite feed showing that it was at the far end?

Anyway, there was no time to contemplate on that.

Ji-hoon had jumped not on to the road below but on to an elevated pathway immediately adjoining the flyover. This pathway merged with the foot over-bridge directly above the Marine Lines local railway station.

'Dammit,' Damini swore to herself. She hadn't thought of this. And clearly Ji-hoon, or whoever was helping him, had.

The Mumbai commuter railway system is one of the busiest in the world. It carries four million passengers every day. And most of these commuters choose the morning hours to get to work.

Damini sighed as she scaled the railing. Ji-hoon Kim was already lost in the ocean of commuters who were using the foot over-bridge. She could barely make out his outline among the crowd.

She gave chase, for whatever it was worth, but Ji-hoon had already hopped on to a crowded local train that was leaving the station.

There was no way she could get to him now.

***

Damini was livid when she got back on radio communication. 'Can someone tell me what the hell just happened there?'

Kunal's tone was not apologetic. 'There were two Ford Endeavours on that bridge. We probably were looking at the wrong one.'

'Probably?' Damini smirked. 'Anyway, this discussion is freakin' pointless. Najeeb, can you try to tail the Ford Endeavour?'

'Am on it,' Najeeb answered. Kunal didn't answer.

Damini buried her head in her hands and slumped to the ground, right there at Marine Lines station in the midst of the Mumbai morning commuters' rush.

She had lost the trail. She was quite sure a search of Ji-hoon Kim's hotel room would yield nothing. The only hope was that Najeeb would be able to interrupt the Ford Endeavour.

***

Damini dialled the Chief's number. She had to own up and bite the bullet.

As the Chief came on line, Damini said, 'I will find him again, sir, that's a promise.'

In characteristic style, the Chief did not lose his cool or let out expletives, but his words were so caustic that she wished he would chastise her outright instead.

'I hope you can make it to your yoga class now.'

Damini had half a mind to rat on Kunal, but the Chief hated it when field agents did not take the onus of a botch-up squarely on themselves. She gritted her teeth and muttered, 'Sorry, sir.'

The Chief had already hung up.

***

Those fifteen minutes at Marine Lines station were the longest in Damini's professional life.

The Ford Endeavour had been abandoned before Najeeb could reach it. The Endeavour, as well as the Honda Civic, whose number Damini had noted outside Kyani, were hired vehicles; thus, checking out their ownership documents would yield nothing.

The ACG could make enquiries about the persons who had hired the vehicles, but Damini was certain that they would have been decoys. It didn't look like the bunch she was dealing with would leave those kinds of obvious clues.

A Honda Civic and a Ford Endeavour. Minutely coordinated to be exactly at certain places at certain times. It was unlikely that Ji-hoon Kim had figured out the intricacies of dodging pursuers through the narrow bylanes of Mumbai all by himself.

She was dealing with some real pros here. And clearly, they had some pretty strong local help.

Then there was the question of how they realised that Ji-hoon

Kim had a tail. And why the control room had given her wrong input about the satellite feed on the Endeavour.

Could it be that someone within ACG had wanted her to fail? Or worse still, was that someone in cahoots with Ji-hoon Kim's bunch?

There was only one way she could find out.

She called Mini privately on her hand phone number.

'What's up?' Mini asked.

Damini spoke fast. 'Mini, I need you to scan every single feed which may give some clue as to what the North Korean guys are up to. Satellite images, surveillance videos, Interpol alerts, intelligence agency intercepts, web chatter, everything. If a North Korean agent as much as opens his mouth or types an email, I want to know about it.'

'Got it, Damini,' Mini said.

'And, Mini…'

'Yes?'

'I need you to make sure Kunal doesn't get wind of any of this.'

CHAPTER 9

Two hours later. . .

Charni Road, Mumbai, Monday, 11 a.m.

Damini, chastened by the morning's debacle, had been busy. She was at one of the ACG's innocuous city offices in a commercial building.

Mini had been feeding Damini details on Ji-hoon Kim as well as on various other North Korean agents—their travel itineraries, bank accounts, families, mistresses, pet peeves, everything. There were also exhaustive transcripts of communications between North Korean agents—tapped phone conversations, decrypted chats, hacked email messages and so on.

Damini paused when she came to the bit about a website that seemed to have been frequented by two North Korean operatives. The website was seemingly innocuous, a support forum for Hepatitis patients. Clearly the North Korean operatives were using the website to exchange messages.

Damini's eyes went to a medical test result—the Serum Glutamic Pyruvic Transaminase, or SGPT— quoted at the beginning of each of the messages from the operatives. Was it a code?

Damini called Mini. 'I need our decryption expert to work on the numbers and messages from the website.'

***

Mini came back with the decoded messages within fifteen minutes. 'The SGPT numbers have used a variant of a prime number code that translates to "Demo". That means anything to you?'

'No,' Damini said. 'But carry on.'

'The latest message reads: "Demo on track for this week."'

Damini whistled. The 'Demo' sounded like some sort of an unsavoury event.

Damini said to Mini: 'I need you to scan all chatter on the web for anything on an event called the Demo, even if the reference sounds innocuous, and rank it in order of suspicion. And once again, this is for your and my ears only.'

'Understood, Damini,' Mini said. She didn't mind keeping stuff from Kunal; she never liked him much anyway.

***

Mini sent Damini a massive file which listed out over twenty thousand references to 'Demo'.

The references were sorted using various parameters, including a sophisticated algorithm for scoring them based on their importance, but there was still no meaningful way to make any sense out of them.

'Let's limit the scans to items posted in the last twenty-four hours, and let's use finer scoring options.'

'I'm on it, Damini,' Mini said over the phone.

Five minutes later, Damini was looking at a substantially truncated list. Top of the list was a message from a person called Jeff on a social networking site that was an underground meeting place for hippies who were planning out the next rave party in Goa.

The message had Jeff boasting about how he rescued a 'bloke' who seemed to have suffered extensive injuries and was in a state of delirium. The 'bloke' apparently kept repeating the words 'Demo' and 'this week'.

The message seemed to have been posted from a cybercafé, but did not contain any details for Jeff. The social networking site itself used multiple layers of security protocols, and masqueraded as an innocuous tourism website.

Damini gave out a slight exclamation as she read the second line of the message. Jeff had signed off saying that he would be 'hitting the scene at Lotus Café' on Monday night.

She took a quick decision and called Kunal at the control room. 'I'm headed to Goa. Will keep you posted.'

'Why the hell are you heading to Goa?'

Damini sounded casual. 'Oh, just checking out some leads. Nothing serious.'

Kunal cursed under his breath. Here he was, stuck in the control room, while his nemesis, Damini, was out in the field, and heading to Goa, of all places.

PART II: DEMONS FROM THE PAST

SAMEER RAJAN

CHAPTER 10

Colaba, Mumbai, Sunday, 10.30 p.m.

The young woman seated at the corner table at Café Royal threw up her hands. 'Relationships scare you,' she said bluntly.

She was around 5'4", wearing an ethnic top and a pair of jeans that outlined her figure, her hair falling lightly on her shoulders. But it was her eyes that stood out. Sparkly and vivacious, they could light up a room the moment she entered. At the same time, they could also convey kindness and sensitivity.

The young man opposite her was the object of her ire, yet he could not help but look fondly at her eyes. For the umpteenth time. They were the first thing he had noticed about her, on a rainy Sunday ten months ago.

The young woman got up from her chair, jolting Sam Rajan back to reality.

'Let me know by tonight. One way or the other,' she said, walking away. 'I need to tell the channel tomorrow.'

***

Colaba, Mumbai, Sunday, 10.45 p.m.

Sam got into the cab with a sigh. The cab seemed to mirror his mood, trudging along reluctantly through the pouring rain.

The rain reminded Sam of the day he had first met Ananya ten months ago.

The sequence of events seemed almost dreamlike in his memory. His realising over a Friday night-out at the Hawaiian Shack bar in Bandra that twenty-eight was not too late an age to reclaim his lost love for the hills. His enrolling for a Sunday trek to the Western Ghats off Mumbai. Then waking up late that Sunday and rushing against time to catch the trekking bus.

Sam couldn't suppress a chuckle. His morning wake-up time had been an abiding source of tension between his dad and him. Colonel Rajan was used to springing out of bed at 4 a.m. and going for his morning run, followed by a game of squash, breakfast at the club, a long chat with his Army buddies and half-an-hour of poring over the morning newspapers. He could never come to terms with the fact that half his day was over by the time his son even got out of bed.

Sam had summoned up all his stamina from his trekking days as he had sprinted to catch the bus. The bus had begun accelerating, but Sam was able to muster up a last-minute burst of energy, notwithstanding the recently added kilos to his otherwise athletic 5'9" frame. When he had finally ended up catching the trekking bus, he had plonked himself onto the first available seat.

That was when he had seen her sitting next to him.

'Hi,' she had smiled. 'Warming up for the trek, huh?'

'Sameer Rajan,' was all that he could manage in return. Involuntarily, he had found himself drawn to those eyes. And the lightly dimpled smile that went all the way up to her eyes.

That was how it had all begun.

A smile formed around Sam's lips as he remembered those days.

Light. Exuberant. Carefree. Like the raindrops on the cab window.

Then her parting line from fifteen minutes ago came to his mind, and the smile vanished.

***

'Relationships scare you.' Sam found the words reverberating in his head.

He couldn't help but feel a tinge of regret.

Their first date, too, had been at Café Royal, over chocolate brownies and ice cream.

Sam remembered the evening vividly. She had looked beautiful in a one-piece black dress. A few strands of hair were falling lightly over her face. Sam had noticed her graceful walk. And her figure.

The chocolate syrup had formed a slight outline around the edges of her lips. She seemed almost like a kid who had helped herself to some chocolate on the sly. And she was oblivious to it as she talked earnestly.

He also remembered their first kiss that night. Hesitating at first, then firmer, then more passionate, until all that remained in the universe was just the two of them, frozen in time.

Sam remembered thinking then that he would not let this relationship go the way of his other, transient dalliances.

And yet here he was, on the verge of letting it all go.

***

Mumbai, Sunday, 11.30 p.m.

Back at his apartment, Sam parked himself on the couch and began preparing for a crucial appraisal meeting with his boss, Ayush.

He desperately needed to concentrate. He was, to put it mildly, in deep shit at work.

The investment banking division at Bancroft Cohen was headed by Ayush Sharma, who was better known by the nickname 'Arsehole Ayush'. The division had severely underperformed under Ayush's watch, and he was looking for scapegoats. The entire team was to have their performance appraisal meetings on Monday morning. The rumour was that many of the staff might be let go.

Sam could not afford to get fired.

He had spoken to the Colonel exactly three times in the last three years. The first time was to inform him about shutting down his education venture. That conversation, from the Colonel's end, had consisted of snorts and an 'I told you so' expression, topped up with an order to 'pull up your socks' and register for an MBA. Sam had no money with which to finance his MBA. So, the second conversation, mortifyingly, was about asking the Colonel for funds. In the third conversation, Sam had informed him that he had got a job at Bancroft Cohen, and that he would pay back the money soon.

Sam did not want the fourth conversation to be about getting fired.

***

Unable to concentrate, Sam found himself picking up the phone and calling Ananya. He disconnected after a few rings.

Why wasn't she picking up the phone? Had she given up on him? Had something happened to her?

Sam closed his eyes and composed himself, trying to get a grip on his emotions.

He had been a bundle of nerves on their first date as well. But as the evening progressed, they had found themselves talking excitedly and yet cozily, almost like lovers meeting after a long hiatus.

Over helpings of ice cream, she had told him that she loved poetry, theatre, Linkin Park, Rahman's music and Anurag Kashyap's films.

He had talked about how city life made him yearn for the serenity of the hills, about how he had spent six months backpacking in the Himalayas after graduation, and how he had gotten the inspiration to start an online education venture after passing by a group of children at a hillside village.

She had told him that she believed in not planning her life, about how she had worked for an NGO, and had then taken up her job at Discovery Channel almost on a whim.

He had told her that he hated office politics and often thought of quitting his investment banking job and doing something more meaningful.

She had asked, 'So what's stopping you from taking the plunge?'

That question had hit him like a bolt of lightning.

Sam bit his lip as the cab swerved on to another lane. Even ten months later, he could feel the same discomfiture.

Sam had sat frozen as a kaleidoscope of emotions had hit him.

The constant shadow of the Colonel's expectations, the pressure to make conventional choices, the grand start to his online education venture, the naïve dreams and aspirations. . . Then the slow route to failure: first the denial, then the seeping realisation that all that the Colonel had dimly prognosticated had indeed come true. And then his finally throwing in the towel and heading for his MBA. And now, all he was left with was the anger—the inescapable anger—and a feeling of failure.

Too much water had flown under the bridge. It was best to let bygones be bygones.

'Huh, did I say something wrong?' Ananya had asked, a bit concerned. She had always had an uncanny knack of sensing his feelings better than he did himself.

He had just shaken his head and looked away.

The cab lurched as the impatient cabbie tried to overtake a bus, bringing Sam back to the present.

Here he was, ten months later, at the cusp of losing a relationship.

Maybe this time he ought to acknowledge his feelings and not look away?

***

Mumbai, Sunday, 11.45 p.m.

Sam called Ananya again. This time she picked up.

'Hi,' she said, somewhat tersely. Clearly the argument was still on her mind.

Sameer could hear the rhythmic noise of a local train passing by in the background, and it seemed to give him a headache. 'Not reached the hostel yet?'

Ananya stayed at the hostel at the National Institute of Social Sciences, NISS. Ananya's employer, Discovery Channel, was producing a documentary series on the Himalayas in collaboration with NISS.

'Nope. Professor Bavdekar was in South Mumbai, so I met up with him to discuss a presentation to the channel tomorrow. We are on our way to NISS now.' She was starting to sound less clipped.

Professor Bavdekar was an expert on Himalayan plant and animal life. He was the professor from NISS that Discovery Channel was collaborating with.

'Oh ok,' Sam said. 'Maybe we should talk later then.'

'No, we can talk now,' she said, sounding warmer, much to Sam's relief. 'The Prof. has stepped out to use the ATM.'

Sam stuttered, but Ananya interrupted him before he could say anything. 'Oops, my battery is running low.'

'Uhh . . . reach the hostel and call me then.'

There was no response. Sameer looked at his handset. It was working fine.

Ananya's battery had probably died out.

***

Mumbai, Sunday, 11.50 p.m.

The phone conversation with Sam left Ananya in deep thought.

The initial few months with Sam had been breezy. Friday night dates at cozy cafes, Saturday street food lunches, Sunday morning treks, and snuggling up in the afternoon over popcorn and Netflix. He had been witty, sensitive and a good conversationalist, not to mention a good kisser.

And then, as things had begun to get more serious and friends began to ask about taking things to the 'next level', she had begun to notice the changes in him. Turning up late for dates, steering clear of intimate conversations, losing himself in work over weekends, and shying away from anything that resembled commitment.

They had gotten close enough for her to understand where this was coming from, so she had laid off. Besides, she was a believer in letting things take their own course. Life was much more beautiful that way.

But now she had a career and relocation decision to make.

The Discovery Channel documentary series on the Himalayas was almost complete. The channel had asked her whether she would move to Brazil for a new documentary on the Amazon.

This meant that Sam and she could no longer be on the fence. She had to know whether their relationship was headed anywhere.

***

Ananya lost herself in rumination for a few moments, and then suddenly sat up with a start as the realisation of where she was hit her.

She looked out of the car window. What the hell was taking Prof. Bavdekar so long?

Probably fumbling around the ATM, she thought. But a sixth sense told her to check.

With mild trepidation, she proceeded to open the door and get out of the vehicle.

She walked towards the ATM. The security guard was asleep in his chair, and Prof. Bavdekar was nowhere to be seen.

There was a small, dark, somewhat dirty lane adjoining the building which housed the ATM. She looked around, hesitated and took a few tentative steps towards the lane.

She heard what she thought was a muffled thud, and then the sound of hurried footsteps. She hesitated, taking a step back.

That was when she heard the sound of footsteps again, this time unmistakable. Then she felt a light blow on the head and her world went dark.

CHAPTER 11

Mumbai, Sunday night/Monday morning, 12.30 a.m.

The vampire took out a Kalashnikov rifle and started shooting just as a bunch of bloodsucking leeches came out of underground caves and started spouting venom from their sticky mouths.

Sameer switched off the TV. His need for escapist entertainment had indeed touched new lows.

He picked up his phone and dialled Ananya's number. It was off.

Ananya ought to have reached by now. Unless she had not yet gotten around to charging her phone.

***

Mumbai, Sunday night/Monday morning, 12.45 a.m.

Sam called Ananya's number again. It was still off.

Something was not right. Ananya should have reached a good half hour ago.

He looked at the living room clock. Traffic snarls did not have a habit of happening at 12.45 a.m.

Sam called the NISS hostel and spoke to Namrata, Ananya's roommate. She was pretty definitive that Ananya had not entered the hostel.

Sam put on his shoes. They probably had a car breakdown on the way. Or maybe an accident?

***

Mumbai, Sunday night/Monday morning, 12.50 a.m.

The cab driver looked sullenly at Sam as he swiftly eased himself into the rear seat.

Sam decided to trace the path that Bavdekar and Ananya were likely to have taken—from Colaba to the NISS hostel in Deonar—and keep a watch out for bank ATMs where Bavdekar might have stopped to withdraw cash. Thankfully, the rains had eased off otherwise the task would have been more tedious.

As the cab driver lazily switched on the ignition, Sam prodded him to drive fast.

***

Mumbai, Sunday night/Monday morning, 1.20 a.m.

After having checked out the seventh ATM, Sam threw up his hands in despair.

He was looking for a needle in a haystack.

The cabbie was getting impatient. ‘Sahib, I need to take the car back to the stand. I am running late,’ he said in Hindi.

Sam tried tempting him with extra money, but the cabbie did not relent.

‘Ok, fine,’ Sam threw up his hands. ‘Just drop me to one last ATM and I will let you go.’

***

Certain memories have a way of hiding themselves below the surface of consciousness, often manifesting just in the nick of time.

Somewhere during his ATM-hopping spree, Sam remembered the noise in the background when he had last talked to Ananya.

The sound of the ubiquitous Mumbai local train.

So he needed to look for ATMs only in places that were close to train tracks.

Within three minutes, Sam thought he might have found what he was looking for.

A WIC Bank ATM. Western India Co-operative Bank. Along D'Mello Road.

Sam got off near the ATM and paid off the cabbie, who had been muttering a steady stream of curses.

***

Sam took a look around.

By day, this was a pretty rough neighbourhood, dotted with old warehouses, steel melting shops, scrap sellers and trucking agents' offices. At this hour of the night, there was not a soul around, not even a security guard at the ATM.

He walked around to the nearby lane. It was dirty, deserted and dark, the sort of place you would not want to visit in the night.

That was when he saw the body on the pavement.

***

For a few seconds, Sam just stood still, shocked and disoriented, even as his mind was suddenly flooded with memories going back many years.

Memories of loss, of a progressively increasing distance from the Colonel, the warmth of love replaced first by the insufferable burden of expectations, and then by coldness and distance. Memories that he had tried to avoid by drowning himself in the din of his job, the allure of short, unfulfilling relationships and the lights of the city.

That night at D'Mello Road, Sam banished the memories once again, and collected himself, bending down to look.

He knelt closer. It was a man's body.

Not a woman. Sameer heaved a sigh of relief, and immediately felt guilty for it.

The man was wearing a security guard's uniform. Probably the guard at the ATM.

But his momentary relief had given way to a sinking feeling in the stomach.

Now there was no question of going with the theory that they had had a car breakdown. Or that Ananya simply didn't get to charge her phone.

Something had clearly happened here. Something bad.

***

Where was she? What had happened to her? What if she was no longer alive?

For a few seconds, Sam was gripped by a seemingly bottomless fear. The sweet scent of Ananya's perfume, the moistness of her lips, her dimpled smile and simply her presence, all seemed to come back to him. And then, in one swift swoop, it all seemed to be on the verge of slipping away from him. Forever.

At that instant, Sam knew that this was somebody he loved more than life itself. And that he had been really, really stupid to have shied away from his feelings all this while.

Somewhere in that tense moment, Sam found himself starting to pick up the pieces. He summoned up all the will that he could muster from everything that he loved, every memory that gave him strength, and made a resolution.

He would never shy away from his feelings again.

He loved her. Deeply. And he would find her. Even if he had to go to the ends of the earth for it.

***

The sub-inspector in the police jeep patrolling D'Mello Road was in a bad mood.

It was his wife's birthday, and he was supposed to have taken her to the movies. But the police had received a warning about impending mafia movement near the docks, relating to a smuggled drugs consignment, and his boss, the inspector, had asked him to stay back late.

As the sub-inspector's jeep traversed the empty roads, he spotted a young man on the opposite side of the road, loitering suspiciously in the by-lane near the Western India Co-operative Bank ATM, bending down and seemingly looking at something from different angles.

***

Sam panicked as he saw the police jeep approaching.

Should he explain things to the police? But he was the only one present on the deserted road right at the scene of a murder. Fat chance he had of convincing them.

Besides, he would lose valuable hours, maybe even days, trying to establish his innocence. He could not afford that.

Sam made his decision in less than a second. He had to flee.

The police jeep was approaching fast. It would be pointless running along the main road.

Sam started running into the by-lane, away from the main road. The late nights notwithstanding, he was still reasonably fit and retained a trekker's stamina.

He hoped that the lane would not finish at a dead end.

He was around fifty metres ahead when he heard the police jeep screeching as it turned into the by-lane.

As Sam looked ahead, he realised that his worst fears had come true. The by-lane abruptly finished into a wall opposite. There was no opening or gate in the wall.

He was at a dead end. There was nowhere to run.

***

Sam's survival instincts took over, his mind racing wildly.

Should he try to barge into one of the rooms in the old building adjacent the wall and take hostages? Even at that chaotic instant, it seemed like a ridiculous idea. Besides, the building seemed deserted. Probably not a residential building.

As he looked up at the floors in the building adjoining the wall, an idea struck him.

He hoped that his trekker's instincts were still reliable. Otherwise it would be curtains for him.

***

In a split-second maneouvre, Sam ran up to the building, jumped up and grabbed hold of a ledge extending from the first floor. He hoisted himself up, and then moved up further to a ledge extending from the second floor.

The second floor ledge was at the same level as the wall, and pretty close to it. In one swift move, he jumped up to the wall, grabbing on for dear life as his hands got badly scratched and precariously started sliding down from the top of the wall.

The police car meanwhile had reached the end of the lane, making another screeching sound as it abruptly braked to a halt. It was now only a few metres away from him, albeit at a lower level.

His heart almost pounding out of his chest, Sam hoisted himself up the wall and jumped on to the other side, just as a policeman got off the jeep and fired a shot from a revolver.

***

Sam fell heavily on to the other side of the wall. A mountain of garbage cushioned his fall, averting a situation where he might have ended up with at least a few broken bones.

Sam was in shock, but not from the fall. He never thought he would ever be shot at by a revolver. He had to touch himself all over to believe that the bullet had indeed missed him.

But there was no time to waste. The policemen might not have his trekking skills, but it would not take them long to figure out a way to scale the wall. Besides, the police jeep might be trying to reach him from the front end. And the policemen would almost certainly have called for backup.

Sam took a look around. He was in a defunct mill, a common feature in this part of Mumbai.

To his surprise, there was a fair bit of activity in the mill building opposite. Sam dusted himself as he got up from the garbage heap and ran towards the place.

It was a bar-cum-discotheque set in the mill building, again a common feature in this part of Mumbai.

As Sam looked at the high-end vehicles in the parking lot and saw the valet leave his post to park a car, an idea struck him.

It was a crazy idea, but then he was a desperate man.

***

Sameer had read that missing persons cases were like heart attack patients.

After a heart attack, the first few minutes were the most crucial.

Ananya had gone missing, and the best time to trace her was in the first couple of hours. After that, the trail would most likely go cold.

Sameer could not spend these hours stuck in a police station, trying to prove his innocence.

Desperate times call for desperate measures. He had to do the unthinkable.

***

Sam walked up to the valet post, snatched a car key from the rack, and pressed the unlock button.

One of the cars in the parking lot blinked.

As luck would have it, it was a BMW 7 Series.

Sam hesitated. A big car would attract too much attention. But then he could do with a car that could take high speeds. And had the ability to accelerate from zero to a hundred kilometres per hour in the shortest possible time.

Sam had already turned on the ignition by the time the valet got back to his post and realised what had just happened.

***

As the BMW raced at over a hundred kilometres an hour on the narrow Mumbai roads, Sam drove to the first destination that came to his mind.

It would have to be NISS. The WIC Bank ATM was out of bounds for him now. The only place where he could even remotely hope to find any clues would be the NISS campus, where Ananya stayed and Bavdekar worked.

The odds of finding any clues did not seem high. The murder of the ATM security guard suggested that it was probably a spur-of-the-moment crime. But he did not have a choice.

Behind him, he could hear what seemed like the sounds of multiple police sirens.

Sam wondered whether his picture would have been caught in the CCTV feed either at the ATM or the bar at the mill. If yes, then he might be a marked man much sooner than he would like. He switched off his mobile phone, just in case it might be tracked.

The BMW's tires screeched as Sam swerved into a lane yet again, desperately attempting to zigzag among a maze of roads to try and lose his pursuers.

He decided to lose the BMW in one of the lanes and get a cab instead. That might buy him some time as the police might lose the trail.

***

Mumbai, Monday, 2.10 a.m.

The bumpy, clumsy ride in the cab was in sharp contrast to the ride in the BMW. On Sam's left, the green campus of the National Institute of Social Sciences came into view.

Sam shivered a little as memories of the man's body on the pavement near the ATM, bloodied and with eyes staring vacantly into space, clouded his mind. Had Ananya met the same fate?

***

Mumbai, Monday, 2.35 a.m.

Sam was inside Ananya's room at the NISS campus, speaking to Namrata, Ananya's roommate.

The room was a typical twin-sharing hostel room. They were sitting in Namrata's half of the room.

Sam struggled to steady himself as he spoke to Namrata. 'What kind of research was Prof. Bavdekar into?'

'Well, he is an expert on Himalayan flora and fauna.'

'What does that mean?'

'His claim to fame is a series of books that he wrote eighteen years ago, comprehensively detailing the plant and animal life of the Himalayas,' Namrata said. 'The books are still held up by the International Council on Climate Change as definitive guides on chronicling the biodiversity of any region.'

'Anything that could have gotten him into trouble?' Sam asked.

Namrata shook her head.

Sam walked across to Ananya's half of the room to check for clues.

He staggered back momentarily as he detected a faint whiff of a familiar scent, and a lump formed in his throat as he realised it was from a bottle of perfume stacked in a corner of her desk.

Elizabeth Arden 5th Avenue.

He had asked Ananya what perfume she was wearing during their first date at Café Royal. That was when she had mentioned that *5th Avenue* was her favourite perfume.

He liked the scent of the perfume. Especially on her. And he would make it a point to tell her that when he met her again.

If he met her again.

***

A worried Namrata took Sam to Professor Bavdekar's office.

'*Professor Shrikant Bavdekar, PhD, Padma Shri*', the nameplate proudly proclaimed.

To their surprise, the room was not locked.

As he turned the knob and entered the room, a chill went through Sam's spine.

The room was in complete disarray. Professor Bavdekar's room had been combed. In a hurry.

***

A search of the room yielded no clues. It resembled an earthquake zone, but it was not clear what the intruder had been looking for.

Sam shook his head as he walked across to the telephone. 'Let's see what we have here,' he said to Namrata as he pressed the redial button.

The last dialled number was a US number starting with 1-510. Probably California, Sam thought as he made a mental note of it.

The phone went through to the voicemail of a person called Professor Hudson. The voicemail recording did not specify any further details.

Namrata said, 'He just got back last week from a trip to the US. Maybe he met Hudson there.'

'Maybe you could check out what Professor Hudson is into,' Sam asked Namrata.

They were just about to leave when Sam noticed a small green light in the corner of the phone handset. Probably an indicator that there was a voicemail message.

Sam pressed the voicemail button on the phone. It asked for a password.

Sam knew that few people bothered to change their voicemail passwords. In a world with too many passwords, it was an unnecessary burden to remember yet another password for voicemails that nobody else was likely to be interested in.

Sam hesitated, then keyed in '1234' on a hunch.

Lo and behold, it worked!

The voicemail message was left at 11.35 p.m., just over two-and-a-half hours ago.

The man who had left the voicemail had a distinctive baritone voice. He could have given Amitabh Bachchan a run for his money.

The message was long and at the same time cryptic. *'Hey, Zico, Pele here. Drop everything and meet me in Goa. 8.30 p.m. tomorrow, Monday. In front of the band at Ephesus Hotel. And watch out for people following you. This is getting dangerous. Very dangerous.'*

CHAPTER 12

Deonar, Mumbai, Monday, 2.45 a.m.

Sam and Namrata stared at each other, incredulous.

'Zico, Pele. Unless the yesteryears' Brazilian soccer team is holidaying in India, these sound like bloody code words,' Sam said. 'What kind of kinky stuff was the Prof. into?'

A bar of chocolate was lying in one of the drawers in the shelf adjoining the main table.

Sam had a sweet tooth, and he liked to nibble on chocolate when stressed. There were only two cubes of it, and Sam took one out.

No sooner had he put it in his mouth than his face contorted into a weird expression. 'Eww, what is this?' he exclaimed.

He took it out of his mouth, taking a disgusted look at it, when suddenly his eyes widened.

The contraption he held in his hand was not chocolate.

It was a USB drive, shaped like a chocolate cube.

That's why the thugs had missed it when they had combed through Bavdekar's room.

***

The Mansion, Monday, 3 a.m.

A micro-transmitter installed under the table in Prof. Bavdekar's room relayed the entire conversation between Sam and Namrata to an ornately decorated room many hundred miles away, in a building known to its occupants as the Mansion.

Bruce made a phone call to a person called Deedar Singh.

Deedar Singh had missed both the voicemail and the USB drive while combing Professor Bavdekar's room. Bruce quivered slightly. The Doc would not be happy with that goof-up. He was on a thin leash now.

***

Sam's attention involuntarily went to a notepad in one of the drawers.

Bavdekar had scribbled 'KaalKoot' in it, with a double underline. A vivid set of images came to Sam's mind from the course on Indian mythology that he had taken while in college.

KaalKoot. The deadliest poison in the universe, with the power to annihilate all of creation.

The ancient Indian texts, the Puranas, talk of a metaphorical churning of the cosmic ocean, undertaken by the deities—the devas—and the demons—the asuras. The goal of this *Samudra Manthan* was to obtain amrit, the nectar of immortality.

Sam clearly remembered the story of the Samudra Manthan. The churning released a number of things from the cosmic ocean, the most terrifying of which was the supremely lethal poison known as KaalKoot or *Halahala*, which was so powerful that it could destroy all of creation. As the devas and asuras started to be felled by the venom, they rushed to Lord Shiva, who redeemed the universe by swallowing the poison himself. In the process, his throat turned blue, earning him the name *Neelkanth,* the Blue-throated One.

Bavdekar had gone on to scribble in the notepad: '*Can we stop KaalKoot?*'

Sam stared at the notepad, wide-eyed.

The abode of Lord Shiva, who had swallowed the KaalKoot, was believed to be in Mount Kailash, deep in the Trans-Himalayas.

Bavdekar was an expert on plant and animal life in the Himalayas.

Was there a connection? Or was Sam's mind simply playing tricks on him?

KaalKoot. The primordial plague, with the power to destroy the universe.

What sort of stuff was Professor Bavdekar into? And how the hell was Ananya linked to all this?

***

Sam's head was whirring. There were too many smoking guns here. Ought he to turn himself in and let the police take over? Should he hang around NISS and figure out what Professor Bavdekar was really up to? Or maybe go to Goa following the crazy voicemail?

He had no idea how to choose between the options. A wrong call on this would mean curtains for Ananya.

The voice message seemed the wackiest of the lot, but it was also the most frantic.

Sam remembered something the Colonel used to tell him as a child, about trusting his instinct.

Namrata and Sameer looked at each other. Both their lips formed the same word.

'Goa.'

PART III:
THE PRIMORDIAL PLAGUE
GOA

CHAPTER 13

Mumbai, Monday, 3.10 a.m.

Namrata and Sam were in Professor Bavdekar's room at NISS.

'We should be informing the police,' Namrata said.

'Err . . . I'm not really on very good terms with the police right now,' Sam stuttered. 'I'll take the USB drive and head to Goa. You file a missing persons' report with the police, inform Ananya's parents and trace out Professor Hudson.'

Sam's heart skipped a beat as he said this. He had met Ananya's mother when she was visiting Mumbai recently. Ananya had considered introducing him as her boyfriend, but he, ever the commitment-phobe, had insisted on being called a 'good friend'.

Sam could not help feeling a pang of guilt. He *had* let things drift with Ananya.

If only he could get a chance to make it all up to her.

He was jolted back to reality by Namrata's voice. 'There's a vehicle rental place right opposite our campus. If you drive fast, you can get to Goa within twelve hours.'

***

Deedar Singh hung up the listening device. He was smarting under the weight of the fact that a bumbling amateur could locate a USB drive for which he had turned a room upside down.

One look at Deedar Singh, and you would know that he was one of those that you did not mess with. It was not his six-and-a-half-foot height, or his wrestlers' build, or the heavy chain that loosely hung around his neck. It was not even his menacing eyes, which he mostly kept covered with dark shades.

It was something far more intangible. Just as certain people exude kindness and envelop their surroundings in an aura of warmth, there are some who have a much darker effect. Such are the people through whom the Devil chooses to do his work.

Deedar Singh had been handpicked by the Devil himself; by the man they called the Doc.

***

Deedar Singh knew that Sam was going to hire a vehicle from the rental place directly opposite the campus. It would be child's play for Deedar Singh to get the car details from the rental agency.

He smirked. He felt almost ashamed trying to tackle a bunch of amateurs; he was used to tougher customers.

Deedar was in Tardeo, around 19 kilometres away from the NISS campus. But his retrofitted Hummer could move fast. If Sam was a slow mover, he might even catch him as he was in the process of renting the vehicle.

Deedar Singh's brown leather jacket glistened in the moonlight as he turned the air-conditioner on to full blast and stepped on the gas pedal, taking the Hummer to 120 kmph.

The speed or the choice of vehicle might not mean much to a person used to the roads and speeds of the West, but in Mumbai, they both made a stark statement. The narrow, pot-holed roads of Mumbai were used to much slower traffic and much smaller vehicles. The objective was to cram everything into as small a space as possible, to economise, to save.

But that was not Deedar Singh's objective. He had clear instructions. And he was prepared, right up to the jerrycan of kerosene needed to dispose of the body.

The Hummer cast an eerie shadow in the moonlight as it thundered towards Deonar, shrouding the road in a dark cloud as it passed by.

***

Mumbai, Monday, 3.15 a.m.

Sameer Rajan was not a slow mover.

Within five minutes, Sameer had swiped his credit card at the car rental outlet and was in a grey Toyota Innova. He mouthed a silent prayer as he turned the key in the ignition.

Thankfully, the rains seemed to have taken a long breather. He could get to Goa within twelve hours if he really stepped on the gas and if he was not held back by traffic on the highway.

***

The Innova had a headstart over the Hummer. But without much traffic at that hour, and at the speed the Hummer was capable of, the gap was narrowing by the second.

Deedar Singh first saw the Innova from a distance, near the toll gate at Panvel that led on to the Mumbai-Goa highway.

He reached out underneath the passenger seat and took out a .32 revolver. That would suffice for the job.

***

Even in the best of days, the Mumbai-Goa highway was a death trap, with bored, often inebriated, truck drivers occupying both lanes. In the late hours of the night and early hours of the morning, though, it was infinitely worse. A deadly cocktail of sleep-deprived drivers and missing vehicle headlights turned the road into a veritable dragon, ready and waiting to snuff the life out of unsuspecting wayfarers.

The young man did have some spunk, Deedar thought. Driving an Innova at 140 kmph on the two-lane highway in the middle of the night was not easy, and he seemed to have the vehicle well in control.

None of that was relevant, though. At best, it would buy the young man a few extra minutes in the land of the living.

The road was largely deserted, except for some wearied trucks plying the route. That would work to his advantage, though he was confident he could have accomplished the task even in broad daylight.

The Hummer was now about sixty feet behind the Innova, and Deedar kept a watch for a nice tree-lined stretch that would suit his need. It was time to test the Innova's collision capabilities.

To his surprise, the Innova slowed as it swerved left towards an eatery off the road.

Deedar Singh did not have much use for luck in his calculations, but he did not particularly mind when it gave him a good break.

CHAPTER 14

Eatery near Karnala, off Mumbai on the Mumbai-Goa highway, Monday, 4.05 a.m.

Sam was feeling groggy. He had been driving at breakneck speed, but needed to take a break and brace himself for the long drive ahead.

He took a look at the menu and ordered a vegetable sandwich and a cup of strong filter coffee.

Four tables away, an unusually tall man wearing dark shades and having a wrestlers' build sat down and looked at the menu.

The eatery was crowded even at this hour of the night. Not that Deedar was unused to using the gun in crowded places, but he was smart enough to not do that when there could be other opportunities. Like when the boy went to use the washroom.

***

'Instincts are often more powerful than logic,' the Colonel used to tell Sam, during the many sermonising sessions that he had been subjected to since childhood. 'They come to your aid first during a crisis.'

As he sipped on his coffee, Sam found himself feeling progressively queasy, almost as if there were some obvious storm clouds that he was overlooking.

He turned to look around, and immediately knew what could have bothered his subconscious mind. There was a rather unusual guy sitting a few tables away, the kind of guy you did not encounter often.

Maybe it was just the fact that he was very tall and well-built, or maybe the fact that he looked slightly menacing. Either way, Sam told himself to calm down. He could not have his mind going on overdrive merely at the sight of a tall guy.

Sam stretched himself, trying to relax, and leaned in his chair, his head tilted back, involuntarily looking out upside down at the parking lot behind him.

That was when he caught sight of the massive tires of the Hummer. Sam abruptly straightened himself. For some reason, this vehicle sent alarm bells ringing in his head.

As he took another sip of his coffee, an image suddenly came into his mind—that of the Hummer being constantly behind him for about five minutes before he had turned into the eatery.

Was he being followed, or was it all a coincidence? He remembered the voicemail message from 'Pele' on Professor Bavdekar's phone, warning him that things were getting dangerous.

Either way, he decided to act on his instinct once again. He would not be taking any chances.

He got up to head to the washroom.

***

Deedar saw the young man get up and head towards the washroom.

This was his opportunity.

He waited for sixty seconds to avoid being conspicuous, and then unholstered his revolver as he, too, headed the same way.

***

A sixty second head-start was all that Sam needed. He still had the split-second decision-making capabilities of a sprinter, and the climbing abilities of a mountain trekker, albeit a somewhat rusty one. He used both of those skills to advantage in those eventful seconds.

He ran into the restroom, got into one of the toilet stalls, closed the toilet seat and climbed on to it.

It was still nine feet up to the window. The partitions between the stalls were about seven feet high.

Sameer braced himself, jumped up to catch the partition, and then used its support to hoist his legs up towards the window.

With one massive heave, he managed to get his legs on to the window. He then propelled himself forward, and jumped off the window on to the outside.

He got up swiftly, steadied himself for no more than a second and then rushed towards a truck that was leaving the parking lot, just as Deedar Singh stormed into the toilet with his revolver pointed.

***

Sam jumped on to the back of the truck just as it left the parking lot. He prayed that his pursuer, if he was indeed that, would not notice the truck leaving.

Sam heaved a sigh of relief as the truck hit the highway. There were dozens of trucks plying at that hour, and there was no way his pursuer would be able to zero in on him. He was safe. For now.

***

Deedar Singh noticed the closed toilet seat, climbed on to the window and looked out. There was no movement outside. The Innova in which the young man had come was still in the parking lot.

Deedar Singh grit his teeth in frustration. He would search the parking lot to see if his quarry was hiding somewhere, but his hunch was that he had got on to a vehicle that would have just left.

He got out of the toilet stall, went up to the washbasin and let out a massive roar of frustration as he effortlessly dislodged it and smashed it to the ground.

The washbasin crashed into a thousand pieces as it hit the floor.

The young man had given him the slip for now. But he would not get far.

***

Mumbai-Goa highway, Monday, 4.30 a.m.

'It's dangerous without a seat belt, buddy,' the well-turned-out man in the red Gap T-shirt told Sam.

'Sure, Vivaan,' Sam said, omitting to mention his recent experience with 'dangerous' as he fastened the seat belt.

The journey in the truck had been nail-biting. First, Sam had caught sight of his pursuer's Hummer not far behind. Then, to Sam's panic, the truck driver had spotted him and stopped the truck in the middle of the road to argue with him. Sam had quickly settled the argument with a hundred-rupee-note, and then desperately thumbed a ride from a Honda Accord, all the while praying that his pursuer would not notice the commotion.

***

The Honda Accord was occupied by a well-turned-out, suave, South Mumbai couple heading to Goa. The husband, Vivaan, was driving, while his wife, Riyaa, moved to the back seat with their Pomeranian puppy, Bouncer. His nerve-wracking escape notwithstanding, Sam could not help but notice the gentle puppy cozily curling up on Riyaa's lap in the back seat. The name 'Bouncer' seemed somewhat inappropriate for him.

'So what sort of work do you do?' Vivaan was asking Sam.

'Err . . . umm . . . I'm into investment banking,' Sam found himself muttering.

'Sounds exciting,' Vivaan said. 'I'm just a boring businessman.'

Sam avoided getting into the details of just how 'exciting' his life had become lately.

He suddenly remembered the chocolate-shaped USB drive from Professor Bavdekar's room that was still in his right pocket. He needed to check its contents urgently. Maybe that was what the tall giant was after.

'Hey, Vivaan, I've already imposed on you guys, but would you, by any chance, have a laptop that you wouldn't mind my using?'

'We do, but it's out of charge,' Vivaan said. 'We'll charge it at a shop when we take our tea break.'

'Thanks, Vivaan,' Sam said.

***

The rhythmic movement of the car had a lulling effect on Sam, shaken as he was by the night's events. Conscious that dozing off would be discourteous to Vivaan, who was driving, Sam struggled to keep awake.

Vivaan patted him lightly on the shoulder. 'It's okay, buddy,' he said, smiling. 'Get some rest.'

Riyaa nodded from the back seat. 'Bouncer and I are getting our naps, too.'

As if on cue, Bouncer let out a contented moan.

Sam experienced a surge of gratitude towards the couple and their display of concern as he let sleep overcome him.

***

Mumbai-Goa highway, Monday, 6 a.m.

Sam woke up with a start as the car lurched while overtaking a bullock cart.

He looked at his watch. He had been asleep for well over an hour.

That was when he remembered that he still had his mobile phone. He had switched it off in the melee of the police chase in Mumbai. He could use the phone to google Professor Hudson and see what he was all about.

Sam took the phone out of his pocked and switched it on.

***

Unknown to Sam, his mobile phone had been added to the list of numbers being tracked by a heavy-set man in an abandoned warehouse, who was sitting behind what looked like an aircraft console with tastefully done interiors.

As soon as Sam switched on his phone, a beep sounded on

Bruce's computer screen, and he let a half-smile escape his lips as the map on the screen converged to a narrow area.

In less than a second, many miles away, Deedar Singh let out a pronounced grunt as he received the coordinates on his mobile device.

***

Mahad, Mumbai-Goa highway, Monday, 6.30 a.m.

As Sam's phone struggled to find Internet connectivity, the car skidded to a stop. 'We've reached Mahad, folks,' Vivaan said cheerfully as he opened the car door. 'Time for a break.'

CHAPTER 15

Mumbai-Goa highway, Monday, 6.30 a.m.

The coordinates from Bruce's computer were forwarded to Deedar Singh's handheld device as a live feed. Sam's phone did not have the GPS setting switched on, so Bruce was using a cell-tower triangulation software that could pinpoint a location within a three hundred-metre radius.

Deedar's eyes burned as his Hummer closed the gap between him and Sam. He could not afford to goof up again. Besides, this guy had been able to give him the slip in just a sixty-second interval. He had a score to settle.

Deedar suddenly let out a start as the phone coordinates seemed to stop and then remained static.

The young man was probably in a vehicle that had stopped. Deedar was now only fifteen kilometres away. He revved up the Hummer for a fresh burst of speed.

***

Vivaan had parked the Accord outside two abandoned warehouses by the Savitri river. The warehouses faced each other, with a courtyard in the middle.

Vivaan headed into the first warehouse by the roadside, while Riyaa stopped to stretch.

Mindful of space, Sam headed to the second warehouse, which was closer to the river.

It was still dark, probably a few minutes before dawn, and the moon looked magical, lighting up the river. For a few moments, Sam stood still, taking in the vista—the almost aesthetic ruins of the warehouse, a couple of fishing boats on the river, a small jetty a hundred metres away, and a few people queueing up at the jetty to board a boat. An almost perfect backdrop for an impressionist painting.

A lump formed in Sam's throat as he remembered a similar morning, six months ago, when he and Ananya had trooped over to Harihareshwar, near Mumbai, and climbed up a hillock with a 270-degree view of the Arabian Sea. Between the two of them, and the timeless expanse of the sea, it had seemed like he had everything he had ever wanted.

Sam stood there for a few moments, motionless and helpless, until the urge to relieve himself brought him back to reality.

***

Sam was in an abandoned urinal in the second warehouse building. To his irritation, his phone was still struggling with Internet connectivity.

He called Namrata. Hopefully she would have found out about Professor Hudson by now.

She sounded a little shaken. 'Professor Hudson was a luminary in the political sciences department at the University of Berkeley. He was one of the world's foremost experts on weapon proliferation and was an arms-control activist. Professor Bavdekar met him when he was in the US last week.'

'What do you mean – he *was* a luminary?' Sam asked.

'You'd better brace yourself for this,' Namrata said. 'Professor Hudson was found dead in his faculty room on Sunday night. The autopsy mentions that he died of a heart attack, though the police have not ruled out foul play.'

***

Bavdekar had met Hudson. Now Hudson was dead. And Bavdekar missing.

Sam's heart did a somersault as he realised that Ananya was somehow mixed up in all this.

His heart still beating wildly, Sam made calls to a few friends to see if he could extricate himself from the mess with the Mumbai police and maybe get the police to do something about Ananya's disappearance.

His lawyer friend, Kaushik, said, 'Dude, I can probably get you cleared with the cops. But you will have to present yourself here for interrogation.'

Sam hung up. He could not afford to go back and get slowed down.

He called a journalist friend, Hanif, to see if he could run a story on the professor's disappearance. Maybe the cops would take notice and try to find Bavdekar and Ananya. Hanif was not optimistic. 'The Mumbai police is burdened with literally dozens of such disappearances every day. You would need to come back and talk to the police.'

Sam hung up again. Now he was really on his own.

***

As Deedar arrived closer to the mark, he knew he was in luck. A red Honda Accord was parked outside an abandoned warehouse very close to the Savitri river.

The young man had most probably been in the Accord. And was now somewhere in the vicinity.

***

Vivaan was heading towards the courtyard where Riyaa was stretching and Bouncer was prancing about. That was when Vivaan noticed the tall man with a wrestlers' build and a brown leather jacket heading towards him.

He looked up enquiringly.

'Police,' Deedar told him. 'We are looking for a young man who might have hitched a ride in your car. He is wanted for multiple crimes back in Mumbai.'

Vivaan did a double take. Had he put his family in danger by giving a lift to a stranger?

But Vivaan was a good judge of people. And his instincts had told him that Sam was not malevolent. On the other hand, just one look at the tall man in front of him told Vivaan that he was up to no good.

'If you are the police, why don't you show me some ID?' Vivaan asked defiantly.

'I don't have my ID,' Deedar was now getting impatient as he stole a glance at the buildings around. 'Are you telling me about the young man or not?'

'Maybe not,' Vivaan said, still defiant.

Deedar Singh could waste no time. Sam was somewhere in the

vicinity, and Deedar needed to get to him fast. He fished out his .32 and pointed it straight at Riyaa. 'Tell me or I shoot.'

Vivaan's eyes widened instantly. He could not risk his family's safety, but he did not want to put Sam in danger either. His voice quivered just a little bit as he cooked up a story. 'He got off our car half-an-hour ago. Said he was going to go back to Mumbai.'

Unfortunately for Vivaan, he did not know that Deedar had tracked Sam's mobile to a three hundred-metre radius of his vehicle, and that he knew Vivaan was lying.

For Deedar Singh, Vivaan was eminently dispensable. He had narrowed Sam down to a three hundred-metre radius anyway. If Deedar let Vivaan go, he could create an unnecessary distraction by alerting the authorities.

Everything happened in a matter of seconds after that. Deedar undid the safety catch of his revolver and fired a shot straight at Vivaan's chest.

Vivaan's body crumpled and fell to the ground as Riyaa let out a helpless, deafening shriek. That triggered off a barking bout from Bouncer as he started running towards Deedar.

Deedar Singh did not want any witnesses. And he did not particularly care for women. Or pets.

He fired one more shot. The woman's shriek abruptly stopped, cut off in its prime. The barking continued.

Then he fired another shot, and the barking, too, stopped.

***

From the broken window of the toilet at the abandoned warehouse, a pair of horrified eyes watched as the last shot was fired.

Sam had run to the window when he had heard the first shot. By the time he realised what was happening and could rush out to help, the next two shots had been fired. It had all happened in a matter of seconds.

A gasp escaped Sam's lips as the magnitude of the evil he was facing dawned on him.

A few images passed through Sam's mind—first the image of Riyaa and Bouncer curled up on the back seat, and then the image of Ananya and the corpse at the ATM—and Sam's body involuntarily shuddered in a way that it had never shuddered before.

CHAPTER 16

Mahad, Mumbai-Goa highway, Monday, 6.45 a.m.

Sam stood paralysed for a second before he pulled himself together. It was over for Vivaan and Riyaa, but he still had to try to get out alive. He would have to keep the surging tsunami of guilt aside for the moment.

The towering giant had gotten into the first building and was combing it swiftly. Sam had no more than maybe a minute before he would enter the second building where Sam was hiding.

He had to act fast. It was still dark, and that gave him an advantage. But the morning light was just about knocking on the horizon.

The surroundings were eerily quiet, except for the pleasant lapping sound of the waters of the river, and the unnervingly loud sound of the gigantic man kicking open the broken, mould-eaten doors in the dilapidated first warehouse building.

There was only one door out of the building that Sam was in, and it directly faced the courtyard. If he tried to get out through that door, he would be spotted in the moonlight. And probably shot in the head with the man's revolver.

He would have to seek another way out. Fast.

***

The answer came to Sam instantaneously. He would have to create a diversion—something that he had seen in many spy movies.

Sam surveyed the surroundings quickly. At a distance of around eighty metres, he could make out the outline of a boat at the river bank, and the silhouette of a few passengers who were probably waiting to board it at the jetty.

He looked around, hoping to find a conveniently sized object that he could throw into the water. There was nothing.

He dug into his pockets. The mobile phone. That's how they had probably tracked him.

Sam took aim, summoned up all his throwing abilities and threw the mobile phone into the water.

Thank God for all those years spent fielding in cricket, Sam thought as the mobile phone landed in the water a good sixty metres ahead of his position, very close to the jetty and the boat.

He was in luck. Almost immediately, the towering man ran from the courtyard, and headed for the jetty in the darkness, assuming that Sam was there.

Sam was quiet—and swift—as he got out of the second building and ran to the courtyard, to the place where Vivaan's crumpled body lay.

***

Things moved pretty quickly after that.

Sam stifled a gasp, and a sharp stab of guilt, as he dug into Vivaan's pockets for the keys to the Accord.

He did not have time to take their bodies to the car. He would have to make an anonymous call to the police later.

Sam ran to the Accord and put it into ignition, hoping that it would be at least a few minutes before the giant realised what had happened. He cranked up the vehicle and headed back in the direction that they had come from—towards Mumbai—instead of towards Goa. If that got the giant confused and bought Sam a few extra minutes, even better.

***

After driving away from the warehouses, Sam abandoned the Accord in a clump of bushes by the side of the road at the earliest opportunity, and hid.

Sure enough, a few minutes later, the Hummer came thundering past, roaring at a dangerously high speed of over 150 kmph.

When the Hummer was safely gone, Sam got onto the road and thumbed a ride from the next vehicle—a Tata Sumo carrying four young men just out of college. They were headed to Shrivardhan, a town located by the sea and accessible by a road that branched off from the main Mumbai-Goa highway.

Sam was grateful that the men in the Sumo did not ask him for any money. It seemed sensible to conserve the cash he had in his wallet.

Shrivardhan might actually be a good idea, Sam reflected. Being away from the Mumbai-Goa highway, it would not be the obvious choice for his pursuer to follow him, and Sam might actually be able to hitch a ride on a boat from there and reach Goa by sea.

After all the activity of the last half-an-hour, Sam felt slightly relieved as he sank into his seat. But he was jolted back up by the realisation that the lifeless bodies of the previous folks who had offered him a lift were now lying abandoned by a dilapidated warehouse. Thanks to him.

***

Shrivardhan, coastal village in Maharashtra, Monday, 8.30 a.m.

The hamlet of Shrivardhan was buzzing with the activity of the morning as Sam got off the Sumo. There were fruit-sellers spreading their wares in the town square, women scurrying past with baskets of fish over their heads, and buses whirring as commuters prepared to head to their place of business.

The bustle suddenly reminded Sam that he was on a sticky wicket at his office. The performance appraisals and employee firings were due to happen today. Not being present in office on such a day would be the equivalent of the American President not showing up in office on 9/11.

At the very least, Sam would need to call Ayush and register his inability to show up.

Sam slowly walked up to a payphone, hating every second of it.

***

Ayush was scathing. Sam was subjected to a rude grilling and warned of 'severe repercussions'.

Sam banged his knuckles in frustration. 'Severe repercussions' probably meant losing his job, accompanied by unflattering commentary in his 'relieving' letter.

He desperately tried to compose himself as he walked towards the jetty. He had heard about the boats which carried goods of questionable legality along the coastline, and he hoped that he would get a lift to Goa in one such boat.

He peered into his wallet. He had around three thousand rupees.

That might be enough to get him to Goa, and maybe to Ephesus Hotel, but would leave him with practically nothing beyond that.

Sam wondered whether he ought to go to an ATM and withdraw some more cash. But given that his pursuers seemed to have been tracking his mobile phone, there was a good chance that they would be tracking his debit and credit cards as well. He would have to manage with the money he had.

***

The boat pulled away from Shrivardhan, creating large ripples as it cut through the water. To Sam, the spray from the water and the ripples seemed to coalesce and form an outline of an image of a young couple holding a small puppy.

They seemed to stare at him forlorn, disappointed in him for putting them in danger; and for the fate that his entry into their lives had invited for them.

Sam closed his eyes to mentally distance the image, but it refused to go away. His heart sank as he realised the images of Vivaan, Riyaa and the puppy would follow him everywhere; this was a lifelong burden that he would have to carry.

CHAPTER 17

Mumbai-Goa highway, 12 noon

Deedar Singh was experiencing a very uncharacteristic series of emotions as he reversed his Hummer for the thirtieth time and made enquiries at petrol pumps and restaurants along the Mumbai-Goa highway.

First there was frustration: at not being able to get any leads into Sameer's whereabouts.

Then disbelief: that an amateur had outwitted him.

And then the overwhelming sense of shame. Back in his village in Haryana, being bested by a city-bred man half your size was not exactly a badge of honour.

And then there was fear. Not just fear, but bottomless, unadulterated terror: of consequences. Of the man they called the Doc.

Fear was a rather unusual emotion for Deedar Singh. But then, the Doc was no ordinary person. Deedar recollected how the Doc dealt with a traitor from within the ranks a few weeks ago. The man's wails had reverberated through the Mansion, and his heart-rending cries for a swift death still rang in Deedar's ears.

The memory of the incident was enough to make Deedar feel queasy. A swift death was a better choice any day.

There was only one thing to do. Deedar Singh barely hesitated as he placed the tip of the revolver into his own mouth and pulled the trigger.

***

Goa, Monday, 6 p.m.

Sam sighed as the boat approached land.

Despite trying his best, he had not managed to sleep even a wink on the boat. The choppiness of the water was magnified by frequent gushes of the monsoon winds, and the rustic crew of the trawler was focused on carrying smuggled goods along the coastline, not on providing a smooth travelling experience. And then there was the guilt; the ever-present guilt.

After parting with two thousand rupees for the boat ride, Sam was still left with one thousand rupees. That ought to be more than enough to get him to Ephesus Hotel, though he would have to find a way to get some cash post that.

He felt fortunate that he was on the verge of completing the journey without being robbed. Or worse, he thought wryly, as he watched a clearly sex-starved deckhand walk past.

Close to twelve hours had passed since Sam's encounter with the giant in the Hummer. Despite being menace personified, the giant had at least represented a link to the guys who were responsible for Ananya's disappearance. He now seemed to prefer that to the radio silence of the past ten hours.

As the boat drew closer to a makeshift harbour in north Goa, he saw a somewhat rusted signboard that said 'Welcome to Goa'.

Sam sighed.

Paradise for many, home for some. Riotous celebration for many, object d'art for some. Weekend getaway for many, pristine slice of heaven for some.

Sam sighed again. He wished he knew what Goa held in store for him. And for Ananya. Wherever she was.

***

The radio was blaring as the cab made its way to Baga beach, one of Goa's most popular beaches.

The announcer was droning on about a Global Security Summit (GSS) in Delhi on Wednesday, the first time ever that the heads of state of the western powers—the US, UK, France, Germany and Australia, along with Japan—were congregating for a meeting in India. The choice of India as the venue was strategic. The GSS would signal the West's strategic 'pivot' towards India, to serve as a counter to China's growing influence. The main agenda of the meeting, aside from the usual platitudes about democracy, was to pass stiff sanctions against China for its aggressive military posturing in the South China Sea.

For obvious reasons, this was not going down well with the Chinese.

The monotony of the radio announcer's voice had a soporific effect on Sam. He had not been able to sleep on the boat, and the sheer featurelessness of the radio commentary was a change from the world of murderers, dead bodies and abductions that he had ended up inhabiting in the last twenty-four hours.

'This is so boring,' the cabbie was muttering as he changed the radio station.

Another radio station was playing an interview with the Indian captain ahead of the India vs the 'Dream Combo' T20 cricket match in Delhi on Wednesday. As a nod to India's status as the premier world cricketing power, it was single-handedly pitted against the combination of the best of Australia and England, who had come together as the Dream Combo.

'Are you nervous?' the interviewer was asking him. 'Everybody from the US President and UK Prime Minister downward are going to be watching the match.'

The Indian captain was all charged up. 'We are going to give the Aussies and the Brits the thrashing of their lives. They are not calling it "Match of the Century" for nothing.'

Sam closed his eyes. Even hearing about cricket seemed like music to his ears, taking him away, albeit fleetingly, from grimmer thoughts.

***

Ephesus Hotel, Baga beach, north Goa, Monday, 8.30 p.m.

As Sam got off the taxi at Baga, he had neither the time nor the inclination to ruminate on the influence of tourism on what used to be one of Goa's most pristine beaches as he headed to his blind date at the Ephesus Hotel with the guy who called himself 'Pele'.

The lobby of the hotel was teeming with people.

Sam took a quick look around. He did not know what 'Pele' looked like, but the guy probably ought to be around the same age as Bavdekar. And he would most likely be alone, in light of his paranoia about being followed.

Sam made his way to the first floor. It was obvious that the band was playing there—the metallic plucking of the electric guitar was clearly audible in the lobby.

He walked up to the bar, and was immediately transported to a different world. The band was belting out 'Rock you like a Hurricane'. The reverberating beat of the drums and the searing intensity of the guitar mingled with the head-banging crowd to create a magical atmosphere. The tension in the room was electrifying. Sam could almost see a ray of lightning cutting across the room.

Pele be damned, Sam thought, as he closed his eyes, forgot about all his troubles and soaked in the atmosphere for a few moments.

There were claps and cheers as the song drew to a close. The band leader took the mike and announced that his next song was going to be a contemporary pop hit.

There were groans from some in the crowd, and shook his head in disgust and walked towards the bar to get himself a drink.

He was probably around sixty years old and was around 5'10", with salt-and-pepper hair and the general demeanour of a professor.

Sam walked up to him as he neared the bar, looked straight into his eyes and shouted 'Pele'.

The look in the man's eyes—a mix of recognition, apprehension and anxiety—told Sam that he had found the man he was looking for.

***

Sameer Rajan and Bhabani Bhattacharya did not exactly start off with a warm hug, to put it mildly.

First, there was the issue of Bani's attempting to flee the scene, countered by Sam's firm hand placed between the bar and Bani's planned flight path. Bani was no stranger to physical combat, having been used to rough street soccer in his younger days, but he did not want to start something which would draw too much attention.

Then, once Sam had tersely given Bani a background of why he was here, there was the issue of boundaries. Bani was a private, almost paranoid, recluse who did not relish having to share details of his secretive quest with a stranger less than half his age.

Sam, on his part, had an innate hostility towards authority figures, starting with his father, and an avuncular professor was as quintessential an authority figure as could be. It did not help that the person in question was trying to be cagey.

'Pele, or whatever your bloody name is, I'm going to say this as straight as possible. My girlfriend is missing, and I don't mind having to kill to get her back.'

Bani just snorted.

Sam continued. 'Your friend, Bavdekar, or Zico, or whatever you kinky guys call each other, is missing, too. You need all the help you can get, because you sure as hell ain't getting anywhere trying to find Bavdekar on your own.'

'It's *Professor* Bavdekar,' Bani interjected, eliciting a murderous glare from Sam.

'Whatever,' Sam said. 'You want him back, don't you?'

Bani was quiet. Shrikant Bavdekar was among the few friends he had, and he was concerned about him.

'If we work together, we might get him back. Along with my girlfriend,' Sam said.

'…hopefully alive,' he added.

***

A muscular Caucasian man, wearing beach shorts and a blue T-shirt, got up from his chair as soon as Sam and Bani went down to the lobby of the Ephesus Hotel.

He was known as Rider among the crew at the Mansion because of his driving skills. He had perfected these skills during his early days as a member of a biker gang in Melbourne. He was around 5'9", but his toned body and six-pack abs would have put professional bodybuilders to shame. He had sharp, observant eyes which missed nothing. All this was concealed beneath a relaxed demeanour and a happy-go-lucky exterior. He did not look out of place among the beach revellers and the Baga crowd.

Rider had arrived in Goa from the Mansion just a few hours ago. Two shooters—an Indian man, Milind, and an Australian woman, Nicole—were backing him up.

Bruce had made sure that the shooters were among the best they had. The goof-up, with Sam giving Deedar Singh the slip, had happened under Bruce's watch. He had to make sure he delivered this time. He did not want to meet the same fate as Andy. Or Deedar.

As Rider swiftly stepped down to the lobby, he spoke into his Bluetooth micro mouthpiece, through which he could reach Bruce and the two backup shooters at the same time. 'I have the targets. They are headed out, probably to the rave to meet Jeff.'

'You know the instructions, Rider. Remain concealed till they lead us to Steve.'

Rider rubbed his hands together. The young man had given the slip to Deedar Singh, of all people. He couldn't wait to get his hands on him.

***

Lotus Café, north Goa, Monday, 9.30 p.m.

Finding Lotus Café was not difficult. You just had to ask the right person in the right manner.

By day, Lotus Café was an innocuous, somewhat grungy convenience store surrounded by a very large but poorly tended lawn.

By night, on certain days of the week, however, Lotus Café underwent a Jekyll and Hyde transformation. The poorly kept lawn metamorphosed into a den of revelry with huge psychedelic lights, trance music and free availability of various questionable substances.

Sam knew that asking the question straight-out would never get them to the rave. He had learnt this while trekking near Malana in the Himalayas. Raves were for the regulars, not for those who might create a nuisance or blurt things out within earshot of the authorities. The unwritten code was to keep the 'tourists' and the 'fuddy-duddy crowd' out.

So he had approached a couple of bike-taxi guys, subtly dropped hints about his knowledge of the 'scene', and got them to ferry Bani and him to Lotus Café.

Sam and Bani walked amongst the crowd in the lawns off Lotus Café, wondering how they would spot Jeff.

Most people at the rave were in a haze, hippies with needle marks all over their arms. They were in their own private Shangri-las, sprawled on hand-crafted mats, hands drooping to the sides, occasionally moving to drag the chillums towards their mouths, eyes glazed with far-away looks.

At the foot of the hill right behind Lotus Café, a flight of stairs led towards the centre of the party from where the music—rhythmic chants—seemed to be emanating. The only person in the vicinity who seemed remotely awake and aware was a Caucasian woman sitting on one of the steps of the stairs.

At last, Sam thought, somebody with whom I can have a semblance of a conversation.

She seemed to be in her thirties, around 5'5", was of slim build and had silky hair that fell loosely over her shoulders. For a moment, her figure reminded Sam of Ananya, and he was immediately hit by a stab of guilt as he remembered what he was here for.

He moved closer to her to ask her a question, but his throat went dry as he smelled what seemed like a delicate floral perfume on her. Probably the same perfume that Ananya had worn during their last meeting in Colaba.

'Yes?' she asked, in a French accent.

'Uh . . . my friend and I are looking for Jeff,' Sam said.

'Follow me,' she said, taking a drag from her chillum.

***

Damini was able to locate Jeff fairly easily at the rave party. His profile on the underground social networking site did not have his photo, but it did have the names of some of his 'friends', and Damini was able to convincingly throw their names around and locate Jeff. Sporting an orange bandanna, a T-shirt littered with esoteric symbols, and a faded pair of jeans, Damini blended in completely.

Jeff fit the hippy profile well. He looked like what a 1960s 'flower child' might look like if he had continued living the same nomadic lifestyle, complete with drugs and rock-and-roll, but without the sense of energy and purposeful revolt that had characterised those times. He had a scraggy beard, unkempt hair, a continuous wheeze, an unsteady gaze and a few syringe marks on his arms.

Damini kept her distance, as she wanted to glean whatever intelligence she could before she tried a more direct approach.

Her antennae went up as she saw two Indian blokes, accompanied by a Caucasian woman, walk up to Jeff.

Damini almost choked with suppressed laughter. The older, avuncular man looked hopelessly out of place in the rave. He would attract as much attention as a red teddy bear in a sombre company board meeting.

She captured the images of the two men using her smartphone's camera and sent them to Mini at the control room. 'I need the download on these two guys,' she said.

***

After suspiciously checking whether Sam and Bani were accompanied by any cops, Jeff eased up.

He walked up to the makeshift parking lot near Lotus Café, and got on a bike. He motioned towards a spare bike and tossed the keys to Sam who nodded, started the engine and glanced at Bani, who had made no attempt to get on the bike.

'I can ride,' Bani said tersely, barely concealing his distaste for taking the backseat to Sam.

'You don't have a bike,' Sam pointed out. 'Or a key.'

Jeff was already on his way, and Bani could not afford to lose the trail over a squabble. He gritted his teeth and climbed behind Sam.

***

Jeff rode through a route that was not a thoroughfare, to put it mildly. Both Sam and Bani felt like they were being put through the blender as they passed through bumpy hillocks, village dirt roads and sandy beaches. Sam wondered how Jeff was managing to ride his bike through all this when he could not even manage a steady handshake through his drug-hardened veins.

More than once, Sam, who possessed a keen sense of sound, paused as he thought he heard a bike somewhere behind them. But Jeff was getting away, and they could not afford to stop and lose time.

Sam stopped his bike abruptly as Jeff reached Solaris Hospital.

***

Damini whistled. The plot was getting thicker.

Mini had sent Damini the brief stats on the two blokes—the young man, Sameer, and the old, avuncular guy, Bhabani—by matching their photographs with her database. The young man's profile matched that of a person who had fled a crime scene in Mumbai, while the professor, according to Mini, was a conspiracy theorist with some bizarre obsessions.

As Damini followed them on her motorcycle, her eyes widened as she saw a man wearing shorts and a blue T-shirt also following them. He seemed to be riding his bike with panache. Even through the dark, she could make out the reflection of the moonlight on the metal of a revolver sticking out of his pocket.

Excellent, she thought. The situation just got more interesting, what with this fast-and-furious acolyte joining the game.

She reached into her holster, fished out her handgun and released the safety catch. This could get ugly.

***

It was difficult to shadow people on a completely deserted, winding path without being discovered.

Rider realised he was being followed.

He spoke into his Bluetooth mouthpiece. 'Bruce, I have a tail, probably a woman, probably on a bike.' He then addressed the two backups. 'Milind, Nicole, Solaris Hospital is the nearest landmark. Meet me at the parking lot. Bring the Land Rover.'

Bruce's instructions were clear. 'Don't make a move on anyone till we have located Steve. Then take the professor. The younger guy I don't care about.'

'Sure,' Rider nodded as he continued on his bike. He knew what the last bit meant.

Bruce added, 'Don't forget to retrieve the USB drive from the younger guy before you kill him.'

CHAPTER 18

Goa, Monday, 10.30 p.m.

Damini was smart and cocky, and a daredevil, but she was no fool.

After the incident in Mumbai when she had lost Ji-hoon Kim, she was wary of sharing too much information with Kunal. But the situation now demanded urgent action.

She would have to take a chance and trust him. If he was partnering with the bad guys, he might deliberately stall. But at least she would be able to confirm her suspicions.

She called the control room. Kunal came on line.

Damini spoke quickly. 'I need backup. Fast. Have them come in an SUV and arrange to rendezvous somewhere near my current path.'

'Mind telling me what's going on?' Kunal asked.

'I will,' Damini said tersely. 'Let me get done with this high-speed chase first.'

Kunal sighed and then said, 'Ok, backup coming your way. I'm sending two agents: Malcolm and Nisha.'

Thankfully, the ACG had a unit in Goa who were aware of Damini's movements. It would not take much time for the backup to materialise. If Kunal wanted to cooperate, that is.

'Mini,' Damini continued. 'I need more info on the two blokes, Sameer and Bhabani.'

***

Solaris Hospital, Goa, Monday, 11 p.m.

Bani and Sam trooped behind Jeff as he made his way up the staircase at Solaris Hospital. Paranoid sociophobe that he was, Jeff did not want to take the lift to get to the intensive care unit on the second floor.

'You seem to be in good spirits,' Sam remarked as Bani bounded up the stairs.

'Can't wait to hear what Steve has to say,' Bani replied.

Sam sniggered. 'You make me sick, man. Steve, who is supposedly your friend, is probably in some trauma-induced state, and all you can think of is your stupid research!'

***

Steve, sure enough, was in delirium. His head and left shoulder were wrapped in bandages, his eyes were heavy with sedation and his hands were limp, though he was conscious.

'No visitors,' one of the nurses on duty told them with a stern look.

The resident doctor stopped briefly to talk to Sam and Bani as he emerged from the ICU. He told them that one of Jeff's friends had apparently dressed Steve's wounds and given him sedatives in Mumbai. Nevertheless, the wounds, including a bad gash on the left shoulder and blows to the head, had acted up further due to the ill-advised train journey from Mumbai to Goa.

Bani, notwithstanding his enthusiasm for what Steve had to say, felt a sharp tug of guilt and concern.

As the two nurses at the ICU station stepped away from their desk to attend to another patient, Sam and Bani grabbed the window of opportunity. They quickly made their way to Steve's cubicle.

Steve showed a glimmer of recognition as he saw Bani, but he was too weak to speak coherently.

With a huge effort, he tugged at Bani's sleeve. His voice was hoarse. 'KaalKoot . . . Demo,' he croaked haltingly.

'What demo?' Bani asked, leaning close to Steve's face.

'Master . . . different . . . l . . . l . . . lo.' Steve paused, his entire face heaving as he struggled to speak.

He was getting progressively agitated as he spoke. 'Torture. Hot, hot . . .'

'Hot what?' Bani egged him on with a sense of urgency. 'Tell me.'

Steve was choking now. 'Ho . . . Ho . . . Hottt,' he continued, as wheezing shook his entire body.

'In . . . s.s.sick,' Steve panted, barely audible, his voice reduced to a croak.

Sam noticed a glimmer of understanding pass through Bani's face. Clearly, Steve had said something that made sense to him.

The last wheeze was particularly bad. Steve's face contorted into a grotesque expression as he spat out blood.

He was now gasping for breath, getting progressively more hysterical. 'KaalKoot. Demo.'

Bani leaned closer. 'What demo?'

Steve had a look of terror in his eyes as he mustered up his last ounce of energy to scream 'Stop . . . it.'.

Clearly, the effort was too much for him. His eyeballs moved rapidly as the left side of his body slumped. The monitors connected to Steve's body pranced about wildly as a nurse rushed in and urgently motioned Bani and Sam to leave the room.

This nurse was fair, tall and athletic, with blonde hair. A fleeting thought about the unusualness of this entered Sam's mind, but there was no time to think.

The blonde nurse hurriedly pushed Bani to the side as she fished out a needle to inject Steve with a sedative. 'You will have to leave the room,' she said with a heavy Australian accent. 'Now.'

Bani and Sam stepped outside the doorway.

They did not notice that the look on Steve's face had twisted into an even darker expression of horror as the Aussie nurse turned towards him.

***

Solaris Hospital, Goa, Monday, 11.08 p.m.

Bani and Sam walked up to the stairwell from the ICU, intending to make their way to the cafeteria on the ground floor.

Jeff was nowhere to be seen. 'Probably scooted off back to the rave, now that his job is done,' Sam snorted.

The two of them were just starting to walk down the stairs when they heard the deafening sound of glass shattering.

The noise of the crash reverberated through the floor. This was followed by the sound of more glass breaking and the almost simultaneous shrieking of people from around the ICU.

Sam and Bani mouthed the same word as they rushed towards the ICU.

'Steve. . .'

***

Solaris Hospital, Goa, Monday, 11.10 p.m.

There was commotion on the second floor of the hospital. It was not every day that a patient got into a scuffle at the ICU. The staff and nurses were swarming around the corridors, while the hospital's security guards cordoned off the area around Steve's lifeless body.

The same resident doctor whom Sam and Bani had spoken to earlier came to talk to them. 'He seems to have had a scuffle with the nurse and overturned the trolley with all the medicines and ampoules. Considering how much blood he had lost, that must have taken a lot of strength. But coupled with the ill-conceived train ride from Mumbai, I guess his heart could not handle the strain, and it gave way.'

Sam noticed Bani sighing loudly as he fought hard to control his emotions.

'So how did he get the strength?' Sam asked the doctor.

'Well, something may have triggered the release of a large amount of adrenaline in his body. A person can muster up that kind of hysterical strength when he is responding to extreme fear.'

Sam and Bani walked up to Steve's bed. The water jug on the bedside table was overturned, and a needle was lying on the floor.

Something about the needle rang a bell in Sam's mind. 'The tall Aussie nurse,' he blurted out. 'She was the one who took out a needle to inject Steve. She seemed out of place here.'

Bani had recovered enough from the shock of Steve's death to nod slowly. 'Let's find her.'

***

Sam and Bani were walking down the corridor when they saw the Aussie 'nurse' at one end.

They had just begun to run towards her when the sight of another person stopped them dead in their tracks.

The Aussie 'nurse' was with a person who wore a doctor's uniform.

Sam and Bani did not know that the person had, till recently, worn beach shorts and a blue T-shirt, and was known as Rider. But the revolver in his hand told them more than they needed to know.

They ran in the opposite direction, desperately looking for an exit.

They entered into the first door that came their way. It turned out to be a housekeeping room, filled with shelves lined with linen and blankets.

But their pursuers were not far behind.

Bani had barely entered the room when a powerful hit to the head knocked him out cold.

The last thing Sam did before a blow to his head rendered him unconscious was to take the USB drive out of his pocket and shove it under the rack of linen and towels in the housekeeping room.

CHAPTER 19

Solaris Hospital, Goa, 11.20 p.m.

While Nicole and Rider had been busy with Sam and Bani, the second backup, Milind, had been assigned to 'take care' of Damini.

Unfortunately, he had no clue where she was.

He had seen her getting into the lift on the ground floor, and had waited right outside the lift door on the first floor for her to emerge.

Bafflingly, the lift door opened and there was nobody inside.

He entered the lift gingerly, looking perplexed, when a kick to his head squarely knocked him down.

Damini had suspended herself below the lift ceiling, balancing herself between the walls. As soon as Milind entered the lift, she had found her opportunity and flattened him.

She was starting to drag Milind's limp body to a safe place when she happened to glance through the corridor window. A man was pushing a stretcher with a limp body across the parking lot to a Land Rover.

It had to be either Sameer or Bhabani on the stretcher, Damini thought with dismay. Or maybe both, considering how big the body looked.

The man dragging the bodies was the same fast-and-furious guy she had been following. And along with him was a tall, athletic blonde woman in a nurse's uniform.

***

A gunfight in the hospital, that too with a guy who could potentially use Sameer or Bhabani as human shields, was a bad idea. Even if Damini fired simply to create a distraction, she would still be hauled up by the Chief.

But then if the guy got away, Damini might lose her main clue. Along with possibly the lives of Sameer and Bhabani.

She had to decide fast.

Damini let go of Milind and ran at breakneck speed towards the window by the staircase.

She fished out her gun, took careful aim at the tyres of the Land Rover, and fired.

***

All hell broke loose. Rider immediately looked up, saw Damini, dived for cover and unholstered his revolver, all within a span of two seconds. Nicole did the same.

They were both crouched behind the Land Rover, on the same side. That was the only narrow spot which gave them cover from Damini's window. The stretcher was lying about fourteen feet away from them, Sam and Bani's limp bodies on it.

Rider was under strict orders to get Bani alive. He could not afford to have him shot. Sam he could dispense with, but only after retrieving the USB drive from him.

Rider sensed that his hands were tied. He could not quite use either Sam or Bani as human shields.

Then a realisation hit him, and his eyes lit up.

His opponent did not know his constraints. She had no clue that he was under orders to get Bani alive.

***

Damini had won the first round, crouched as she was at a vantage point, with the fast-and-furious guy and the blonde nurse both constrained in terms of moving space.

But she also knew that this advantage would not last for very long. The bad guys, who had nothing to lose if a couple of innocents died, were always at an advantage when there were bystanders around.

For one, the guy might get nervous and fire at Sameer or Bhabani. Hospital staff or patients would almost certainly arrive on the scene and complicate matters.

She had barely finished thinking this when the fast-and-furious guy fired at the windows of the hospital's casualty department on the ground floor.

There was pandemonium as a cacophony of wails and shrieks accompanied the sound of the department's windows smashing into a thousand pieces.

***

Damini exhaled sharply. Her gambit had backfired. The guy was shooting at civilians now. She had no option but to capitulate.

She had just finished deciding on this when luck—and Kunal—lent her a helping hand.

The ACG backups that Kunal had promised—Malcolm and

Nisha—arrived on the scene just then. Damini sprang into action, barking orders on her microphone.

'Nisha, flank them from the left side of the parking lot. I have the right side covered.'

'Copy that,' Nisha's voice sounded clearly on Damini's earpiece.

'Malcolm, take the two guys on the stretcher to safety. I will provide cover fire for you.'

***

Rider knew when he was outnumbered. With Damini and Nisha firing at him alternately, he took the only option he had—he jumped into the Land Rover, followed quickly by Nicole, and they drove off as fast as they could, flat tyre notwithstanding.

Damini tried following on her bike, but with patients, nurses, doctors and helpers all streaming into the corridors and parking lot, and running helter-skelter, she lost the trail even before it began.

***

Damini went back to the lift. The guy she had overpowered was gone.

She sighed. At least she had Bhabani and Sameer in her custody.

And now she knew that Kunal was not deliberately trying to sabotage her effort. Maybe he was not partnering with the bad guys after all.

She called Kunal on her smartphone. 'Thanks,' she said tersely.

Kunal used the opportunity to rub it in. 'You're welcome, boss,' he said, with an emphasis on 'boss', and then, inexplicably, burst out laughing.

The lightness was infectious, and Damini, too, laughed, the tension between them infinitely reduced.

She said to Mini: 'I took a picture of the bloke I clobbered in the lift. I'm forwarding it to you.'

Mini replied, 'Ok, Damini. Do you have a picture of the guy driving the Land Rover?'

'No,' Damini said. 'He's been consistently on the move. But check the hospital CCTV records for the guy. And run a search on the Land Rover license plates, too.'

'On it, Damini. And I'm sending you more info on Sameer and Bhabani.'

***

Damini gave a low whistle as she read Sameer and Bhabani's file on her smartphone.

Sameer did not exactly fit the profile of a terrorist. His father, Colonel Rajan, had served in the Indian Army with distinction, winning many medals for meritorious service. He was on the verge of being promoted to Brigadier when he had retired.

The dossier also mentioned Sameer's mother, and how Colonel Rajan had never really come to terms with things; how he had turned progressively aloof and brooding, and how the relationship between father and son had turned frosty over the years.

She turned to Bhabani's file. A once-brilliant professor, whose mind had apparently given itself to senility. He now spent most of his days obsessing about a conspiracy theory regarding some hidden secrets dating back to the Quit India Movement.

Damini paused, frowning, somewhat irritated. She ought to warn

Mini not to jump to conclusions too fast. One of the first things she had learnt from the Chief was that no conspiracy theory was too ridiculous to be dismissed without proper investigation.

***

Damini bit her lower lip in irritation.

The profile search on the guy in the lift turned up a blank. He did not figure in any crime database.

The hospital CCTV records also drew a blank on him. The fast-and-furious guy seemed to have clobbered the control room security staff and deactivated the CCTV feed before he got away.

The license plate numbers of the Land Rover revealed that it had been hired by somebody who had given a fake set of name, address and identity papers. No luck there either.

Damini would have to get whatever information she could directly from Sameer and Bhabani.

She chuckled. This one would be interesting.

***

Solaris Hospital, Goa, 11.50 p.m.

To the police inspector and the two sub-inspectors who arrived at the scene at Solaris Hospital, it was pretty clear who the culprits were. The resident doctor told them that two men—a young man named Sam and an old, professorial-type guy whose name he did not catch—had been asking a lot of questions about Steve. And now they were nowhere to be seen.

The inspector asked the sub-inspectors to flash the descriptions of the two men to all police check posts, train stations and the airport in Goa.

CHAPTER 20

ACG safe house near Dabolim, Goa, Monday night / Tuesday morning, 12.45 a.m.

Sam and Bani had no idea where they were being taken. They were being transported in a van that did not have rear windows.

As the vehicle came to a halt, the rear door was opened by a burly man.

They were in a small farmhouse of sorts. The burly man ushered them into a sparsely furnished room. A tall, athletic woman was seated on a couch.

The woman looked up as they trooped into the room. 'I'm Damini. This is a safe house. Only a few people know of its existence. You'll be out of harm's way here.'

'…for now,' she added, somewhat ominously.

Sam and Bani presented quite a sight. Their clothes were covered with layers of mud, thanks to the bike ride behind Jeff through slushy roads. Being unceremoniously dragged through the hospital housekeeping room floor had not helped matters. They looked like they had just been put through the wringer.

'I need to shower,' Bani said, somewhat defiantly. 'Now.'

'No such luck,' Damini said. 'You guys need to start talking, and fast.'

She turned to Sam. 'You first. Why is the Mumbai police looking for you?'

***

After thirty minutes of hearing Sameer narrate his story, Damini took a break to freshen up.

Bathrooms in ACG safe houses were not exactly epitomes of luxury, but they were practical and functional. Safe houses were places where ACG agents could lie low, or where various people, often of dubious antecedents, could be brought to 'cool their heels' for a while. Nobody outside the ACG knew the locations of these safe houses.

Sameer Rajan's story added up, Damini had to admit. Right down to the smallest detail.

Through her years of being involved in undercover operations and constantly looking over her shoulder, Damini had developed a sharp instinct for figuring out whom she could trust. And Sam figured on that list.

But the professor made her feel uncomfortable. Damini was sure he was not a crook, but he seemed to be a harder nut to crack—somebody who lived inside his own head; somebody who would not take kindly to being questioned by her.

***

Damini went back into the room, and found Sam and Bani arguing.

She wasn't surprised. Right at the outset, she knew that Sam and Bani wouldn't quite get along.

Sam was talking animatedly. 'Enough of stone-walling, buddy.'

'It's professor,' Bani said coldly. 'Not buddy. You're less than half my age.'

'Whatever. One of your friends is dead, the other has been kidnapped, and we almost got killed ourselves. Time to start spilling the beans. What the hell was it that you and Bavdekar were researching?'

'Innocuous stuff,' Bani said with disdain. 'About some historical artefacts.'

'Innocuous stuff, my arse!' Sam's face turned red as blood rushed to his head. He was desperate for clues on Ananya's disappearance, and the lack of sleep was not helping his mood. 'Why the hell would people kidnap and kill for some historical mumbo-jumbo?'

Bani made a face and looked away.

That was it. It was war now. Sam brought his face really close to Bani's, and breathed into his face.

'Why did I see that nod of recognition in your voice when Steve mumbled something in the hospital?'

Bani pushed Sam away gruffly.

Sam caught Bani's hand as he was being pushed, and twisted it behind his back.

'I'll ask you one last time. What're you hiding?'

Bani swung his free hand and was about to bring it down on Sam's face when he found it being stopped by Damini's taut, muscular arms.

Damini freed Bani's other arm from Sam's grip. 'That's enough. I'm going to knock you both unconscious if you even think of starting a street fight here,' she said.

Bani and Sam retreated. Both of them had had enough of being knocked out for one night.

Damini then turned to Bani. 'But Sameer is right. You do have some explaining to do. And you'd better cut out the attitude.'

***

Bani knew he couldn't be completely uncooperative. With Steve dead and Shrikant kidnapped, he, too, needed some answers. Besides, he could tell them whatever he had told Mukhshuddi. That was all in the public domain anyway.

So, for the next thirty minutes, Bani spoke. About the Imperial Guard and their invisible hand in imperial policy during the British Raj; about the Bengal Famine of 1943-44 and how the Imperial Guard might have had a hand in it; about Manohar Rai and his suspicions about the Imperial Guard's plot to destroy the iconic treasures of Indian civilisation. He also spoke about the mysterious Yogyaveer—the Worthy, Brave One—who was to preserve the ancient treasures of Indian civilisation in the Gupt-Kandara, the Hidden Cave.

Sam was the first to speak, much to Bani's irritation.

'So basically, twelve years ago, you discovered this kickass Imperial Guard thing, and then you got sucked into some fantasy story.'

Bani just snorted.

'And you believe that this Yogyaveer guy might still be around somewhere in a cave? If he was twenty in 1944, he must be in his nineties now.'

'I didn't say I expect him to be alive,' Bani grunted.

Sam was continuing to talk. 'What were you collaborating with Steve on?'

'I had asked him to help find further clues about the Gupt-Kandara.'

Sam butted in again. 'What did he tell you in the hospital?'

'He was incoherent. It wasn't making any sense. He said something about a Demo.'

Damini kept quiet. She didn't want to reveal that the connection to the 'Demo' was what had brought her to Goa in the first place.

'He said something about KaalKoot,' Sam persisted. 'That's the name of the mythical plague in the Samudra Manthan story, isn't it? The poison that had the power to destroy the entire universe? What was that about?'

Bani nodded. 'Steve was probably hallucinating.'

Sam did not relent. 'Why then did Bavdekar's notepad have KaalKoot scribbled on it?'

Bani looked at Damini. 'Does this guy really think I can get into other people's heads and know what they were thinking?'

Sam ignored the barb. 'Steve said something about a "different master" and about torture and something being "hot" and then about him being "sick". What the hell was the connection?'

'I told you. It didn't make any sense to me,' Bani replied. 'Seemed like incoherent rambling.'

Damini could sense when a person was lying, but she knew when not to push.

She changed the topic. 'What were you collaborating with Bavdekar on?'

'He is a friend and collaborator. I thought I'd get him along to see what Steve had to say.'

Bani almost heaved a sigh of relief as the questioning ended. He had blurted out about the second leg of the Imperial Guard plot when talking to Mukhshuddi. He did not want to slip up again.

***

ACG safe house, Goa, 1.40 a.m.

Within a short span of time, Sam had developed an informal working equation with Damini.

He looked at her as they were alone in the adjoining room. She had all the panache of a secret agent, yet did not have the detached, deadpan demeanour of the quintessential spy. Her enthusiasm and passion were childlike and somewhat infectious. It was almost as if she were born for this line of work.

'You have only one life; you might as well do what you love,' Damini laughed when Sam asked her about it. 'We become what we repeatedly do.'

Sam could not help feeling a dash of envy. He wondered where his destiny lay. Was it in the education venture that he had given up on? Or maybe in rediscovering his love for the hills? Possibly setting up a trekking school?

One thing was certain: his destiny did not lie in a stuffy job with Bancroft Cohen.

He suddenly felt guilty. Here he was, ruminating on his career, while Ananya was missing and Vivaan, Riyaa and Bouncer were dead.

He was suddenly struck with dread. Was Ananya, too, dead?

Meanwhile, sitting opposite Sam, Damini was experiencing a rather unfamiliar emotion. Something about what she had said to Sam had disturbed her.

'We become what we repeatedly do.'

Damini was somewhat surprised at herself. She was not prone to feeling disturbed easily.

She tried to shake off the feeling, but it did not leave her.

We become what we repeatedly do.

***

ACG safe house, Goa, 1.45 a.m.

'That's a lot of stuff to digest,' Sam said, referring to Bani's story.

'I'm not impressed,' Damini said, pointing to the smartphone dossier on Bani that Mini had sent. 'He didn't reveal anything that is outside the public domain.'

'Yeah. He clearly gleaned something from Steve's ramblings in the hospital that he's not telling us.'

'Maybe some clues about the location of this cave, the Gupt-Kandara…' Damini said.

Sam shook his head. 'This whole cave thing just seems like the imagination of a couple of professors running wild. I can't see why anybody in their right mind would want to kidnap or kill for this information.'

Damini's smartphone beeped. It was an encrypted message from Mini on the ACG app.

Mini had sent Damini a dossier with Bavdekar's itinerary of the preceding few weeks. As always with Mini, the file was very detailed. It even included CCTV footage from a café he had frequented while in the US, and nuggets such as 'Bavdekar checked out a waitress named Ruth at the café a couple of times.'

Damini smiled. Sometimes the ACG's work did infringe on people's privacy. But then they had lives to save. And the end always justified the means.

Mini's dossier corroborated Sam's story that Bavdekar had met Professor Hudson in the US.

The mention of Professor Hudson suddenly brought a memory to Sam's mind. 'Oh shit,' he blurted out. 'The USB drive! I completely forgot about it.'

'What USB drive? And where?' Damini asked, leaning forward.

'A USB drive I found in Bavdekar's room. That's what the crooks were probably after,' Sam said. 'I had hidden it in the hospital housekeeping room just as we were being abducted.'

Damini had already picked up the phone to call her agents. 'Tell me exactly where you hid it.'

***

ACG safe house, Goa, 2.10 a.m.

Damini's smartphone beeped as she received an email from Mini. It was the decrypted file from the USB drive which the ACG team had retrieved from the hospital.

Sam leaned over as Damini opened the email.

The USB drive contained two files.

Damini clicked on the first file. It was an MS Word file which went by the uninteresting title of 'Notes', but as soon as she opened it, the first sub-heading itself had her riveted.

It was titled: What are Biological Weapons?

CHAPTER 21

ACG safe house, Goa, 2.10 a.m.

Why the hell was a boring expert on Himalayan plant and animal life taking notes on biological weapons?

Sam and Damini looked at each other incredulously for a moment and then continued reading.

The notes were written almost like a primer. It was all new for Sam, though not for Damini who had dealt with this subject at the ACG.

Biological warfare. Germ warfare. Bio weapons. Bio agents. Apparently, this stuff went by different names. What was common was the use of living organisms or biological agents such as bacteria or viruses, known as pathogens, in order to harm humans, plants or animals, known as hosts.

The world powers were well aware that biological weapons were a two-edged sword—any weapons that were lethal for their enemies were likely to be lethal for them as well. So various international treaties had attempted to ban their production and stockpiling.

The professor had underlined a sentence that highlighted the chilling menace of bio weapons.

> *Biological weapons can potentially cause mass destruction at a level well in excess of that caused by conventional weapons and, when seen in the*

context of cost and ease of development, maybe even in excess of that caused by nuclear weapons.

Sam's eyes widened. Bavdekar's and Ananya's disappearance did not seem like a random event anymore.

***

The notes also detailed various countries' weapons programmes. One section mentioned about alleged stockpiling of biological weapons by the US after World War II, and also an alleged secret Soviet bio weapons programme called 'Biopreparat', though nothing much was known about what happened to this programme after the collapse of the Soviet Union.

As if to add to the dubiousness surrounding Professor Bavdekar's interest in bio weapons, he had underlined the question: What are the attributes of an effective bio weapon?

He had listed four attributes. Bavdekar likened these attributes to the 'Four Horsemen', after the biblical legend about four horsemen who are to be harbingers of the apocalypse, the end of the world.

The first two attributes—or Horsemen—are infectivity and virulence. Virulence is a measure of the severity of the disease caused by the pathogen, while infectivity is the proportion of exposed persons who become infected, and denotes the ease with which the disease agent can spread. Another related concept is pathogenicity, the proportion of infected individuals who develop the disease.

The third attribute is treatability: whether the disease is difficult, or impossible, to treat, especially at short notice, and whether there are any vaccines available.

The fourth attribute is scalability. This means that the pathogen underlying the bio weapon should be suitable for mass production, storage and weaponisation. This would determine the level to which it can cause mass destruction.

The professor went on to note that most known bio weapons' agents meet only two or three of the attributes of what he called the Four Horsemen.

Anthrax has high virulence; it is often fatal and can be effectively delivered against a target. But it has a limitation of not being contagious.

The plague, which was a big killer in medieval times, is now controllable by using insecticides to kill fleas, which are the transmitting carriers, and is treatable using antibiotics if detected early. So, it did not meet the third attribute.

The dreaded Ebola virus is high on virulence—the ability to harm, even kill, the host; and it does not have a documented cure. However, infection from one human to another requires physical touch, so it is difficult to use for mass destruction.

The file 'Notes' also contained a list of items at the end that Professor Bavdekar needed to follow up on. The last item in the list sent shivers down Sam's spine.

It said 'Reminder: ask Ananya for introduction to Professor Hudson'.

What did Ananya and Professor Hudson have to do with biological weapons? What kind of stuff had she gotten mixed up in?

***

Sam waited with bated breath as Damini opened the second file, called 'Discussions with Prof. Hudson'.

Background to the meeting: used Ananya's contacts in the NGO world to get an introduction to Prof. Hudson. He is one of the few experts who openly profess to know about biological warfare, while the rest of the scientists mostly work for covert government programmes. He exposed weapons programmes in the Soviet Union (in the 1980s), the US and, more recently, Syria.

Sam paused for a second. At least he was now beginning to know how Ananya fit into the whole thing.

Objective of the meeting: to understand KaalKoot. What sort of pathogen might have been involved in the second leg of the Imperial Guard plot mentioned in the verses?

Sam and Damini stared at each other, intrigued. So the Imperial Guard plot had a second leg, probably using pathogens. And mentioned in some 'verses'. And then there was KaalKoot again. This was getting interesting. And crazy.

After much prodding, Hudson revealed some information that he had received from one of his contacts deep in the CIA; information that was apparently so heavily classified that it would be impossible to verify independently.

He talked about a secret US project called 'Project Darkworm', which was rumoured to have conducted extensive research on bio weapons. This project was supposedly after the ultimate bio weapon, a pathogen that could achieve all four attributes of an effective bioweapon—the 'Four Horsemen', as I called them.

There were murmurings that they had actually achieved some measure of success in finding the ultimate bio weapon. It was a toxin, code-named Toxin Z, produced by a pathogen, code-named Pathogen Z.

Damini let out a low whistle.

Was there any clue about the identity of Pathogen Z and Toxin Z? Hudson hazarded a guess.

The prime suspect would be the most poisonous substance known to mankind—the dreaded botulinum toxin—responsible for a disease called botulism. This toxin is produced by a bacterium named Clostridium botulinum, or C.botulinum. According to a paper prepared by a Working Group on Civilian Biodefense and published in The Journal of the American Medical Association in 2001, a single gram of this toxin, evenly dispersed and inhaled, would kill more than one million people.

So theoretically, a few kilograms could wipe out the earth's population, subject to effective dissemination. Not surprisingly, covert programmes of many countries have focused on harnessing the deadly power of the botulinum toxin. But they have all met with technical limitations in weaponising it. Is it possible that Project Darkworm somehow found a way around these limitations, maybe by developing a genetically modified variant of the bacterium?

Damini and Sam continued reading pensively.

Pathogen Z, and probably Toxin Z, could apparently be transmitted through air, enabling it to be delivered effectively at a gigantic scale. This possibility for airborne infection, along with its virulence, and resistance to treatment and scalability, could make it potentially the most lethal pathogen known to man; more lethal than existing versions of the botulinum toxin.

Without an antidote, such a bio weapon would be potentially disastrous because it could annihilate not only the enemy but also the US itself. If and when fully developed, it could indeed be a weapon of mass destruction, maybe even a weapon of ultimate annihilation of the world.

Rumour has it that Project Darkworm was disbanded just after Obama's election in 2008.

Sam's eyes widened. This was serious stuff.

The next sentence was in bold letters.

> **HERE COMES THE SHOCKER**
>
> *When I described the symptoms of KaalKoot mentioned in the verses, Hudson said they are strikingly similar to the symptoms said to have been noticed in the testing of Toxin Z!*
>
> *Drooping eyelids, double vision, loss of control over facial muscles, weakness and loss of sensation in the arms, skin on the arms turning purple, laboured breathing, and difficulty talking and swallowing. The affected person progressively becomes paralysed and turns fearful, then delusional and finally dies a torturous death. The symptoms matched to a tee.*
>
> *Could it be that KaalKoot is the same as Toxin Z, and that Manohar and the Yogyaveer had stumbled upon it, even as the Imperial Guard were close on their heels, searching for it? The scientist in me is fascinated with the thought, even as the humanist in me is terrified.*

Damini had begun pacing up and down the small room. This was the type of challenge that she lived for.

Bavdekar was on to bio weapons, and he was missing. Hudson had clearly caught on to something, and he wound up dead. The third, a nutty professor, was in the next room at the safe house. And they were all on the trail of something that could apparently unleash destruction on a gigantic scale.

KaalKoot. The mythical plague that could destroy all of creation.

Botulinum toxin. A few kilograms of which could wipe out the earth's population.

Toxin Z. Probably an even more lethal variant of the botulinum toxin.

And somehow a bunch of professors were mixed up in all this.

They needed to talk to Bani. Now.

CHAPTER 22

ACG safe house, Goa, Tuesday, 2.15 a.m.

Bani bit his lip as he faced a belligerent Sam and a stern Damini. So they had gotten to know about KaalKoot, and the second leg of the Imperial Guard plot. Unlike with Mukhshuddi, he could not fib his way out this time.

Maybe he could play this to his advantage. Maybe he could sound cooperative and reveal just enough to make them co-opt him. That was still his best bet to find Bavdekar.

'All right, all right; I'll fill you guys in,' he said, palms open defensively.

'How very kind of you,' Sam smirked, settling into a chair.

Bani took a deep breath as he started. 'For many centuries, going right back up to medieval times, a terrible legend has been doing the rounds among the locals in the upper reaches of the Himalayas. About the most lethal poison ever known to mankind.'

'KaalKoot,' Sam said slowly.

Bani nodded. 'Kaalkoot. Named after the mythical poison that was unearthed during the Samudra Manthan, the churning of the cosmic ocean, mentioned in the Puranas. The legend among the locals is that any person who even inhales the air around an infected person develops a series of violent symptoms and dies within hours.'

Damini quoted from Shrikant Bavdekar's file. 'Drooping eyelids, double vision, loss of control over facial muscles, weakness and loss of sensation in the arms, skin on the arms turning purple, laboured breathing, and difficulty talking and swallowing. The affected person progressively gets paralysed and turns fearful, then delusional and finally dies a torturous death.

Bani nodded again. 'Professor Bavdekar and I had heard the legends but there was nothing documented, so it did not fall in the radar of government authorities and was not mentioned in any records. And then during Steve's travels, he did come across a few ravaged villages with not a single soul alive, and we started wondering whether the legends might be true.'

He continued: 'Professor Bavdekar put together the legends and concluded that that the toxin—KaalKoot—was probably produced by a bacterium which thrived in the low-oxygen environment of the upper Himalayas. The bacterium, or its dormant spores, might have been transmitted to humans by the bite of a certain type of tick, possibly belonging to the *Ixodidae* family, which might exist in the upper Himalayas.'

'Ticks?!' Sam exclaimed. 'They seem like harmless insects.'

'Ticks are technically arachnids, like spiders, not insects,' Bani snorted. 'And they are far from harmless. For instance, Lyme Disease, caused by a bacterium *Borrelia burgdorferi* and transmitted by a tick bite, is quite common.'

'Anyway,' Bani continued, 'when a human was bitten by this Ixodidae tick in the upper Himalayas, he would carry the bacterium, possibly in the form of dormant spores, back to the village. While the bacteria were largely dormant at very high altitudes, something dangerous would happen to them if the temperature became even marginally warmer.'

'And that was. . .?' Damini asked.

'The spores, which were harmless in themselves, would germinate into active bacteria, start to multiply rapidly and produce the deadly KaalKoot toxin. As the infected person breathed or sneezed, the pathogen would get aerosolised and get lifted up into the air inside tiny droplets or even dust. It would then spread through the airborne route, and infect anybody who inhaled this mist. A single infected person would be enough to infect his family, and through air currents, the entire village. Villagers still talk about KaalKoot in hushed tones, almost as if mouthing the word itself might invite the pestilence to their homes.'

'What's all this got to do with the Imperial Guard and the second leg of their plot?' Sam butted in.

Bani ignored him. 'In the nineteenth century, the British Regent in the court of the king of Nepal, Brian Houghton Hodgson, who was also an avid naturalist, heard about these legends, and took it on himself to investigate. He even documented a few insects or ticks which might be the carriers of the bacterium which produced the toxin KaalKoot.'

'Many decades later, in the 1940s, some members of the Imperial Guard seem to have gotten hold of some of Brian Hodgson's papers, and they realised that this tick and therefore KaalKoot, if discovered, could be a valuable tool for their unholy ends,' Bani said.

'How so?' Damini asked, skeptical.

'Because an airborne pathogen can literally spread like wildfire. It can kill people in the tens of thousands, if not hundreds of thousands. If discovered, Britain could have used it in their fight against the Nazis. And certain sections of the Imperial Guard felt that it could be used to accomplish something else.'

'What was that?' Sam asked, his curiosity overtaking his scepticism.

'To leave a "parting gift" for the Indians,' Bani sniggered. 'KaalKoot would fit in neatly with the Imperial Guard's intent to wreck India before the Empire left. The "Scorched Earth" policy. If they could not hold on to India, the Imperial Guard would reduce it to rubble before they left.'

Sam nodded, slowly comprehending.

'The first leg of the Imperial Guard plot—to destroy or desecrate iconic symbols of Indian civilisation—was somewhat metaphorical, aimed to strike at the country's pride. Testing KaalKoot on Indian territory, on the other hand, would be a real, deathly blow. It would leave the fledgling nation tottering on its knees, without leaving a clue about who had unleashed it. The trail of mass destruction would be impossible to erase for generations to come.'

Damini let out a groan, shocked. 'Would the British have sanctioned such a dastardly attack against the Indians?'

'Well, in a different context, Churchill is on record that he was "in favour of using poisonous gas against uncivilised tribes". He said that "it would spread a lively terror". While we do not have any evidence of Churchill being a member of the Imperial Guard, it is conceivable that the Imperial Guard might have gone ahead with their plans irrespective of government sanction,' Bani explained.

'How real was this plot? And how did you get to know about it?' Damini questioned.

Bani inhaled slightly. He would have to be careful now.

'Manohar seemed to fear that it was real. He and the Yogyaveer apparently visited multiple villages ravaged by KaalKoot, trying to find out more. And the Imperial Guard was close on their heels.'

'Did the Imperial Guard actually succeed in finding KaalKoot?' Sam asked.

'Obviously not, Einstein,' Bani sneered. 'If they did, they would have used it against the Nazis, right?'

'You still haven't answered how you got to know all of this stuff. It wasn't in the publicly available information in your papers,' Damini prodded.

Bani's face went pale for a second. His more recent discovery—the scroll that contained the verses—was known only to Steve and Bavdekar. Was there any way Damini had gotten to know about it?

But he recovered and played along. 'From another letter of Manohar's that I discovered. It is not in the public domain.'

Damini had noticed the momentary draining of colour from Bani's face. What was he hiding?

'What were these "verses" that Bavdekar referred to in his notes?'

Bani's heart skipped a beat as he answered. 'Manohar's letter was in the form of verses, that's all.'

***

Sam and Damini were back in the other room.

'The bastard is evading again,' Sam says. 'We now need to up the ante with him.'

Damini frowned. Bani did not seem the kind of guy with whom upping the ante was likely to have the desired effect. He was more the kind who might reveal things if put at ease.

'Is there somebody who can tell us more about this Project Darkworm?' Sam asked.

'There is,' Damini said tersely. 'But I am not sure I want to call him.'

***

Damini sighed as her memory went back to the events of two years ago.

She had first met Bob on an Interpol anti-terrorism exercise. He was a data mining specialist with the CIA—a tall, wiry guy; brilliant and witty, while also being nerdy. He had a certain offbeat kind of handsomeness and intensity, and that had attracted her.

Hacking was Bob's passion. During their tenure in Lyon, he had hacked with equal ease into the French intelligence network, into the records of the torrid deliberations of the European Central Bank in the months following the Lehman crisis, and into private videos of an English soccer league team having group sex following a home win.

If there was somebody who could tell her about Project Darkworm, it was Bob.

Damini frowned as she realised she would have to call him.

She had always known that their relationship would never work out. They were too far apart—she with the ACG, and he with the CIA. A life together was inconceivable. Yet, at a personal level, they were alike—creatures of the shadows, haters of mundaneness and conformism.

They were, to quote the Mahabharata, like logs of wood in a stream, destined to travel together for some distance, and then be separated when the time came.

With a sigh, she picked up her phone and switched on an encryption app. She could not risk Kunal, or the Chief, getting to know that she had contacted an external agency.

***

Tuesday, 2.55 a.m.

Bob called back within ten minutes with details on Project Darkworm.

It was a biological weapons' programme started around fifteen years ago. It was so deeply classified that no official records existed. It was not even clear whether the project had the sanction of the CIA top brass, or whether it was spearheaded by a bunch of rogue elements within the CIA. Bob had managed to get the information from a source deep inside the CIA.

This project was led by a mysterious guy of Eastern European origin, known in rarified intelligence circles as the Doc. In his early days in Europe, this man was apparently known as the 'Maestro'. But there were no records of the Maestro, not even of his name.

The rest of what Bob said rhymed with what Hudson had said: that it was rumoured that this group apparently had found some measure of success in finding the ultimate bio weapon, code-named Toxin Z, produced by a bacterium, Pathogen Z.

'However,' Bob said, 'they could not find an antidote to the pathogen. Without the antidote, the weapon cannot be effectively deployed because the pathogen can spin out of control and devour even those who unleash it.'

Bob continued: 'Now for the interesting part.'

'Huh?'

'All the key guys associated with Project Darkworm are now dead. One guy had a heart attack. The main guy—this guy they called the Doc or the Maestro—died in a bomb blast. One guy went mad, was lodged in an asylum and committed suicide, and another guy died in a car accident.'

***

Tuesday, 3 a.m.

Bob continued: 'Most details relating to these guys have been wiped out. Social security numbers, insurance details, police files, everything. It's almost like these guys never existed.'

'Then I suppose it would be too much to ask for some more info on this Maestro guy?' Damini asked, tentatively.

Damini's question tickled Bob at that precise place in his psyche where curiosity, masculinity and self-worth intersected.

'Give me some time,' he replied.

***

3.30 a.m.

Bob called back in half-an-hour. Damini put him on the speaker phone so that Sam could listen in.

'I have a photo of the Maestro.'

Damini cursed in exclamation.

'I'll take that as a compliment,' Bob continued. 'In five minutes' time, you can download it off an encrypted online storage box.'

Bob continued: 'I have a few sketchy details on the Maestro's background. Nobody knows his real name. He apparently hails from a princely family in eastern Europe. He seems to have had an alcoholic father whose misadventures came to an abrupt end when our boy, who went on to become the Maestro, impaled him with a dagger.'

'Wow,' Damini said. 'How old was the Maestro then?'

'He was a young boy of ten or eleven,' Bob said, eliciting an exclamation from Sam.

He continued: 'He was brought up in the Soviet Union, probably by a relative. He seems to have been a brilliant student who, after graduation, joined the Soviet government's bio weapons' programme—Biopreparat. His prowess at what he did earned him the moniker "Maestro". But over the years, he gradually got disillusioned with communism, especially when government officials back in his country colluded with his cousin to control his family estate. Incidentally, the cousin was subsequently found dead, also impaled on a dagger.'

Sam's face went pale. Deep within, his mind's eye conjured up an image—of Ananya, falling deeper and deeper into an abyss, dragged irreversibly down by the stuff of his deepest nightmares.

Bob continued: 'Post the fall of communism, the Doc, as he was known by then, was hired formally by the CIA. His vast experience with bio weapons was unparalleled in the US, and he quickly attracted the attention of officials at Langley. Meanwhile, he was apparently quite the connoisseur: he had exquisite taste, and was an aficionado of single malts, Cuban cigars and the like.'

'Seems to have been quite a character,' Damini mused.

'There is one more thing. There are allegations that he conducted experiments on human subjects in the Soviet Union, and there were hushed whispers about human experiments in Project Darkworm, too.'

***

Damini downloaded the Maestro's photograph from the online storage box whose codes Bob had given her.

She could send the picture to Kunal for comparing with the ACG's databases, but she decided against it. She did not want to answer questions about the source of the photograph.

She decided to grab a coffee. Bani and Sam, meanwhile, were both in adjoining rooms, continuously being monitored on CCTV by Gautam, the ACG guard at the safe house.

As Damini stirred some sugar into her coffee, she became aware of a knot in her stomach. Something was bothering her about the photograph of the Maestro.

Maybe it was his cold eyes. There was something very dark and evil about them. They reminded her of Bella Lugosi in the movie *Dracula.*

Or maybe it was the subtle twist of his upper lip, a twist which portended greater horrors, a window into the devious personality of someone who had crossed very far into the dark side.

Damini sunk into a chair. She had not even taken a sip of her coffee when her eyelids started drooping.

***

3.45 a.m.

Damini, asleep on her chair, was dreaming.

She dreamed that a North Korean nuclear bomb expert was

having breakfast with her and abruptly his face morphed into the Maestro's face and then the face of a dragon. Suddenly, the dragon grew bigger and bigger, and was about to engulf and smother her.

Damini woke up in cold sweat.

And then it struck her.

Monday morning, when Ji-hoon Kim was having breakfast at Kyani Bakery.

The man was stockily-built and somewhat short for a Caucasian. He had a sunken face and a thick mop of black hair. But there was another feature that had caught Damini's attention through the melee of Mumbai's morning crowd and the anxiety about tailing the North Korean.

It was his eyes. There was a deep, cold and sinister look about them that had made her quiver a bit, even in the bright glare of the morning sun.

The Maestro had been there that morning at Kyani Bakery.

CHAPTER 23

The Mansion, Tuesday, 4 a.m.

The man with the dark, sinister eyes and eerily calm voice took a sip of tea from his cup and savoured it lightly with his tongue.

The loud Americans were responsible for the appellation 'Doc', but he personally preferred the more sophisticated moniker from his days in Europe: the Maestro. For he regarded his work and passion no less profound than that of an artiste, musician or philosopher. Just as he preferred the mythological rich Indian name 'KaalKoot' to the drab name 'Toxin Z' given by the Americans.

The tea was Darjeeling's finest, personally sourced for him by one of his minions who had spent two days scouring tea estates across the length and breadth of Darjeeling. The minion in question was standing in a corner of the room, trembling as the Maestro took his first sip.

He let out an audible sigh of relief as the Maestro nodded slowly and took another sip.

'Update?' the Maestro asked a deeply tanned man who was standing in the centre of the room.

'All on schedule, sir. The kick-off will happen this evening. The midfielders have already got the balls from the defenders, and they in turn will set it up and pass it on to Sylvan.'

The tanned man was shaking slightly as he spoke. The Maestro was not physically imposing; he was around 5' 6" and a little stocky. But there was something about the effect he had on people. Just one look at his deep eyes, one word of his eerily calm voice, and the other person knew that he was dealing with an evil force.

The soccer euphemisms 'midfielder', 'ball' and 'defender' were at odds with the Maestro's suave, rather refined exterior, but they gelled well with the beast within him. A beast that was finally about to be unleashed.

CHAPTER 24

A missing scientist who was sticking his nose into secret bio weapons' research. A crackpot professor with a fantasy tale. A pathologically dangerous bio weapons' expert who had faked his death, was now in India, and was socialising with the choicest pick of the world's most dangerous people.

Damini rubbed her hands in anticipation.

She *loved* her job.

Along with the euphoria came the same strange feeling of unease that she had experienced when giving career advice to Sam a couple of hours earlier.

We become what we repeatedly do.

What about that was so disturbing?

***

Sam had been let into Damini's room by Gautam, the guard at the safe house. She was reading from a series of documents and papers that Mini had sent her, including the 2001 paper by Stephen S. Arnon, Robert Schechter, et al, that Bavdekar had referred to in his notes.

'Botulinum toxin seems to be a credible threat,' she said. 'During World War II, the US apparently produced botulinum toxin, and there were reports that Germany, too, had weaponised the toxin.

The Soviets, too, tested the toxin on Vozrozhdeniye Island in the Aral Sea. After the 1991 war, Iraq admitted to the United Nations inspection team that they had produced over 10,000 litres of concentrated botulinum toxin. That is many times the amount needed to kill the entire human population by inhalation.'

'Phew,' Sam said. 'Why then was it not used in the war?'

'Looks like most countries encountered technical problems in weaponising and disseminating it,' Damini said. 'The Aum Shinrikyo cult actually dispersed the toxin in Japan thrice during the 1990s, but the attacks failed.'

Sam exhaled. 'And somehow, the Maestro and his gang may have synthesised a version that can be more effectively weaponised. That does not seem like good news.'

***

Goa, Tuesday, 4 a.m.

'What the hell is this bio weapons' expert doing with the North Koreans?' Sam was saying as he paced around the room. 'More importantly, what is he doing in India?'

Damini offered Sam some coffee from the safe house espresso machine. She did not extend any such courtesy to Bani. His room was locked from the outside, a fact that Bani discovered when he tried to visit the restroom.

'I'm sure whatever Steve was mumbling in the hospital has something to do with this. He said something about a Demo,' Sam was saying. 'Possibly of KaalKoot?'

Damini hesitated. She had not told Sam about the Demo. 'I'll let you in on some classified stuff, Sam,' she said, haltingly.

'You'd better,' Sam said, his voice cracking a little. 'I have to find my girlfriend.'

Damini carried on: 'We intercepted some communication between North Korean agents on coded channels, about an event called the "Demo", scheduled for this week. Meanwhile, a whole bunch of questionable characters—representing syndicates ranging from a Colombian drug cartel to the Slav Gang to a North African dictatorship—have been spotted in Mumbai over the last couple of months.'

Sam was pacing up and down. 'Maybe the Demo is some sort of demonstration of this bio bomb, based on KaalKoot, or Toxin Z. And based on this Demo, maybe the North Koreans will decide whether to sponsor and support this Maestro guy in developing bio weapons. And maybe the other members of this cast of baddies are people that he is negotiating with.'

Damini nodded. Sam was making sense.

'So the Demo has to be big enough to demonstrate how lethal this bio bomb is,' Damini said. 'Going by what we heard from Bob, even a Demo could be as lethal as a nuclear bomb.'

Sam exhaled perceptibly, and said, 'That's scary. Especially since you said it's supposed to happen this week.'

***

Damini was thinking aloud. 'Why is this Maestro guy's base in India?'

Sam snapped his fingers as he had a burst of realisation. 'The Global Security Summit—GSS—in Delhi on Wednesday. The heads of state of the US, UK, France, Germany, Australia, Japan and India will all be in one place. If I was the Maestro and I wanted to give a "Demo", that's where I'd look.'

'Bingo,' Damini nodded appreciatively. 'But then, how about all of the above plus forty-five thousand other people?'

Sam's eyes widened as he slowly comprehended. 'You mean the T-20 cricket match—the match of the century—immediately after the GSS that same evening?'

Damini nodded.

'All the heads of states are planning to attend the match as a goodwill gesture,' Sam said, letting out a low whistle. 'The leaders of the free world, besides forty-five thousand people, dead in one single swoop.'

Damini nodded again. 'That's what I'm talking about.'

CHAPTER 25

The Mansion, 4.30 a.m.

The Maestro allowed himself the luxury of a mild smile. It had been a long, frustrating, multi-year wait since that evening in 2008 when he got to know that Project Darkworm was being shut down by the CIA. If things went according to design, he would be back on the map soon.

And the Demo would be just the first step of his larger plan.

The Maestro found himself reminiscing.

It had been an eventful journey.

He had always known that Botulinum toxin would be a good place to start his quest for the most powerful bio weapon. The toxin acted very effectively. By blocking the release of acetylcholine, a crucial neurotransmitter that is responsible for muscle activation, it rapidly led to paralysis of muscles, eventually culminating in respiratory failure and death.

But there were issues. Botulism as a disease has been around for centuries, and results from eating contaminated food, from wounds, or from direct inhalation. There exist antitoxins which would be effective in treating it if administered at the right time. The toxin itself could be destroyed at high temperatures. The spores, dormant versions of the bacteria Clostridium botulinum, are harmless in themselves and are fairly common in soil and sediments.

By modifying the genetic structure of various bacteria by using a combination of techniques including gene splicing, a process by which genetic information from one organism is introduced in another, the Maestro had developed a variant, called Clostridium dystolinum, as part of Project Darkworm.

Clostridium dystolinum produced the dystolinum toxin, an even more lethal variant of botulinum toxin. Unlike in the case of C. botulinum, the spores of C. dystolinum were not harmless. They would rapidly germinate into bacteria once in the human body, and the bacteria would then produce the toxin. The ease with which the pathogen could be aerosolized into extremely tiny particles gave it a powerful edge. And so did the fact that exposure to even the tiniest amount was enough to cause an infection. These traits enabled it to be more effectively dispersed over a large area through the airborne route. The pathogen would form spores easily, which could stay in air for long periods and infect human hosts. Compared to botulinum toxin, dystolinum toxin had a lower incubation period, and harsher symptoms, including disruption of mental faculties.

The Americans had insisted on giving the code-name Toxin Z to the dystolinum toxin, though he would have preferred a name like *Ragnarok*, the destruction of the world in Norse mythology, or *Pralay*, the final apocalyptic end of the world in Indian mythology. Free from the clutches of the Americans now, he could call it KaalKoot, after the identical toxin found in the upper Himalayas.

***

He still remembered the euphoria of those days.

Toxin Z always killed. In the absence of an antidote, every single person infected by it would die.

It acted fast. People exposed to it would start showing symptoms within an hour. It would kill some of its victims in an hour and all within sixty hours, much quicker than other biological weapons.

It could be produced and stored easily, making it scalable. It could be delivered effectively, making it easy to weaponise.

It was more infectious than other biological agents, and could be transmitted lethally through the airborne route. Through air currents, it could infect people over a wide area.

The Maestro still remembered the triumphant jubilation with which he had presented his findings to his benefactors. Even today, his hair stood on end as the memory overtook him.

***

The Maestro went over the details of the plan in his head.

The euphemisms of 'midfielder', 'ball' and 'defender' fitted the context well. The 'balls' were containers holding spores, dormant forms of the bacterium Clostridim dystolinum, which produced the toxin KaalKoot. The 'defenders' were the ones who had kickstarted the Demo by carrying the 'balls' into Delhi as part of a large food products shipment. The 'midfielders' had the job of setting it up—putting the 'balls' together into the final three pairs of two cylinders each that would be passed on to Sylvan, the person who was supervising the operation.

KaalKoot would kill those directly affected by the primary airborne infection in the stadium, some in an hour, and all within sixty hours. By then, through interpersonal contact—especially breath and sneezing, which would result in aerosolization into very tiny particles—it would spread to others and kill them, too. But the potency would be lower in secondary infected people, so rather than becoming a chain reaction, it would gradually die out by the time it reached the seventh or eighth degree host. By then, tens of thousands would be dead.

The International Cricket Stadium could seat forty-five thousand people. Many of these people would infect others outside the stadium. The Maestro's statisticians had estimated the death toll at eighty thousand.

But it would be a potent eighty thousand, including as it would the heads of state of the seven most powerful countries of the world who had gotten together to censure China and Russia.

Enough to point giant needles of suspicion at China and Russia. Enough to bring the world powers to the brink of a war, possibly the worst confrontation since World War II.

Good enough for a start, and to put him back on the map. Before he could execute his grander plan.

CHAPTER 26

ACG safe house, Goa, Tuesday, 4.30 a.m.

'Dammit. This is serious business. Can't you alert your agency?' Sam asked.

Damini shook her head. 'This is still just a hunch. Without tangible proof or at least strong pointers, the information will lack credibility.'

Sam's mind was racing. 'Assuming that the Maestro is planning something for Wednesday, there's one thing that does not make any sense. Why would he kidnap Bavdekar and go after Bani? What do they have that he wants?'

Damini wondered. 'It can't be to find KaalKoot; he has probably synthesised the bacterium which produces the toxin in the laboratory anyway.'

And then it hit Sam.

There was one common thread between Bavdekar's notes on the meeting with Professor Hudson and Bob's account of Project Darkworm.

'The antidote,' he blurted out. 'The goddamn antidote. That's the one thing Project Darkworm failed to develop.'

Damini let out an exclamation. 'Wow!'

Sam continued: 'Bavdekar said in his notes that without an antidote, the bio weapon could not be used at a global scale because it could spin out of control and annihilate not only the enemy, but also the person who unleashed it.'

Damini nodded. 'And Bob, too, mentioned that the Project Darkworm gang could not find the antidote to the toxin.'

'Somehow, these two madcap professors have some way to get to the antidote, and that's the one thing the Maestro—and probably his friends, the North Koreans—don't have.'

Damini continued the train of thought. 'Maybe that's why a Demo is needed. It is more like a proof of the concept. Not the full thing.'

Sam nodded. 'The Maestro is probably seeking state sponsorship, maybe from the North Koreans, so that he can develop an antidote and commercialise KaalKoot to unleash destruction at a much larger scale.'

Damini frowned. 'How exactly would two senile professors have some way to get to the antidote?'

Sam spoke animatedly. 'The Yogyaveer. The Gupt-Kandara. Maybe Manohar and the Yogyaveer somehow came across the antidote. And maybe the secret to it is contained in the Gupt-Kandara.'

Damini's eyes widened as Sam continued: 'So, maybe this Hidden Cave really exists. Maybe this villain is after Bavdekar and Bani to be able to lead them to it. To find the goddamn antidote; because that's the only thing that stands between KaalKoot and being able to unleash worldwide destruction with it.'

Sam paused to catch his breath. 'The thing that Bani was hiding—

these mysterious verses that Bavdekar referred to in his notes—I think they contain some clues to locate the Gupt-Kandara. That's probably what Bani was working on with Steve—Steve doing the exploring, and Bani trying to crack the clues. And when Steve called him, it was probably because he had found something definitive about the location.'

Damini nodded.

'And that's what the villains kidnapped Steve for. But he somehow escaped. And yet Steve managed to retain enough sanity to divulge something to Bani from his hospital bed.'

Damini looked at Sam. 'So, our only bet to get to the Maestro is to get to the location of the Gupt-Kandara. And there is only one guy who can help us get to it.'

'Bani Bhattacharya,' Sam nodded, baying for blood.

***

Tuesday, 5 a.m.

Bani's heart was pounding even as he stared defiantly at Damini and Sam.

How the hell had they learnt about the antidote? How much had Bavdekar revealed in his notes?

He would have to go with guesswork for now, and reveal only as much as he really needed to.

'An antidote,' he said slowly, 'called *Prativisha* in Sanskrit. Something that could be administered to neutralise the effect of KaalKoot.'

'How did Manohar and the Yogyaveer find it?' Damini asked.

'The plant life in the Himalayas is a rich source of both poisons and cures. Our mysterious Worthy One—the Yogyaveer—was apparently an expert in these secrets, starting right from the time he learnt yoga and meditation from a guru in the Himalayas as a teenager. He knew both about KaalKoot, and the antidote, the Prativisha.'

'What kind of antidote was this?'

'Some sort of powder extracted from a type of mushroom,' Bani replied. 'Fungi can produce certain compounds which can be effective antidotes to infections.'

From the papers Mini had sent her, Damini knew that botulinum toxin binds itself to a receptor at the neuromuscular junction. It then enters the neuron and blocks the release of the crucial nerotransmitter, acetylcholine. Acetylcholine is responsible for activating muscles, so the toxin is able to prevent muscle contraction all over the body, eventually causing paralysis and death. The antidote in this case was probably a substance that could somehow react with the binding sites and neutralise the toxic activity.

'So, the Yogyaveer basically found KaalKoot and the antidote, while the Imperial Guard didn't,' Damini said.

Bani nodded. 'This was the secret he was supposed to guard, along with all the artefacts and manuscripts, in the Gupt-Kandara. So that in case the Imperial Guard did indeed discover the pathogen and unleashed it on the unsuspecting masses, the Yogyaveer could use the antidote—the Prativisha—to prevent a death toll of hundreds of thousands, maybe even millions.'

'Would it not have been better to just make the antidote public?' Damini asked.

'Not really,' Bani answered. 'Sometimes it is best to let sleeping dogs lie. As recently as 2013, when some researchers in the US claimed to have discovered a new variant of Botulinum toxin, they refused to reveal its gene sequence, fearing that it could fall into the wrong ends. Certain things are best kept secret.'

'And this secret is still hidden somewhere, in the Gupt-Kandara,' Damini finished.

***

'What did Steve tell you at the hospital?' Sam asked.

Bani smirked. 'Nothing really. I thought I told you that already.'

'You need to refresh your memory,' Damini said sarcastically. 'You can take your time about it while you cool your heels in this safe house.'

Bani sighed. He had not come this far to reveal his life's work to a bumbling amateur investment banker and a cagey secret agent. But it looked like he didn't have a choice.

Or did he?

'I always take a morning walk,' he said. 'Helps clear my mind.'

'You can walk inside the room,' Damini said.

'Not the same,' Bani replied. 'Not once have I missed my morning walk in ten years.'

Damini knew about Bani's fanatical dedication to his morning walk from Mini's dossier. Maybe the morning walk would help the professor make peace and cooperate?

And then another idea struck her, and she decided to play along.

She pretended to hesitate, then murmured a reluctant 'Ok, but my security guard will follow you.'

As she walked out of the room and passed by the corridor, she whispered something discreetly to the safe house guard, Gautam.

***

Tuesday, 5.20 a.m.

Bani's mind was far from calm as he took his morning walk. His hands quivered in excitement as he remembered the verses from the scroll.

He was right at the cusp of the discovery of a lifetime. He had to flee from here. At any cost.

He sneaked a look behind him. The safe house guard, Gautam, was unarmed, lagging behind and seemed somewhat inattentive as he talked on his mobile phone. Nearby, a bus was just leaving from a bus stop.

Bani acted quickly. He hoped that he could run at least half as fast as he could as a youth during his soccer days.

***

Tuesday, 5.40 a.m.

'How the hell did Bani dodge past your security guard?' Sam yelled.

Damini smiled. 'Relax, I was the one who instructed the guard to let him escape.'

Sam looked at her incredulously, then calmed down sheepishly as he understood. 'Ah, the idea is to let him think he's free, then tail him surreptitiously. Maybe he'll lead us to the Gupt-Kandara.'

Damini simply nodded. She had also had the Goa police remove their alert on Bani.

'You secret agents are devious,' Sam laughed.

For some reason, Damini did not find Sam's comment funny. The same disturbed feeling came back to her.

We become what we repeatedly do.

***

Dabolim, Goa, Tuesday, 6.45 a.m.

Bani took a moment's rest to take in the morning sun after he called Souvik-da from a payphone asking him to email a flight ticket from Goa to Kolkata under a fictitious name.

He needed to refer to a couple of books from his home in Kolkata in order to make full sense of Steve's utterances at Solaris Hospital, but he knew that his home would be under surveillance by the villains.

There was no way to find the books in Goa. He would have to ask Mukhshuddi to get the books from the Asiatic Society Library in Kolkata.

***

Kolkata, Tuesday, 7 a.m.

'Samuel Beal's translation of the *Si-Yu-Ki: Buddhist Records of the Western World*, by Hiuen Tsang,' Mukhshuddi said, as he jotted down the name of the fourth book.

'I will be in Kolkata soon,' Bani said. 'I need you to get these books and meet me at Olly Pub.'

'Olly Pub, aha. That sounds like a plan!' Mukhshuddi replied. He did not probe further.

***

Goa, Tuesday, 8 a.m.

Damini hung up after speaking briefly on her smartphone.

'The old man is at the airport. He has managed to check-in for a flight to Kolkata via Mumbai without an ID,' she said. 'Though a discreet word from my team to the airline staff helped with that.'

Sam said, 'I assume you have folks in Kolkata ready to follow him when he lands.'

'One of my men is getting on the same flight as him,' Damini replied.

***

Goa, Tuesday, 8.10 a.m.

The Chief was on the line with Damini, and he was livid.

'I had said no contact with foreign intelligence agencies. I didn't make any exceptions for ex-boyfriends.'

'How did you find out?' Damini asked, incredulous.

The Chief smirked sarcastically as he said, 'We have our ways.'

It must have been Kunal who must have given her away, Damini thought bitterly. He must have somehow gotten to know; maybe from Mini?

Damini made a desperate attempt to argue her case, but it seemed like her assignment was split into two separate worlds.

There was the world of the visit of the baddies to India—Ji-hoon Kim and the characters from the Slav gang, the Cali Cartel, ISIS and the African dictatorships. Then there was the other world: Bavdekar's kidnapping, Professor Hudson and Project Darkworm.

Only Damini and Sameer believed in the connection between the two worlds—a connection predicated on Damini's memory of the Maestro's presence at Kyani Bakery that morning.

But she did not have a shred of evidence to support her case. No records of Project Darkworm existed. At Kyani Bakery, Damini had not been able to pan her pendant-camera to the Maestro. It was just her word.

'We have tight security at the GSS and the cricket match,' the Chief thundered. 'Not even a rat can slip past, leave alone a goddamned bio weapon. I will not compromise my credibility by raising some false alarm based on some irrelevant missing professor.'

'But Chief…' Damini tried to explain, but she was abruptly cut short.

'I am removing you as lead agent from this case. You are to return to Mumbai. From now on, Kunal will lead the investigation, and you are to cooperate with him. Is that clear?'

Damini grit her teeth. 'Yes, sir,' she said tersely.

***

Sam checked out the news on the television at the safe house.

The Asian stock markets were on a tailspin ahead of the Global Security Summit on Wednesday evening, as the GSS was to call for strict sanctions against China for its expansionary activities in the South China Sea. The Hong Kong and Shanghai markets were both down by 8 per cent, while the Nkkei was down by 6 per cent.

The US President, never one for controlling his words, had tweeted that the GSS was 'an opportunity to kick China's butt in public,' stirring up more than a hornet's nest. The Chinese had lined up long-range ballistic missiles along the border with India, Japan and South Korea.

Meanwhile, Russia was not happy either. A reprimand to Russia for its activities in Ukraine was also part of the agenda of the GSS, though this was only a token censure without any new sanctions.

Russia and China had closed ranks and lined up a Nuclear Energy Summit in Beijing where their defence ministers were due to discuss 'cooperation on nuclear warheads'.

In response, the US had stationed aircraft carriers close to Chinese waters. NATO bases in South Korea and Japan were on high alert. US bombers were staging trial runs as part of joint military exercises with South Korea and the Philippines.

And then it struck Sam. The Demo would do more than just cause a few thousand deaths in Delhi.

It might actually trigger off a world war.

***

Goa, Tuesday, 9 a.m.

Damini looked into the bathroom mirror, and found a distinctly downcast face staring back at her.

The means justify the ends, she had repeatedly told herself. Yet, here she was, deprived of the means to prevent a global catastrophe.

Being a natural rebel, she was no stranger to rebukes and reprimands, but she had never let them get to her. Back home in Mirzapur, a number of framed motivational quotes adorned the walls of her room. 'Impossible is nothing,' screamed one quote, with the Adidas logo underneath it. Another was an excerpt from a Nike ad: 'Failure is not an option.'

A whiff of meaninglessness had sneaked in on her in a couple of previous assignments, but it had never been this pronounced.

For some reason, the phone call with Bob lingered in her mind and took her back to their time together.

She had never had any illusions about the future of their relationship. Yet she seemed unable to let go of the faint memory of the warmth and intimacy she has shared with him. Was it the only redeeming feature in a life filled with adrenaline rushes and transient highs?

The greatest good for the greatest number. Somehow, it all seemed so empty now.

***

Even as Damini stared into the mirror for a long moment, her survival instinct started to kick in.

She might be constrained, but she would still figure out a way to prevent a catastrophe.

Impossible is nothing! The words echoed in her mind. *Failure is not an option.*

It was cheesy as hell, but she did not give a damn. She never did.

For a brief moment, she contemplated making a run for it. But with the ACG's tentacles spread far and wide, it would be pointless. She was better off cooperating and staying within the system and using the ACG's infrastructure informally.

She picked up the phone to make a few calls. She had built up a fan following among various sections of the ACG. This was the time to encash it and call in all the favours she could.

***

Goa, Tuesday, 9.45 a.m.

'I'm grounded,' Damini said to Sam. 'But I have made arrangements to get you to Kolkata on an Air Force plane. I will get you real-time info on Bani's whereabouts so that you can follow him to the Gupt-Kandara.'

Thankfully, the few ACG agents Damini had called were willing to help her informally. That list included Gautam, the safe house guard.

Damini gave Sam some cash, a fake identity card and a satellite phone. 'I'm sure the Chief is tapping into my main phone, so I'm giving you my satellite phone number. If it's a routine update, leave a missed call and hang up after two rings. If it's an emergency, then wait till four rings and I will call you back.'

'Buddy, I will help you as much as I can,' she said. 'But from now on, you're basically on your own.'

***

Sam breathed heavily.

Bani's theory about the Gupt-Kandara might be no more than a shot in the dark, but it was the only lead he had to the Maestro, and possibly to Ananya.

But what if Ananya's disappearance had nothing to do with the Maestro? Was she even still alive?

What if she was actually in cahoots with the Maestro's crew? Was there a side to her that he was not aware of?

Sam's mind, already reeling from lack of sleep, was throwing up progressively uneasy questions like an excavator digging up the earth.

Sam closed his eyes, trying to calm himself. Through all the doubts and the worries, there was only one feeling that lingered: that of love. For the woman whose smile went all the way to her eyes.

He would gladly go to the ends of the earth to find her. Even if he had to swallow the deadliest poison, much like the Lord Neelkanth himself.

'Kolkata,' Sam told himself gently. 'Just get to Kolkata.'

CHAPTER 27

The Mansion, Tuesday, 7 a.m.

After Bani hung up on his call with Mukhshuddi, a tall, heavy-set man at the Mansion, who was listening in on Mukhshuddi's phone calls, heaved a sigh of relief.

Bruce knew that he was on thin ice with the Maestro the moment his men lost track of Bani at Park Hotel on Sunday night. Bruce had fervently hoped that the rave party in Goa would give him a chance to retrieve the trail of Bani, Sam and Steve in one shot.

However, the Goa trail had gotten botched up. Rider and his crew had been unable to control the situation at Solaris Hospital. Bani and Sam had escaped, and Steve had died.

Bruce had panicked and kept the details of the botch-up from the Maestro, desperately hoping to somehow recapture the trail in the interim.

With Bani's call to Mukhshuddi's phone, maybe he had just got a golden chance to redeem himself in the Maestro's eyes?

***

The Mansion, Tuesday, 7.15 a.m.

As Bruce narrated the details to the Maestro, he felt a deep chill spreading across the room.

The Maestro, adept at understanding body language, had sensed the situation quite quickly.

Bruce's act of treason did not warrant a verbal firing. The Maestro anyway regarded angry verbal outbursts as the preserve of lesser, unsophisticated mortals.

He turned to an underling, his expression not betraying any sign of volatility, exuding instead an ominous undertone of quiet menace. 'Ask everybody to gather,' he said.

The powers of evil and darkness were about to focus themselves on the room.

The Maestro was sorry that he would have to lose Bruce. He was largely swift and efficient.

But an example had to be set. One of the Maestro's favourite quotes was from Machiavelli: It was more important for a leader to be feared than to be loved.

Meanwhile, a dozen other members of the Maestro's team had gathered in the room.

Bruce was quivering like jelly as the Maestro delicately opened his toolkit—his 'playbox', as he called it—with a sensitivity that would do an artiste proud.

Somehow, whenever he opened his playbox, an image from his childhood would come to the Maestro's mind.

He still remembered it vividly. His father had come home drunk, as usual, and in a foul mood. He, a young boy then, had hidden himself behind a couch and watched, frightened, as his mother trembled and suffered as she had done for years.

That night, somewhere in the midst of the shouts, the insults and the violence, something had suddenly snapped inside him. Something that unleashed a force that he struggled to comprehend, even to this day.

He had pushed his father, who fell down the stairs, hit himself on the head and cried out in pain. That was when he had taken the family's heirloom—a ceremonial dagger—and impaled his father with it.

Even now, as he thought of the incident, a ferocious energy overcame him, unleashing a kaleidoscope of emotions which included rage, a recognition of his own power, and a hunger for control. A hunger so deep that it could not be satisfied by mortal trappings of money and fame.

As Bruce's face twisted into an expression of unadulterated terror, the Maestro opened his playbox and took out a pair of pliers and an object which resembled an electrical drill.

It was time to have some fun.

CHAPTER 28

Delhi, Tuesday, 8 a.m.

The view of Lutyens' Delhi from Sylvan's hotel was spectacular. The placid green lawns of the Connaught Place central park stood out against a backdrop of beautiful Georgian buildings. The monsoons had not yet hit Delhi, so the city was still bathed in a warm, sunny glow.

Sylvan had woken up with his usual mix of alertness and purposefulness. Today was going to be a big day. He needed to do a recce of the site one final time, and report back to the Maestro.

He glanced at the view as he neatly combed his hair and put on a jacket that draped well over his athletic frame.

Below the hotel, office denizens were queueing up at a bus stop to head to their workplaces; like a swarm of ants. Going to work in a mindless herd every morning, and crowding back in the opposite direction every evening.

He wondered what the bus stop would look like after KaalKoot was unleashed tomorrow.

***

Delhi, Tuesday, 9 a.m.

In the car, en route to the International Cricket Stadium for the recce, Sylvan skimmed through the newspapers. They were filled with stories about how China was saying that the sanctions being proposed at the GSS were an 'act of war' and that they would have to 'respond appropriately'.

Sylvan went over the plan in his mind.

It was all quite simple, really.

The 'midfielders' had already received the 'balls' containing spores, dormant forms of Clostridium dystolinum, the bacteria that produced the toxin KaalKoot. Employed in industrial units in the city, they would subject the contents of the 'balls' to certain temperature, pressure and pH conditions. They would then pass on three pairs, each containing two sealed cylinders, to Sylvan that evening.

Sylvan's associate, Yash, had secured a job in the floodlights and generator maintenance room at the International Cricket Stadium eight months ago. He would have no problem smuggling in the cylinders into the stadium on Wednesday. He would keep one pair of cylinders with himself and hand over one pair each to Sylvan and another associate of theirs, Yuko.

Sylvan, Yash and Yuko would carry large backpacks, specifically designed to gradually release the contents of the cylinders through nozzles. As the three of them would briskly walk across the stands, the potent, finely aerosolised mix of live bacteria, bacterial spores and toxin would disperse widely across the stadium through air currents.

Sylvan, Yash and Yuko were under the impression that the Maestro already had the antidote and that they had been injected with it. They would realise the deception only when it was already too late.

KaalKoot was so highly reactive that it would quickly cause infection in those exposed. The spores, too, once they entered a human host, would rapidly germinate into bacteria, which in turn would produce toxin. Breathing and sneezing by affected people would result in aerosolization into very fine particles, and would help in spreading the pathogen further through air currents. The net result would be that within an hour, KaalKoot would have spread like wildfire across a large area. The analogy was that of a thin fuse lighting up an entire nuclear bomb. Just the three pairs of cylinders would be enough to contaminate the air in the entire stadium.

The people in immediate vicinity would all die, some within an hour and all within sixty hours. Through breath, sneezing and contact, these people, in turn, would infect others too. The potency would be lower in secondary infected people, and the outbreak would gradually die out.

But by then, eighty thousand people would be dead. And the countries who led the civilised world would be like headless chickens.

PART IV: THE DESTROYER OF WORLDS

KOLKATA

CHAPTER 29

Kolkata, Tuesday, 12 noon

The yellow cab belched smoke as it careened through the crowded Kolkata streets. Nearby, a long-suffering public transport bus lurched and sputtered as it lugged its fare for yet another back-breaking journey. All around, the sweat and chatter of people merged with the cacophony of horns and brakes into the giant melting pot that was Kolkata.

But Professor Bani Bhattacharya barely registered any of this. He was in another world, reminiscing about that fateful evening four months ago when he had discovered the Yogyaveer's scroll at a monastery.

The monastery was in a remote village in Nepal on the hilly slopes of the Himalayas. Bani had come across it while retracing various routes that Manohar and the Yogyaveer might have taken.

The sun was starting to set over the mountains, and the intricately carved wooden façade of the monastery was silhouetted against it, forming a mystical backdrop to the scenario inside.

The middle-aged priest at the monastery was very sick, and he had been able to narrate the story to Bani only haltingly.

Apparently, a couple of years ago, he had come across a charismatic old man when he was traversing a remote mountain pass while on a trip. Being lone travellers on the icy slopes, they had struck up a conversation. The old man was probably in his nineties, yet had a striking presence—a sparkle in his eye, a swing in his step, a countenance that exuded calm authority and a demeanour that immediately commanded respect.

Unfortunately, they had encountered a sudden, rough snowstorm, along with a deadly avalanche. As the priest himself was almost crushed by the ice, the old man rescued him, but in the process, ended up fatally injuring himself.

As he sensed his life-breath leaving him, the old man told the priest that he had the weight of a serious responsibility on his shoulders. He had been guarding a valuable secret for over seventy years, and was keen that the secret should not die along with him. Saying this, the old man had handed the priest a scroll with some verses in Sanskrit. The verses on the scroll would apparently lead the seeker to the secret.

The middle-aged priest was to find a way to disseminate the contents of the scroll to the wider world. If fate willed, someday somebody who was a *Yogya Dayada*, a 'Worthy Heir', would unlock the key to the secret using the verses on the scroll. If fate willed otherwise, however, the secret was destined to remain hidden forever.

The middle-aged priest in Nepal narrated the story to Bani amidst coughs and wheezes. He himself had been seriously ill since then, and had found no way to 'disseminate the contents of the scroll'. His only fear was that he himself might die before he could keep this promise to the old man.

Bani remembered vividly the kaleidoscope of emotions that he had experienced in that moment. The first emotion had been shock. Despite all the years of searching, Bani's logical mind had still not fully believed that the Gupt-Kandara and the Yogyaveer had survived all this while. And yet, here was proof.

The shock, however, was soon replaced by childlike excitement as Bani realised that the verses on the scroll represented a code to get to the Gupt-Kandara.

***

True to form, the Yogyaveer had indeed ensured that only a Worthy Heir should access the secrets of the Gupt-Kandara. The clues in the verses required a potential seeker to know intricacies of India's history and legends, besides having an expert's knowledge of Sanskrit and Pali.

The crowning glory seemed to be the architecture of the Gupt-Kandara itself, designed by the mechanical genius of the Yogyaveer. A series of obstacles—the Great Agonies—inside the Cave would test the seeker to breaking point. Only a person who displayed extraordinary mental capabilities could get past them.

Bani still remembered the moment when he read the verses for the first time. His hair had stood on end. In particular, he remembered the fourth verse.

The secret shall be revealed only to the Worthy Heir

That person alone, of supreme faith, courage, stillness and compassion

Shall be able to conquer the Agonies

And prevent KaalKoot from striking again.

Bani sensed an enormous weight on his shoulders. The meeting with the priest in Nepal had been serendipitous. If it had not been for that, the scroll, and the secret of the Gupt-Kandara, would have been lost to the world forever.

But if there was anybody who could be the Worthy Heir, it would have to be him. He would share the glory with no one else. And certainly not some upstart banker or snooty secret agent.

***

The scroll was now in, of all places, Bani's bank locker.

That was when Bani had enlisted Bavdekar's and Steve's support to crack the verses and locate the Gupt-Kandara, given their familiarity with the Himalayas.

Bani knew that Steve had only half-believed his theories. But this story had been too compelling for Steve to resist.

And that had made all the difference.

CHAPTER 30

Kolkata, Tuesday, 12.30 p.m.

A tingle of excitement ran through Bani's spine as he replayed the verses from the scroll in his head.

The scroll first gave an account of the story of Manohar Rai and the Imperial Guard's plan to destroy iconic symbols of Indian civilisation, and to unleash mass destruction in case they found KaalKoot.

It talked about how the Yogyaveer knew about KaalKoot from his teenage years under the tutelage of a guru in the Himalayas. He also knew its antidote—the Prativisha—which was a powder extracted from a mushroom that grew in the mountains. The Yogyaveer went into hiding at the Gupt-Kandara with a meaningful quantity of the Prativisha with him.

The scroll went on to describe that many years had passed, with India gaining Independence and the world order changing. The Yogyaveer observed all this from a distance, and kept abreast of developments on his occasional trips to civilisation.

Meanwhile, he was getting on in years, and his health was beginning to falter. However, true to his promise to Manohar Rai, the Yogyaveer had waited till all the members of the Imperial Guard had died; till 'the last of them was gone' and 'the danger was no more', so that the secret was now ready to be passed on.

In order to prevent it from falling into wrong hands, the Yogyaveer decreed that the secret would have to be discovered only by a Worthy Heir, a Yogya Dayada.

This account was then followed by the verses.

There were ten verses, with four lines per verse. Bani had translated the verses into English and numbered them in his notes.

The first three verses contained clues to the location of the Gupt-Kandara. The fourth and fifth verses detailed the qualities that the Yogya Dayada—the Worthy Heir—needed to have to be able to crack the Great Agonies. The next five verses—numbers six to ten—gave clues on how to handle the Great Agonies once inside the Gupt-Kandara.

***

Bani chuckled as he remembered the first two verses. True to form, the Yogyaveer had included references that only a person with a deep knowledge of Indian history could understand.

Verse 1

Many may seek to find the Gupt-Kandara

Some for the treasure, some for Kaalkoot or its antidote

But the Yogya Dayada will look beyond the obvious

Towards the land the Master visited with hesitation at the end of his journeys.

Verse 2

Seven yojanas from the origin of the river the Master had to cross

Eight yojanas from the Courtier's second home

There exists a settlement with the ten noises complete

Ten yojanas away lies the Gupt-Kandara.

The 'Courtier' in the second verse was probably Brian Houghton Hodgson, the British resident at the court of Nepal in the nineteenth century. Brian Hodgson was the same person who had heard about the legends of KaalKoot and had tried to locate the tick from which it originated. It was his writings on the subject that had got the Imperial Guard interested in KaalKoot.

'The land the Master visited with hesitation at the end of his journeys' . . . Bani had inferred that the 'Master' meant the Buddha. Before his *parinirvana*—his final exit from this world at the age of eighty—the Buddha had visited Kushinagara, in modern-day Uttar Pradesh.

But what was the bit about the Master having been hesitant about that last journey? There was no such record. And what was it about 'looking beyond the obvious' in the first verse?

Bani did not have all the answers when he had discovered the scroll four months ago. But he had had no doubt that all the signs pointed to Nepal.

Nepal was not far from Uttarakhand, where Manohar Rai had lived. Nepal was also where Bani had found the scroll at the monastery. And Kathmandu in Nepal was where Brian Hodgson had made his second home.

***

As the Kolkata cab snaked past the halting traffic, Bani shook his head in disbelief.

He had been totally on the wrong track the last four months. It was not Nepal.

That was what Steve had wanted to tell him at Solaris Hospital.

Steve had said: 'Master . . . different . . . l . . . l . . . lo.' The 'Master' referred to in the first verse was 'different' from what Bani had presumed. Not the Buddha.

Hiuen Tsang, also known as Xuanzang. The Chinese pilgrim who had travelled to India in 630-645 CE to learn more about the Law of the Buddha. Hiuen Tsang had written detailed accounts of his travels. Hiuen Tsang was respectfully known as the 'Master of the Law'.

'Law,' not '. . . l . . . l . . . lo'.

The Master in the verse referred to Hiuen Tsang, not the Buddha. Bani had not 'looked beyond the obvious'.

The land that Hiuen Tsang had 'visited with hesitation towards the end of his journeys' in the first verse was Kamarupa, which corresponds to modern-day Assam and north Bengal. Not Kushinagara. Hiuen Tsang's initial hesitation was well documented.

Damn, Bani thought. To think that he had missed this interpretation. It now seemed so clear.

The references in the second verse now fell into place.

The 'origin of the river the Master had to cross' referred to the river Karatoya, which Hiuen Tsang had to cross to get to Kamarupa. It is now a small stream known as Phuljhur, but it was once a great river, a branch of the mighty Teesta. The origin of the Karatoya is in the Baikhunthpur jungles in Jalpaiguri district of Bengal.

The 'Courtier's second home' was Brian Hodgson's second home. Bani had mistakenly assumed this to be Kathmandu, with England being his first home. But it actually referred to Darjeeling, which is where Hodgson retired to, if Kathmandu were to be considered his first home.

So the second verse said that seven and eight yojanas from these two places respectively was 'a settlement with ten noises complete'.

Yojana was an ancient Indian unit of distance, measuring around thirteen kilometers. 'A settlement with ten noises complete' was a euphemistic way of referring to a city in ancient Pali literature.

So, this city had to be around eight yojanas, or a hundred kilometres, from Darjeeling, and around ninety kilometres from the origin of the river Karatoya.

Probably Gangtok, capital of Sikkim.

Damn, Bani cursed again!

It was not 'In . . . s.s.sick' that Steve had meant to say. It was 'in Sikkim'.

And 'Ho . . . Ho . . . Hottt' was Hodgson. Hodgson, during his retirement in Darjeeling, had spent a lot of time trekking in Sikkim.

Bani whistled in excitement.

So the Gupt-Kandara would be ten yojanas, or a hundred thirty kilometres, from Gangtok. He needed to consult his books for a narrower fix on the location, but it was pretty clear he needed to head to Sikkim.

Steve's last utterances were not the blabberings of a delirious mind. They were the desperate outpourings of a soul who knew that time was limited. And that he needed to convey the maximum possible details with each breath.

Bani sighed heavily as he took off his glasses and wiped a tear from his eye.

The tear was for Steve. God bless his soul.

CHAPTER 31

Dabolim airport, Goa, Tuesday, 12.05 p.m.

Sam sunk into his window seat in the Sukhoi Air Force aircraft. He had had exactly five hours of sleep in the preceding forty-eight hours, and was struggling to focus.

It all seemed surreal now. The last two days had been a blur, and he just longed to rewind the clock, back to Mumbai, back to when things with Ananya had been lighter.

He remembered a particularly lazy Sunday afternoon when they had hung out at his apartment, exchanging light banter as he made coffee. He also remembered them kissing that afternoon—the passionate kiss of two souls who loved each other.

He sighed. All that was gone. A chain of events had now been set in motion from which there was no turning back.

The aircraft began its steep ascent from Dabolim airport. As the gigantic vista of the Arabian Sea dominated the view, Sam could see a few ships dotting the surface of the waters. Insignificant. Miniscule.

It reminded him of a time from very long ago. He must have been around eight years old when the Colonel had taken him on his first of many treks up the Himalayas. He remembered being awed by the sheer vastness of the mountains and the dots that were the towns far below. Man's handiwork, irrelevant and infinitesimal compared to the enormity of nature.

A part of his being was beginning to yearn for those times when sleep consumed him.

***

Kolkata, Tuesday, 1 p.m.

Bani got off the cab with a spring in his step.

He needed to figure out a list of places in Sikkim—ten yojanas from Gangtok—which might contain the Gupt-Kandara. To do this, he needed to refer to the books that Mukhshuddi would have hopefully borrowed from the Asiatic Society library.

Bani could feel his heart beating in anticipation. He could not wait to meet Mukhshuddi at Olly Pub.

***

Olly Pub, Park Street, Kolkata, Tuesday, 2.30 p.m.

'Dada, you seem anxious. Everything okay?' Mukhshuddi asked Bani as he slurped down a drink.

'Nothing, Mukhshuddi, all fine. Just a little preoccupied,' Bani replied. 'Anyway, I have to go now. I will trouble you again if I need anything more.'

***

Dum Dum airport, Kolkata, Tuesday, 2.45 p.m.

Sam heaved a sigh of relief when he finally exited Dum Dum airport. With alerts out for him everywhere, it helped that the ACG agent escorting him had bypassed security and whisked him out.

***

Park Street, Kolkata, Tuesday, 2.45 p.m.

As Bani stepped away from Olly Pub and walked down the street, a sixth sense told him that something was not all right.

He whirled around and looked at the sea of commuters. Among the dozen or so faces that he saw, one seemed vaguely familiar. It was lean, with a big nose and slightly shifty eyes.

The same sixth sense reminded him that the face was that of a man he had seen sitting at one of the tables in Olly Pub.

Bani stopped dead in his tracks. He could not resist looking back again, even though one corner of his mind warned him that this could alert his pursuer.

One glance back, and the hint of recognition on the lean man's face told Bani what he needed to know.

He needed to get away from here, and he needed to do it fast.

***

It was a crowded street, filled with pedestrians, and the crowds were preventing a swift escape.

Bani looked at the traffic signal, and it was red at the moment. An idea struck him.

He braced himself for a run without giving out any outward signs of inching towards the road.

As the signal turned orange, Bani abruptly turned and commenced his sprint across the road, hoping to pull a fast one on his pursuer.

Unfortunately, the driver of a red Honda sedan was in a hurry, and had set his car in motion before the signal turned green.

The last thing Bani saw before the searing pain hit him and he lost consciousness was the crowd of people rushing to his aid. Even in this age of apathy, Kolkata is one place where people step forward to help.

With the last vestiges of consciousness, Bani helplessly took in the crowd of people. The man with the lean face and big nose was among them, and moving towards him quickly.

CHAPTER 32

The Mansion, Tuesday, 2.30 p.m.

The Maestro whistled softly. So his man was on Bani's trail. Would Bani lead him to the antidote?

The antidote would be the key to his larger plans. The Delhi Demo, after all, was just the beginning.

***

After going underground post the shutdown of Project Darkworm, the Maestro had managed to take things to the next level. He and his team—working in the shadows, and wedded to no country—developed a version of Pathogen Z that had an even more deadly characteristic.

Unlike the original Pathogen Z, which decreased in strength as it spread, this version would actually get stronger as it moved from primary to secondary to tertiary hosts, as the bacterium mutated by acquiring new genetic material from the host which enhanced its ability to multiply. This made it self-perpetuating, causing a chain reaction. This had been his second eureka moment. He had called the version Pathogen Z2.

Unfortunately, the Demo in Delhi would have to be a controlled one using the original Pathogen Z, not a chain reaction involving Pathogen Z2. A chain reaction using Z2 could spiral out of control, and eventually infect entire continents, including possibly his own team and the North Koreans.

In the absence of an antidote, he could not risk it. So the Demo was only phase one of his plan.

***

The Maestro's statisticians had calculated that if a critical mass of the self-propagating Pathogen Z2 was let loose simultaneously in thirty carefully chosen cities, possibly using helicopters, then things would be very different from Delhi. Pathogen Z2 would, like a snowball gathering momentum, become progressively more infective and virulent as it spread. It would proliferate uncontrollably, affecting more and more people in larger and larger areas, forming an ever-widening circle of influence and unleashing a gigantic bio weapon chain reaction which would spread far and wide across the globe.

None of the known biological or chemical weapons, such as sarin or anthrax, could match up to even a millionth of this impact.

The damage would be far more than from a single nuclear bomb. The appetite of this bio weapon chain reaction—the bio bomb—would increase as it spread, much like a demon getting hungrier and deadlier with every kill. The only comparable effect would be from a series of nuclear bombs detonated across the globe.

The entire world order as we know it would be brought down to its knees, leaving a power vacuum that could be filled by the right individual, supported by the right weaponry and the right infrastructure.

That would be phase two of the Maestro's plan.

The objective was not to just cause mayhem. Nor was it about the money. Despite living among the Americans for many years, he never did imbibe their single-minded devotion to it.

He was about bigger things—about a vision for the world; about power being in the hands of the intelligent and the ambitious; about the right place in history for connoisseurs who understood nuances of science, history and human behaviour.

But there were still some hoops to be crossed before he could execute phase two of his plan.

***

The Maestro needed infrastructure to mass produce and weaponise the pathogen, and he needed a sponsor. Not just a splinter group with money, but a nation that could partner with him in his rise.

That's why the shopping around—meetings with the Colombian drug cartel, the Serbian mafia, the North Koreans and the African dictatorships.

He had finally settled on the North Koreans. But the Maestro first needed to show them what he could do. The Demo would do exactly that.

The North Koreans had an axe to grind, and that always helped. They were still seething from their betrayal by the Chinese—their erstwhile friends—who forced them into a humiliating peace settlement with the Americans. The primary suspicion—and wrath—of the US for the Demo would be directed at China, and that would be sweet revenge.

Ji-hoon Kim had left India on Monday night after having committed North Korean support, subject to the Demo being successful.

Once the North Koreans had bitten, the Maestro could start to execute phase two of the plan.

But one thing stood between him and the realisation of his grander dreams.

The antidote.

***

Through all the years of testing, the Maestro had still not found the antidote.

Sylvan had been made to believe that he had been vaccinated with the antidote, but this deception would not suffice for a thirty-city operation that needed to be executed flawlessly. Besides, a thirty-city attack using Pathogen Z2 would almost definitely spiral out of control and eventually threaten his sponsors—North Korea—and the Maestro himself. The only protection would be the antidote.

And that was exactly what he did not have.

***

It was serendipitous that he had gotten on to Bani's trail.

When he heard a few months ago that a well-regarded Indian professor was discreetly checking with bio weapons experts on a mystery toxin called KaalKoot from the Himalayas, he had ordered the wiretaps to be put on him. Through Bavdekar, they had latched on to Bani as well.

The Maestro's ears had perked up further when the wiretaps mentioned effects of KaalKoot on humans that seemed remarkably similar to those of Toxin Z, the dystolinum toxin.

And then the Maestro's mind, ever alert, worked it out. The

atmospheric conditions in the Himalayas were likely to be conducive to the propagation of certain ticks from the Ixodidae family that were likely to be carriers of Clostridium dystolinum, or Pathogen Z. The low oxygen and temperature conditions in the Himalayas might mean that the bacteria would exist as dormant spores at high altitudes, but the moment an infected person reached even a marginally higher temperature zone, the bacteria would start multiplying, producing the toxin and spreading through air.

Could it be that Manohar Rai and the elusive Yogyaveer had indeed stumbled on Pathogen Z decades ago?

Implausible though it seemed, the symptoms described matched too closely for it to be a coincidence.

The Maestro had people travel up to the Himalayas, complete with hazmat suits, and test for sub-species of Ixodidae ticks that might be carriers of Pathogen Z. Sure enough, the results were positive.

So, the Yogyaveer had indeed stumbled on to Toxin Z. Or KaalKoot. The Maestro liked the latter name better. There was so much more character to it.

This presented an even more fascinating possibility. That Manohar and the Yogyaveer had knowledge of the Prativisha, the antidote to Toxin Z, whose prescription was preserved in a hidden cave.

A cave which was out there somewhere, waiting to be found.

***

The Maestro knew, better than anybody else, that there was no room in history for those who almost won.

There had been enough goof-ups already—Steve's disappearance,

Bani's escape, and the botch-up up in Goa. Yet, he was still hot on the trail of Bani and the Prativisha, the antidote.

Again serendipitous. But this time he could not take any chances. He called one of his men. 'I want more people in Kolkata. Get them to organise ammunition and mountain transportation gear.'

He continued: 'And keep arrangements ready in case I, too, need to go.'

CHAPTER 33

Kolkata, Tuesday, 3.30 p.m.

Sam's satellite phone rang. It was Damini, who was now at the ACG office in Mumbai, telling him that Bani was in Family Hospital in Kolkata. Two ACG agents, to whom she had made a discreet personal request, had been tailing Bani, and had witnessed the accident. In fact, unknown to Bani, it was an ACG man who had taken him to the hospital.

The other ACG agent had chased and managed to apprehend the man with the lean face and big nose, but a bullet from behind had got him within seconds of that. The lean-faced man had died a swift death on the crowded Kolkata street.

The man had clearly had accomplices—accomplices who were tailing him and had unambiguous instructions to shoot and kill if any of their compatriots were in danger of being compromised.

***

Family Hospital, Kolkata, Tuesday, 4.30 p.m.

Bani had fractured his leg and had lost some blood. It took the doctors an hour to stem the bleeding, stabilise the bone and bring him back to consciousness.

Bani struggled to focus as he stared at the ceiling in the intensive care unit.

Despite being on painkillers, he could feel the searing pain. Yet, he paid scant attention to it, consumed as he was by a sickening realisation.

He was not going to be the Yogya Dayada, the Worthy Heir.

The opportunity of a lifetime, the moment for which he had let go of everything—his fame, his laurels and even his family—was almost upon him, and yet here he was, immobile.

For the first time since the night Muneera had left him, he felt his eyes moisten.

***

As Bani felt the tsunami of despondency begin to engulf him, a distant memory came back to him. Of that fateful day, many years ago, when Professor Mitra had first taken him to the Asiatic Society of Bengal.

Even in his current state, the memory of that afternoon gave him goose bumps. He could still remember the quiver in Professor Mitra's voice, and the awe with which a young Bani had listened to him as he realised that he had found his life's passion.

It had never been about the accolades and the recognition. It had always been about the love of history.

And today, that same love of history required that he should place getting to the Gupt-Kandara and its contents above any selfish considerations.

Bani sighed. Distasteful as it was, he knew exactly what he had to do.

He had to marvel at life's irony.

Here he was, having given up everything in single-minded pursuit of his goal; yet, the cocky upstart investment banker and the unsubtle secret agent represented his only hope to get to the Gupt-Kandara.

Between the young man and the secret agent, however, he somehow felt a kinship with the young man, despite all the outward animosity.

Bani sighed again. Maybe destiny had willed it this way so that it could test Bani's passion.

Ignoring the stabs of pain shooting through his leg, Bani braced himself for handing over the fruit of his life's labour to the young man.

He had barely registered that he had no means of actually contacting the young man before he passed out from the effect of the sedatives.

***

It was a further thirty minutes before the doctors reluctantly allowed Sam to meet Bani in the ICU.

Sam did not say anything. He just went and sat by Bani's bedside.

Bani spoke feebly. 'Thanks for not giving me the smug look.'

Sam threw up his hands in a placatory gesture. 'Nothing personal, Prof. I'm just a guy trying to find his girlfriend.'

Sam felt a lump in his throat as he used the word 'girlfriend'. How much he had resisted using that word when Ananya was around. Would he get a chance to make amends?

'You might want to get to the Gupt-Kandara fast, then,' Bani said weakly.

'What do you mean?'

Bani had a resigned smile. 'I'm finished now. Totally stranded. I might as well tell you everything before the villains get to it.'

His chest heaved as he squirted out the next few words. 'But promise me you'll not chicken out.'

***

Taking short breaks for rest, and with the nurses periodically reprimanding him for straining himself, a mellowed Bani told Sam everything, starting from the story about the dying Yogyaveer handing over the scroll to the priest from the Nepalese monastery, to Bani's interpretation of the first few verses based on Steve's clues at Solaris Hospital.

'Whew, that's a lot of stuff,' Sam whistled. 'You sure keep your cards close to your chest, don't you, Prof.?'

'Occupational hazard, buddy,' Bani began laughing, and then bit his lip as pain shot through his body.

Sam nodded, and then he, too, started laughing. Bani was the last guy he expected to call him 'buddy', and not just because of the age difference. Funny how the absence of choices made the unlikeliest of people shed their inhibitions.

***

Bani had passed Sam a sheet of paper with the verses from the scroll written on it.

'So, these verses are supposed to provide clues to find the Hidden Cave, and also to crack the traps inside it, huh?' Sam asked.

'The ancient Indians were masters at allegory, at describing man's inner struggles through colourful external imagery,' Bani replied. 'The verses are not to be interpreted at face value. You need to look for deeper meanings in them.'

Sam read the second verse out aloud.

Verse 2

Seven yojanas from the origin of the river the Master had to cross

Eight yojanas from the Courtier's second home

There exists a settlement with the ten noises complete

Ten yojanas away lies the Gupt-Kandara.

'What is a settlement with ten noises complete?' Sam asked.

'That's a euphemistic way to refer to a city in ancient Pali literature,' Bani replied. 'The ten noises of a flourishing town, according to the texts, are elephants, horses, chariots, drums, tabors, lutes, song, cymbals, gongs, and the sound of people crying "eat ye, and drink".'

'These ancient dudes sure had a sense of humour,' Sam muttered.

Bani continued. 'This city being talked about here is Gangtok. So, ten yojanas away from Gangtok lies the Gupt-Kandara. That's a hundred thirty kilometres. You have your task all cut out.'

'Really?' Sam exclaimed. 'A hundred thirty kilometre radius is over eight hundred kilometres of circumference, amidst snow-clad peaks, inaccessible dirt tracks, dense fog, treacherous mountains and zero visibility. I would rather take a chance finding a needle in a haystack.'

'Easy, hero,' Bani motioned, as he suppressed a dart of pain from his wound. 'The third verse contains more clues to the location.'

Verse 3

Climbing unwaveringly up the path beyond the Garden of Heaven

Walking by the river through blinding mists

Crossing the greatest moat of them all

The lion's mane shall meet the scorpion's claws.

'What in hell's name is this?' Sam exclaimed.

'From Gangtok, you need to follow the path to some place called "the Garden of Heaven". Then you need to walk by a river.'

'I got that bit,' Sam interjected. 'But what is the "greatest moat of them all"?'

'A moat is typically a water body surrounding a fort, to guard it against attackers. Some Sanskrit texts talk about human fear as forming the greatest moat.'

'Fear?' Sam queried. 'You mean, like people are afraid of going to a place for some reason, and that itself keeps them away, and forms an effective moat?'

'Yes,' Bani replied. 'So you need to walk along the river towards some place that people are afraid of going to.'

Sam read the last line.

The lion's mane shall meet the scorpion's claws.

'Pray, explain,' he said.

Bani wheezed a little. 'No clue. I have not found any references to this in the ancient texts.'

'Maybe the answer is not to be found in the texts. Maybe it's a local legend,' Sam said.

Bani looked at Sam with sudden respect. 'Maybe you're right.'

'Maybe…' Sam pondered, as he looked at the fifth verse.

Verse 5

The Worthy Heir shall reach the sanctum

Only after enduring the four Great Agonies

Through faith, fearlessness, stillness and silence

Shall the Worthy Heir conquer the Agonies.

Sam's eyes widened. The only way to enter the inner sanctum of the cave, which was where the Prativisha was presumably preserved, was to go through this obstacle course: the four Great Agonies. He looked at Bani questioningly.

Bani looked a little sheepish. 'Er . . . Ashoka had set up a "Chamber of Torture" during his reign where transgressors were put through the "Five Great Agonies". The Gupt-Kandara is probably modelled on this.'

Sam winced as Bani continued. 'There are some interpretations which refer to the hard reality of death as the fifth agony. Maybe that's why there are only Four Agonies in the Gupt-Kandara.'

Sam breathed hard as he realised the significance of what he was hearing.

The Gupt-Kandara was no ordinary cave. It was a death trap for anybody who would be foolhardy enough to attempt to clear the four Great Agonies.

CHAPTER 34

Kolkata, Tuesday, 5.30 p.m.

Sam was just about to ask Bani some tough questions about the Great Agonies when a stab of pain shot through Bani's body, causing sharp convulsions.

Sam shouted for the nurse, alarmed.

The nurses and doctor rushed in to take charge. 'You need to leave now,' the nurse glared at Sam. 'He's already strained himself too much.'

***

Sam walked slowly towards the cafeteria.

Garden of Heaven.

People afraid to go somewhere. The greatest moat of them all.

The Chamber of Torture.

Sam paused for a moment as he walked. Somehow these images seemed oddly familiar.

He dismissed the thought. His mind, short on rest, must be playing tricks on him. There was no way an esoteric historical puzzle should seem even remotely familiar.

Yet, the potpourri of words swirled around unforgivingly in Sam's head, creating a cacophony.

There was some association with all this, but it seemed to be from Sam's distant past, a past which he had tried hard to bury.

He decided to go for a walk to clear his head. He walked out of the hospital, hailed a cab, and got off at the Kolkata Maidan. It was starting to rain lightly, but Sam did not mind.

He was too engrossed in his thoughts to notice a somewhat grungy man getting off a bike behind him.

***

ACG office, Mumbai, Tuesday, 6 p.m.

Back in Mumbai, a somewhat chastened Damini had continued her efforts at being heard. But, as with her previous attempts, her entreaties had fallen on deaf ears.

Damini was desperate. She picked up her satellite phone and started to dial Bob's number. Maybe she could warn the US contingent instead.

No sooner had she dialled Bob's number than a couple of ACG agents walked into the room and held out a pair of handcuffs.

The last thing the ACG agents did before Damini was sent to a detention cell was to confiscate her satellite phone, the one that she had asked Sam to call on in case of any emergency.

***

Delhi, Tuesday, 6 p.m.

The cricket match would start in exactly twenty-four hours.

Sylvan had a satisfied look as he inspected the three pairs of sealed cylinders in his possession.

The mechanism to unleash the pathogen was very simple. There were only two steps.

First, Sylvan would have to lock the two cylinders together and wait for thirty seconds. In which time, the contents of the two cylinders would mix and form a toxic cocktail of spores, live bacteria and toxin, primed to kill.

Then all Sylvan would have to do was press a trigger, and KaalKoot—the deadliest toxin known to man—would be released into the atmosphere.

***

Kolkata, Tuesday, 6 p.m.

Sam was walking around the Maidan, oblivious to the grungy man tailing him, when the first flash of realisation came to him.

Seventeen years ago . . . he must have been eleven then. His father, the Colonel, was still in his forties; still young. Unknown to them then, just a few months later, they would receive news that would change their lives forever.

That evening, unmindful of the turn that fate was about to take, they were in high spirits. Colonel Rajan was with his son on their fourth trek together. This trek was in north Sikkim, and they had hiked from a town called Lachung to a place called Yumthang, known as the 'Valley of Flowers of the East'.

Yumthang valley was lush green in the spring, with a gazillion flowers covering it like a delightful, multicoloured carpet. There were red rhododendrons, pink primroses, yellow poppies, pink louseworts, yellow buttercups, and a dozen other varieties.

The Colonel had remarked that the place seemed like a playground of the gods.

The Garden of Heaven.

There was a Valley of Flowers in Uttarakhand as well, but it was Yumthang that fitted the description in the verse.

The rest of the stuff then fell into place.Yumthang was around a hundred thirty kilometres from Gangtok. The Gupt-Kandara, too, was supposed to be around a hundred thirty kilometres from Gangtok.

Sam felt a surge of excitement. He was close to cracking the third verse.

Verse 3

Climbing unwaveringly up the path beyond the Garden of Heaven

Walking by the river through blinding mists

Crossing the greatest moat of them all

The lion's mane shall meet the scorpion's claws.

The river Lachung Chu passed via Yumthang. So, he would have to continue uphill and follow the course of the Lachung Chu or one of its tributaries.

That was when Sam had his second flash of realisation.

Some locals at Yumthang had mentioned a legend about terrible things happening to those who attempted to traverse the treacherous, inhospitable mountains west of Yumthang.

Sam had not fully understood the local legend then, but now it all made sense. This was the greatest moat of them all; the moat of human fear, more effective than any weapons or rivers.

So he would have to go to Lachung, then to Yumthang, and then walk in a westerly direction along the Lachung Chu river, or maybe one of its tributaries, up the snow-clad hills.

And there the lion's mane shall meet the scorpion's claws.

Whatever that meant!

***

Sam's mind was made up. He had to get to Sikkim. Fast.

He hopped into a cab to get to Bani's hospital. On the way, he dialled Damini's satellite phone number.

A terse 'Hello' from a male voice came through the line.

Sam hesitated. This did not make sense. Damini had been clear that she would not pick up the phone. He was to leave two rings and then she was to call him back.

Sam quickly hung up. Clearly, Damini was in some trouble.

He switched off the satellite phone's power button. He could not afford to be tracked by whosoever it was that had gotten hold of Damini's phone.

He called Dev, a resourceful acquaintance from his college days, who was based in Darjeeling and specialised in Himalayan treks.

After the usual pleasantries and 'long-time-no-see' stuff, Sam got straight to the point. 'Dev, I need some permits to travel around Sikkim. And I need to get to Gangtok quickly, from Kolkata.'

'Bro, I will arrange for the permits. But getting to Gangtok quickly will be a problem. There has been a sudden onset of strong winds and heavy rainfall in north Bengal and Sikkim, apparently triggered off by a high pressure zone over the Tibetan plateau. Gangtok airport is closed, and flights to Bagdogra airport, near Siliguri, are delayed. Meanwhile, a passenger train en route to Jalpaiguri has gotten derailed, so all train traffic to north Bengal is running at least eight to ten hours late.'

'What then?' Sam asked, frowning.

'Your best bet is to take a rocket bus from Esplanade bus terminal in Kolkata. It will take you to Siliguri, from where I will arrange an SUV to get you to Gangtok. You'd better hurry; I think there's a rocket bus that leaves Kolkata at 7 p.m.'

Sam looked at his watch; it was 6.05 p.m. 'Rocket bus, huh?'

'Let me warn you . . . it's not the most pleasant of rides, but it will get you there. Fast.'

***

Bani was still woozy, but conscious enough to understand that Sam had cracked the riddle.

He spoke with a huge amount of effort. 'Hats off to you,' he croaked. 'Though we still need to figure out the bit about the lion's mane meeting the scorpion's claws.'

Bani coughed, lightly at first, but then as he coughed again, he could not get back his breath.

Sam's eyes widened in horror as Bani's face turned progressively blue. He rushed closer to Bani, thumping his chest loudly as he shouted for the nurses.

Thankfully, Bani had only fainted. The nurse gave Sam a stern look. 'I thought I told you not to talk to him.'

Sam backed off from the ICU and went into the waiting area.

The TV was showing some 'breaking news'. China had tested an intercontinental ballistic missile, while the US had conducted military exercises precariously close to Chinese waters. Meanwhile, a German private aircraft had mistakenly entered Russian airspace and had been shot down. Five civilians were dead.

'The world is on a knife's edge ahead of the GSS tomorrow, to be followed by the cricket match in the evening, and the press conference at the International Convention Centre on Thursday.' The news anchor spewed out the entire sentence without breaking breath.

Sam sighed. Even assuming no delays due to the rains, it would take eleven or twelve hours to get to Siliguri, a further four hours to Gangtok, then over five hours to Lachung and then heaven knew how many hours after that to get to the Gupt-Kandara near Yumthang and crack the Agonies.

The world might go up in fumes before then.

Sam could not wait for Bani to regain consciousness. The rocket bus would leave Kolkata at 7 p.m. It was already 6.20 p.m. He barely had time to pick up some supplies for the trip.

***

ACG office, Mumbai, Tuesday, 6.45 p.m.

A livid Damini clenched her fists and brought them down crashing against the door of the detention cell at the ACG office.

She knew that she would end up being confined to this cell till the GSS got over. She felt a surge of anger against the Chief, but could not feel too righteous about it. After all, many a times, she had herself subjected others to exactly the same routine.

Was it Kunal who had given her away? She never did like him. Or was she just being her usual, suspicious self?

She was angry with the Chief. And with Kunal. And with society. And with her relatives in Mirzapur. And with patriarchy. And with authority. And with things in general.

Damini let out a scream.

She could not believe that it had come to this.

She was just a fireball of rebelliousness and anger. Was there anything else to her at all?

She found that disturbed feeling coming back to her once again.

We become what we repeatedly do.

***

Kolkata, Tuesday, 6.58 pm

A breathless Sam reached the Esplanade bus terminal just before 7, with a heavy backpack complete with climbing boots, woolen clothes, lip balm and medication for acute mountain sickness.

'Are you going to Mount Everest, dada?' asked the clerk at the ticket counter.

'Something like that,' Sam replied tersely.

***

Kolkata, Tuesday, 7 p.m.

Sam took a look at the passengers in the rocket bus.

There was a craggy, tramp-like guy who seemed to belong either in a prison or a de-addiction centre. There was a couple who seemed to have just had a really bad argument. There were only two other passengers—a boy who seemed to be in his teens and a pot-bellied man with a roving eye.

Not a particularly inspiring bunch. Sam wondered how the rocket bus company managed to make ends meet.

He did not know that the grungy, tramp-like guy had been shadowing him from the time he had shown up at the hospital to meet Bani. Or that, with Damini now grounded and incommunicado, the ACG men in Kolkata had gotten off his trail.

Sam was assailed by a splitting headache and a nauseating feeling in the stomach as the images of Vivaan, Riyaa and the puppy, the corpse at the Mumbai ATM, and the photo of the Maestro, all churned rapidly in his head. He seemed to be stuck in a maze; there was no escape from it, and he was no closer to finding Ananya either.

Sam decided to use the night on the rocket bus to get some sleep. He needed to have his wits about him if he had to crack the Great Agonies.

I hope this bus doesn't rocket me straight to heaven, he murmured as he closed his eyes.

'…or hell,' he found a voice in his head completing the sentence.

PART V: WHERE THE LION'S MANE MEETS THE SCORPION'S CLAWS

EASTERN HIMALAYAS

CHAPTER 35

North Bengal, Wednesday, 4 a.m.

The rocket bus rocketed through the highway, subjecting its hapless passengers to an extreme version of the bump-and-grind routine. The rains had abated, helping the bus maintain a high speed.

Sam was dreaming about a ferocious lion chasing him through a jungle of trees and hills. As with many dreams, the world of reality intersected seamlessly with the world of his subconscious mind. Each bump of the rocket bus coincided with Sam jumping over a bush or hurtling down a hillock in the dream.

As Sam ran through the forest of his dreams and made his way up a hill, the lion snapping its jaws close to his heels, his ascent was rudely stopped by a horrifying sight ahead. A gigantic scorpion, almost the size of an elephant, was positioned right along his path. It had an eerily perfect set of claws.

If Sam wanted to avoid the scorpion, he would have to break step immediately and risk being mauled by the lion. As his mind wavered for a split second, he tripped on a boulder and fell to the ground.

The lion continued at its momentum and overshot him, heading right towards the massive scorpion. For a second, the lion's mane met the scorpion's claws, and then, suddenly, everything froze over, covered in snow.

The impact of Sam's crash over the boulder in the dream was mirroring the rocket bus actually stopping with a massive gush of deceleration. Sam awakened from his dream just as the lion's mane and the scorpion's claws froze in the snow.

Bleary-eyed, he looked around. It was the hour before daybreak. All the passengers were asleep. The bus driver was heading towards a small chai shack by the roadside.

And then it struck him.

The lion's mane shall meet the scorpion's claws. Frozen in snow.

Maybe this line in the verse referred not to a local legend, but to the physical appearance of a hill or rock formation.

He would have to go to Yumthang, walk along the Lachung Chu river or one of its tributaries, and look along the westerly direction for a rock formation resembling a lion's mane meeting a scorpion's claws.

That was probably where he would find the Gupt-Kandara.

***

Delhi, Wednesday, 6 a.m.

On the D-Day, Sylvan woke up as usual, freshened up and headed down to the hotel coffee shop for breakfast.

A half-amused smile spread across his face as he read the morning newspaper. News about the GSS and poor Chinese economic data shared space with actress Megha's preference for 'men with taut butts' and an expose about yet another cricket match-fixing scandal.

He wondered what tomorrow's headlines would read like.

An ancient verse from the Bhagavad Gita came to his mind. Sylvan had first seen it in a calligraphed version at the Maestro's office. This was the same verse that Oppenheimer was supposed to have quoted to describe the first nuclear test in Los Alamos many years ago.

I am become death, the destroyer of worlds.

***

Rocket bus, Wednesday, 6.15 a.m.

The rocket bus rocketed Sam into Siliguri at 6.15 a.m., well ahead of schedule, complete with a sore back, a churning stomach and a feeling of having been mauled by a bear.

Not exactly my idea of a holiday, Sam thought as he tried stretching his aching back.

He spotted the Land Rover arranged for him by his acquaintance, Dev.

As Sam got into the Land Rover, he stole a look around in all directions, checking for any obvious tails. There were none.

He was not aware that the craggy guy had planted a micro GPS-cum-audio transmitter in Sam's backpack when he had gotten off the bus that morning during the driver's tea break.

***

ACG office, Mumbai, Wednesday, 8.30 a.m.

Damini had not been able to sleep in the detention cell, having spent the entire night feeling frustrated and angry.

She looked up as she heard the sound of the key turning in the lock of the cell.

It was Kunal, and he had come to surreptitiously let her out of the detention cell.

'Why are you disobeying the Chief's orders?' she asked defiantly.

Kunal gave Damini back her satellite phone. 'Much as I hate your guts, I think you might have a point about the bio weapon stuff.'

Damini's jaw dropped in surprise.

'I need your help to get to the bottom of this shit,' Kunal continued. 'Now get cracking.'

He added, 'I'm the lead agent, so I'm authorised to offer you the use of the ACG's resources. But you'll still need to lie low. I don't want the Chief grounding me, too.'

'Maybe I'm not such a jerk after all,' Kunal added.

Damini, overcome by surprise, was tongue-tied.

'Spare me the thanks,' Kunal grinned. 'I'm still going to take credit for your work.'

And with that he walked away, leaving her open-mouthed.

Damini felt a wave of guilt and self-doubt creep up on her.

She had been quick to suspect Kunal, and equally quick to accept his act of generosity when it suited her.

What did that say about her?

***

Along the road from Siliguri to Gangtok, Wednesday, 8.45 a.m.

The Land Rover was speeding along the narrow mountain road from Siliguri to Gangtok. It was raining lightly, and the weather had gotten distinctly cooler as Sam proceeded towards higher altitudes. The view was breathtaking even through the mild fog, with green hills on one side and a steep drop to the roaring Teesta river on the other.

But Sam was not quite enjoying the view, consumed as he was by a burning impatience to get to Yumthang and take a shot at finding the Gupt-Kandara.

Desperate to find an anchor for his anxiety, he was tempted to call Damini. Should he take a chance and try to reach her through the satellite phone again? Or would that be walking straight into a trap, considering that somebody was probably tracking the satellite phone signals?

Sam's itchy fingers got the better of him before he could even finish his ruminations. He ended up switching on the phone and dialling Damini's number.

To his surprise, she picked up.

'What the hell are you doing near Sikkim?' she asked, her tracker registering Sam's location.

Sam brought her up to speed on the verses and the presumed location of the Gupt-Kandara.

Damini did a quick calculation in her head. From her location in Mumbai, she would take at least six hours to catch up with Sam.

She did not have the luxury of that much time. The cricket match in Delhi was to start in ten hours.

She could not use the ACG's resources openly, so she could only discreetly rely on contacts with other agencies, such as the Army. Her best bet was for Sam to go ahead and find the Gupt-Kandara and Prativisha before she caught up with him.

Sam was, to use ACG lingo, her *asset*, and she needed to *use* him carefully.

Somehow, the words rankled in Damini's head.

***

'You'll need permits to get to the protected areas in Sikkim,' Damini said. 'I'll have somebody speak to the government department there to expedite it. Do you want some Army folks to accompany you?'

'No need,' Sam replied tersely, squirming. If the Army got involved, the control would slip out of his hands. He could not afford that, especially if Ananya was in the Maestro's clutches.

Damini sensed Sam's discomfiture. Sam was obviously keen to avert the Delhi Demo. But if he had a chance to barter the Prativisha with the Maestro in exchange for Ananya, would he yield?

Either way, she would have to ensure that Sam's feelings did not get in the way and botch this up.

'We need to have a chat on what you do once you find the Prativisha,' Damini said.

Sam fidgeted uncomfortably. 'Let's find the goddamn Prativisha first.'

Damini did not prod further. Maybe this was not the best time to rake up this issue. Over years of *manipulating* assets, she possessed the tact required to *handle* them.

CHAPTER 36

ACG office, Mumbai, Wednesday, 8.50 a.m.

Damini got off the phone with the folks at the Army base in north Sikkim.

She had been very specific in her request.

The surveillance would have to be very discreet. Only one well-trained Army person could shadow Sam. She was certain the Maestro, too, would be following him and she could not risk alerting him.

The Maestro was the fish that she wanted to catch. Sam was only the bait.

She again felt a stab of guilt, but she quickly quelled it.

After all, she had a job to do. She needed to save tens of thousands of lives in Delhi.

The greatest good of the greatest number.

She hated that it had to turn out this way, but what had to be done had to be done.

We become what we repeatedly do.

***

Delhi, Wednesday, 10 a.m.

The International Cricket Stadium erupted in a flurry of activity as final preparations were underway for the match of the century between the Indian team and the Dream Combo XI. The pitch was being inspected, and the staff fervently hoped that the game would not be marred by rain. It was not yet time for the monsoons to reach Delhi, but the rains had hit Mumbai rather early this year; thus, the staff were understandably nervous.

The choice of a cricket match was an exercise in smart politics. The US wanted to demonstrate its 'pivot' towards Asia, and that it wanted to keep China's political ambitions in check by aligning with India. There was no better way to make a statement of political affiliation with India than through a cricket match.

The GSS would conclude by 4 p.m., after which the foreign delegates, including the heads of state, would be escorted to the International Cricket Stadium. The match was to start at 6 p.m., and would probably finish around 9 p.m.

Yash double-checked the timings and sent an encrypted message to Sylvan. The message was clear and simple: 'Demo on track.'

***

Gangtok, Sikkim, Wednesday, 9.45 a.m.

Despite the sharply winding mountain roads and the continuous, albeit light, rain, the hundred twenty kilometres from Siliguri to Gangtok were covered in three-and-a-half hours, thanks to Dev's Land Rover and the skilled driver, Bikash.

Sam could not help but enjoy the view. The majestic mountains, the lush valleys, the roaring rivers, the rich local legends and the vibrancy of the local culture combine to make Sikkim a veritable Shangri La.

Bikash stopped briefly in Gangtok to fill some forms and pick up their permits.

Damini had clearly put in a word to the folks at the government department. Sam got the paperwork completed in ten minutes and Bikash and he were on their way to Chungthang, the next halt on their route.

***

En route from Gangtok to Chungthang, Sikkim, Wednesday, 10.45 a.m.

As the Land Rover sped along the winding mountain roads, the temperature fell noticeably, and so did the visibility. A thick layer of fog covered the road like a shroud.

Sam was acutely conscious of the ticking time. The GSS would conclude by 4 p.m., and the cricket match would start by 6 p.m.

He would have to get to Chungthang, then to Lachung, and then to Yumthang, all by road. After that, it would be an arduous trek through tough mountains and treacherous weather to locate the Gupt-Kandara.

He needed to get the Prativisha—the antidote—before people in Delhi started dying.

But he also needed to figure out how to free Ananya. How would he do that? Would he need to bargain with the Maestro? Maybe hand over the Prativisha to him?

But that would clear the last obstacle for the Maestro to unleash worldwide mass devastation.

Would it be morally right to condemn millions to their deaths for the sake of saving Ananya? Was Ananya even alive?

Sam remembered her eyes, and the smile that went all the way to her eyes, and his heart fluttered and sank at the same time.

He hoped fervently that the burden of making the choice would be taken away from him.

Anyway, it was already 10.45 a.m. It all seemed like a hopeless quest.

'Faster, dada,' he egged Bikash on.

Bikash did not acknowledge. He was already driving way faster than what was prudent in the narrow, winding mountainous roads. The fog was getting thicker by the minute, and visibility was dropping rapidly. One wrong turn, and their Land Rover would hurtle down many hundred feet to the ravine below.

***

En route from Gangtok to Chungthang, Sikkim, Wednesday, 11.15 a.m.

As they reached a small village en route to Chungthang, Bikash stepped on the brakes. The Land Rover screeched to a noisy halt.

It turned out that they had passed a small outlet selling momos—dumplings with an assortment of stuffings—staple fare in the Sikkim Himalayas.

'Dada, we are in a hurry,' Sam said.

'I've been driving non-stop through this,' Bikash said, gesturing at the fog outside. 'The least you can do is let me have breakfast.'

'Okay,' Sam said. 'But no more than ten minutes.'

CHAPTER 37

En route from Gangtok to Chungthang, Sikkim, Wednesday, 11.17 a.m.

The momos at the roadside eatery looked delicious, but Sam knew what the treacherous mountain roads and hairpin bends could do to a stuffed stomach, so he chose to abstain.

Sam started to look at the fifth to tenth verses which dealt with the Great Agonies and gave clues on how to overcome them.

Verse 5

The Worthy Heir shall reach the sanctum
Only after enduring the four Great Agonies
Through faith, fearlessness, stillness and silence
Shall the Worthy Heir conquer the Agonies.

Verse 6

You lose your faith once, it will slow you down a bit
You lose your faith twice, you still have a chance
If you lose your faith thrice, the doors of heaven
Will be closed to you forever.

Verse 7

The human race spends a lifetime running from fear,

That is not the way of the Worthy Heir

He who stares fear directly in the face

Shall pass gracefully from one world to the next.

Sam's heart sank, He could not bring himself to read the remaining three verses. This stuff seemed really abstract. What had he gotten himself into? Did this Kandara place really even exist? Or was he on a wild goose chase, believing in some crazy fantasy of a madcap historian when Ananya was possibly already dead somewhere?

He had to call Bani. This was bullshit.

His mind agitated, the momos seemed even more irresistible to Sam now. He ended up gorging on them.

***

Sam used the phone at the eatery to call Family Hospital in Kolkata. He managed to get through to the Intensive Care Unit, but hit a dead end there.

'He is scheduled for surgery later today,' the attendant at the ICU reception said. 'Tomorrow would be the earliest that you can get to speak to him.'

Sam grit his teeth as he hung up the phone.

Were the verses really a guide to cracking the Agonies? Each of the verses seemed to demand that the seeker exhibit a specific quality. The sixth verse, for instance, demanded that the seeker exhibit faith. Did the Yogyaveer use his mechanical engineering acumen to design traps that somehow test these qualities in the seeker?

With renewed enthusiasm, Sam looked up the eighth to tenth verses.

Verse 8

He who is still in the face of the most intense motion

He who observes the flow of the universe with equanimity

For that person, the waters shall not pose a danger

He shall reach his destination without much effort.

Verse 9

He who survives the torrent of fear and gets past the ocean of despair

Keeping at bay the ever-lingering insanity

He shall find the rhythm of stillness

And finally hear the sound of his heart.

Verse 10

Silence is the language of the gods

Silence is the deliverance of the soul

What is inaudible to a layperson

Is audible to the seeker who is one with the silence.

Sam smirked. It still did not make any sense. The easier explanation was that this was all just a sick joke.

He could not even speak to Bani to vent his frustrations. He was now basically on his own.

***

Delhi, Wednesday, 1 p.m.

The area around the International Convention Centre was abuzz with activity as the GSS began.

Roads around the venue had been cordoned off since the morning as the most powerful people in the world had made their way to the GSS venue.

The Indian TV channels were having a field day, alternating between reporting on the US-China and US-Russia tensions, the stock market crash, the upcoming cricket match and how India was at the centre of everything. A series of news vans were parked outside the security perimeter, and eager reporters were swarming around, hoping for sound bites from any foreign delegates who would care to talk.

Among the reporters was a wiry man with probing eyes, named Yuko. He had a news van of his own, and complete press identification papers. He sat calmly in the van, surveying the scene and reporting to Sylvan.

***

Chungthang, Wednesday, 12.45 p.m.

After crossing the growling Teesta river and passing through spectacular views of waterfalls, a colourful array of fluttering prayer flags signalled that they were at Chungthang, around eighty kilometres from Gangtok, at an altitude of 5,870 feet above sea level. This was the place where the Lachung Chu and Lachen Chu combined to form the river Teesta.

The journey from Gangtok was covered in three hours despite the dense fog, thanks to Bikash's skillful driving.

'Well done, Bikash,' Sam said.

'Save your thanks, dada,' Bikash replied. 'The weather is getting worse. We may have to halt en route.'

Sam sighed. They could not afford to get slowed down.

Sam read out the altitude: '5,900 feet'.

Their next stop would be Lachung, at 9,600 feet.

Sam let out a low whistle. Things were going to get tougher.

***

En route from Chungthang to Lachung, Wednesday, 1.15 p.m.

The Land Rover ascended steeply over the next half hour. The weather got colder, the roads got rougher and the surroundings got mistier. The steep ascent, coupled with hairpin bends, started playing havoc with Sam's sense of balance.

He took out a shawl from his rucksack and draped himself with it. His breathing was beginning to become laboured and his stomach was starting to churn with the winding roads.

They were not even halfway to Lachung when Sam yelled sharply. 'Stop.'

A startled Bikash stepped on the brakes as the Land Rover swerved dangerously in the middle of a hairpin bend before coming to a halt.

Sam opened the door and rushed out, barely managing to reach the road's edge as he vomited.

He came back to the car, borrowed a water bottle from Bikash to wash himself, and then sheepishly returned to his seat.

Sam took out a pill and swallowed it with some water. Eating the momos had clearly been a bad idea.

He needed to make sure he did not come down with altitude sickness.

***

En route from Chungthang to Lachung, 1.20 p.m.

As the fog cleared a little, Sam saw a small waterfall giving rise to a stream which gently intersected their road and passed on.

Even in the midst of feeling disoriented because of the steep climb, Sam could not help but admire the view of the valley and the hills. For a few moments, his mind went back to the treks of his childhood, and then his six-month journey through the Himalayas, after graduation.

How much simpler those times had been.

Sam was quickly brought back to reality as the urge to throw up overcame him again.

***

En route from Chungthang to Lachung, Wednesday, 1.30 p.m.

A sulking Bikash slammed on the brakes suddenly, throwing Sam momentarily forward.

Sam looked at Bikash and frowned. He did not want a demotivated driver.

As a silent Bikash simply pointed ahead, Sam slowly realised what had happened.

The fog had returned with a vengeance, accompanied by strong winds. They could barely see a few feet ahead.

Sam breathed deeply, struggling to maintain his sense of balance in the low oxygen environment.

He did the math in his head. Considering the weather, they could aim to reach Lachung not earlier than 2.30 p.m., and then they would need at least a further hour to get to Yumthang. He would then have to hunt through the snowy, cold hills on foot, hoping against hope to find the Gupt-Kandara. Thereafter, he would have to attempt to clear the Agonies.

The cricket match was starting at 6 p.m. He had no time to lose.

Besides, they were now at 7,500 feet, and they had ascended pretty quickly, with no time to acclimatise. Even for a seasoned trekker like Sam, it was proving to be difficult to deal with the rarified air and the sharply changing altitude. With a further climb ahead, he had better get to his destination fast before his body gave up on him.

Sam egged Bikash on. 'Arrey, dada . . . I'm sure you've driven through worse.'

If there is a way to kindle a man's vanity, it is to praise his driving skills. Bikash drove on, albeit reluctantly.

***

The fog got worse as they drove on. Visibility dropped to almost zero as Bikash ended up driving more on instinct than on actually being able to see ahead.

The road passed through treacherous bends with steep drops to the valley below. More than once, Sam held his breath as the Land Rover skidded on the wet road, making screeching sounds.

Bikash valiantly plodded on, but the engine coughed and sputtered as he drove, finally grinding to a halt.

Bikash looked at Sam, shook his head and pointed to the engine.

Sam, meanwhile, jumped out of the vehicle and puked uncontrollably by the roadside.

***

Every man has a limit to his endurance. For Sam, already reeling under the beginnings of altitude sickness, and having had only a few hours of sleep in the preceding three days, that limit seemed to have been reached.

He had probably already lost his job. There was no point even bothering to call the office to check.

His photo was most likely featuring on the 'wanted' list in dozens of police stations across Maharashtra and Goa.

His vehicle was stranded in the middle of heavy fog on a desolate hill. Making it out of here alive would in itself be a challenge, especially considering the icy winds.

If he chose to follow the crazy riddles in the verses, he was going to land up at a dead end if the professor was wrong. And the trail to Ananya would be over. Finito.

His fate could be worse if the professor were right. He would be welcomed by the Great Agonies, modelled on an ancient Torture

Chamber, with only some obscure verses for company.

He had promised himself that he would find Ananya, wherever she was, but he had failed. Once again. Just as he had failed at his education venture.

A farrago of thoughts churned inside Sam's mind as he doubled-up by the roadside. A giant-sized visage of the Colonel seemed to come up in front of him, mocking him, reminding him that he was good for nothing.

Yet, somewhere between the throwing up and the dizziness, another visage came to mind—the earnest face of somebody that he had felt close to. And now missed deeply.

And then there was the thought of the tens of thousands who might die in Delhi.

Sam found himself telling Bikash, 'Let's figure out a way to move ahead, dada.'

CHAPTER 38

In a room inside the Mansion, Wednesday, 1 p.m.

Ananya let out a light groan as she stretched herself. Professor Bavdekar looked up from his chair placed opposite her with bloodshot eyes.

They had slept only around six hours out of the last sixty, and that had begun to take a toll on them. Not to mention the emotional roller-coaster of being abducted, blindfolded, transported through bumpy roads, and being holed up in this room for the last two days.

Things could have been worse. By kidnapping standards, the suite they were in was the epitome of luxury. They each had separate bedrooms, albeit small, windowless ones, while the central study area had a table, a clean bathroom and was actually air-conditioned.

At first, this didn't seem to make any sense. But then, as the abductors had tersely explained what they were after, it all added up.

What they wanted was for Bavdekar to crack the verses which would lead them to the Gupt-Kandara and to the antidote. The objective was to provide him with a conducive atmosphere to work on what they wanted, not to physically inconvenience him.

The first thought that had struck Ananya was rather grim. She realised she was completely dispensable to the abductors.

***

Bavdekar had saved her, for the time being, by telling the abductors that she was indispensable to his research for cracking the verses.

Ananya, not one to give up easily, had spent the first few hours of their captivity trying to look for ways to escape. She had tried loosening the tiles in the bathroom ceiling, climbing up to the air-conditioning vents, and attempted to worm out information from the persons who delivered food to them. But with CCTVs and listening devices all over, and no loose objects, there was little she could do.

Their best bet was to try and help the abductors crack the verses.

Although Ananya had introduced Professor Hudson to Bavdekar, she was not aware of the entire background of what Bavdekar was after. So Bavdekar had to surreptitiously bring Ananya up to speed on everything—the Imperial Guard, the Gupt-Kandara, KaalKoot and the verses. He had to slip in details into casual conversations, supplemented with scribbled notes. With the CCTVs and listening devices, they could not afford to alert the abductors that Ananya was not actually in the know of things.

Ananya's heart sank as Bavdekar came to the bit about Project Darkworm and the bio bomb. The bunch they were dealing with did not seem like people who would let them out alive even if they succeeded in cracking the verses.

***

Ananya's mind went back to Sunday evening, and to the argument with Sam.

She missed him now. She longed to be back with him, maybe at his apartment, cozying up on the couch, drinking coffee, looking into his eyes.

And then her mind came back to the present, to the stark interiors of the study, and to Professor Bavdekar's forlorn expression, and she found herself despairing that she might never see him again.

***

Meanwhile, Bavdekar was having no luck with the verses. His background was in botany and zoology, not in history. The only crutches he had to help him were the smatterings of information that Bani had shared with him.

And now, time was running out. The masked man who had come in last had ordered their bedroom doors to be locked. They were now confined to the central study.

They had to come up with results. Soon. Otherwise the comfortable surroundings would disappear very rapidly. The masked man had been clear on that.

He had also mentioned that they were working on alternative ways of cracking the verses, including tailing Bavdekar's collaborator, Bani. If Bavdekar and Ananya did not deliver soon, they might just end up making themselves redundant.

And now their time was almost up.

CHAPTER 39

En route to Lachung, Wednesday, 2.15 p.m.

'Lachung should be around four kilometres away,' Bikash said. 'But there is a village maybe a couple of kilometres from here. We have no option but to hike up to it. And avoid losing our fingers to frostbite.'

The constant urge to throw up made Sam feel out of balance.

He held his head in despair.

Four kilometers did not seem like a lot, but with icy winds, near-zero visibility and his nausea, it was pretty dicey.

Tens of thousands dead in the nation's capital. Chaos in the civilised world. Looked like there was no way to prevent it.

He longed to be back with Ananya, maybe at his apartment, cozying up on the couch, drinking coffee, looking into her eyes. He wondered if she was thinking the same thing, wherever she was.

Sam sighed as the cold winds bit into his face. He was stranded in the middle of an icy hell, on the verge of coming down with altitude sickness. This was no time for rumination.

***

Delhi, Wednesday, 3.30 p.m.

Sylvan switched on the television set in his hotel room as he got up to change.

The global stock markets were in free fall. The Asian stock markets had closed sharply down. China had arrested four American journalists and charged them with spying, just as three British businessmen in Shanghai were gunned down by 'unidentified assailants'.

The US responded by seizing assets of a few Chinese companies in the US. Meanwhile, in London, the Chinese ambassador's residence had to be cordoned off by police as angry protesters ended up hurling bricks and bottles into the compound.

As the GSS concluded, the governments of the US, UK, Germany, France, Australia and India had issued a joint press release stating that the GSS was a success and that the 'largest democracies of the world' had decided to pass stricter sanctions against China. There were also reprimands against Russia for its activities in Ukraine, but no sanctions.

Russia, meanwhile, turned the tap off on gas supply to Ukraine, and consequently, to Europe. Europe would be headed for a serious energy crisis soon. Meanwhile, a Russian reporter was found dead in Washington, a possible victim of a hate crime.

Sylvan looked at his watch. The chaos right now was nothing compared to what was going to happen later that evening.

In exactly three hours, the mayhem would begin.

***

En route to Lachung, Wednesday, 3 p.m.

Sam was perched uncomfortably on a yak.

The villagers had been kind, offering them hot soup and warm clothing, along with a homegrown herbal medicine for Sam's altitude sickness. Sam and Bikash were now headed to Lachung on yaks provided by the villagers.

The ledge they were passing through was so narrow that if the yak were to take one wrong step, they would plummet thousands of feet down into the ravine.

Sam's yak swayed to and fro as it trudged along, lurching precariously close to the edge.

'My yak seems to be a bit restless,' Sam said to Bikash. 'I'm hoping it doesn't have a death wish.'

***

Sikkim, Wednesday, 3.45 p.m.

The handheld device came to life as the Maestro tapped his finger on the touchscreen.

He was on his way from Gangtok to Chungthang, around three hours behind Sam. The GPS micro-transmitter planted in Sam's rucksack by the craggy, bearded guy from the rocket bus was continuing to send signals, albeit intermittently because of the rough weather.

The announcer on Fox News was talking in rapid-fire sentences as he gasped: 'The international situation is on a knife's edge. The arrests and shootings in China have tipped the already volatile global geopolitical potpourri to boiling point. Meanwhile, Chinese business confidence numbers were weak and equities tanked further today, with investors losing a cumulative four trillion dollars in value over the last two weeks.'

The announcer, as usual, said all this in one single breath, causing a flurry of words. He swallowed at the end of it, exhausted from the effort.

Americans, the Maestro snorted as he shook his head. Always high on speed and action; always low on discernment and thought.

But he could not suppress a smile. Things were going according to plan.

***

Lachung, Wednesday, 3.30 p.m.

After what seemed like an eternity, Sam and Bikash reached Lachung, roughly a hundred twenty kilometres from Gangtok, at an altitude of 9,600 feet, thanks to the yaks who did not have a death wish after all!

Sam's brow was knit with anxiety as they got off at what looked like a small inn.

With the dense fog, high-speed winds and icy cold weather, there was no possibility of them getting any transport to Yumthang. And while they had come this far and ascended to almost 10,000 feet in a span of just a few hours, Yumthang was a further 2,000 feet higher.

And then Sam needed to follow the clues in the verses and find the Gupt-Kandara amidst the snowy mountains and biting winds in fading light. It was, quite literally, an uphill task.

The saving grace was that the homegrown herbal medicine the villagers had given Sam had worked wonders. His nausea was gone, and he had actually begun to feel energised.

The Himalayas held many secrets, Sam ruminated. Would he be able to find the one he was looking for?

***

Lachung, Wednesday, 4 p.m.

Sam had managed to hire a battered old Sumo from the innkeeper, the transaction being helped by a hefty down-payment which more than covered the salvage value of the sorry vehicle. This meant that Sam had used up most of the cash that Damini had given him in Goa, but he had no other choice. Getting to the Gupt-Kandara was priority right now.

He could, obviously, find no driver willing to risk his life. He would have to fend for himself.

'Driving through this storm is suicide, dada,' Bikash said. 'The road to Yumthang has a steep drop to the ravine on one side and hills on the other.'

With good intentions, the innkeeper put in his two cents worth. 'There were a couple of guys last month who were as foolhardy as you. Their bodies were found at the bottom of the ravine two weeks later.'

***

Bagdogra, Wednesday, 4 p.m.

Damini was boarding a helicopter which would take her from Bagdogra airport to Gangtok. Visibility beyond Gangtok, however, was low, so she would have to cover the journey from Gangtok to Lachung by road, and that, too, after an indeterminate wait in Gangtok for the weather to improve.

She bit her lips impatiently. She would prefer to be as near the scene of action as possible when Sam hopefully discovered the Prativisha. But here she was, at least six hours behind.

Her satellite phone rang. It was the officer in-charge at the Indian Army's post in Lachung.

'This young man that you wanted followed—Sameer Rajan—appears to be embarking on a suicide mission of sorts. Visibility is almost zero . . . not the kind of weather in which you would drive an old Sumo on a slippery mountain road. I refuse to let any of my surveillance men follow him towards certain death.'

'But officer…' Damini started, but was interrupted mid-sentence by the agitated officer.

'We can't let the young man proceed either. We have the right to detain by force any person who is trying to commit suicide.'

Damini sighed. She was in a bind.

If the Army detained Sam now, any prospect of finding the Prativisha before the Delhi Demo would evaporate into nothingness.

But if she allowed Sam to proceed, he would be hurtling towards certain death.

***

The niggling sense of guilt and self-doubt that Damini had been experiencing, ever since she had realised that she needed to use Sam as a bait, had been building up slowly but surely. Waves of self-doubt had now grown into a full-blown torrent.

Sam was more than just an *asset.* He was a living, breathing person, someone she had gelled well with just thirty hours ago. How could she so casually send him to his death?

A thousand innocent lives in Delhi need to be saved, screamed a desperate voice within her. Even if it means sacrificing Sam.

The greatest good of the greatest number. She had lived out her entire tenure at the ACG based on that simple premise.

But was it really that simple? Did the ends always justify the means?

Damini brought herself back to reality. She could not afford to go soft now. There was a maniac—the Maestro—on the loose, and she had to get him. There was no ambiguity about that.

Yet, somewhere from within her, a memory revealed itself to her conscious mind.

It was a quote from Nietzsche that her English teacher in school had read out. 'Beware that, when fighting monsters, you yourself do not become a monster . . . for when you gaze long into the abyss, the abyss also gazes into you.'

We become what we repeatedly do.

Had she, too, become a monster?

***

Damini's voice was quivering as she spoke to the officer. 'You can drop the surveillance on him. But I need a favour. Just let him proceed. Detaining him will mess with the ACG's plans.'

'Don't say I didn't warn you,' the officer replied. 'There's no way he's going to survive a drive through this weather.'

***

Lachung, Wednesday, 4.05 p.m.

Sam walked up to the fireplace, where a few logs had been put together to make a cozy fire, and warmed his hands.

He turned to Bikash, and handed him a tip from the cash that he had remaining. 'Thanks for everything, dada.'

Bikash was looking pensive. 'Dev babu will kill me for letting you go.'

'Relax, dada,' Sam said. 'Look outside. The skies have begun to clear up a bit.'

A couple of locals who were sitting by the fireplace retreated in horror as soon as Sam mentioned that he intended heading up the westerly direction from Yumthang along the Lachung Chu river. One of them got up and left.

Clearly, human fear was indeed the 'greatest moat of them all'.

According to legend, an ancient king had supposedly once established a chamber of torture there, where men were subjected to the vilest of suffering. These tormented souls were rumoured to still wander the hills, waiting for any passers-by that they could prey on.

Then there were strange occurrences. The innkeeper joined in the conversation as he brought Sam's chai. He talked about stories of men who had gotten lost forever in the treacherous hills, never to return. Others returned deranged and disoriented, blabbering about strange creatures in an underground cave, and of ghosts who preyed on men.

Sam shook his head. He had had enough of naysayers. He got up to pay for his chai.

'No need,' the innkeeper waved his hand. 'It's bad karma to take money from someone who is doomed anyway.'

As Sam walked towards the door, one of the patrons of the inn whispered to the person sitting next to him: 'Another one hurries to his grave.'

CHAPTER 40

Sikkim, Wednesday, 4.30 p.m.

The Maestro looked at his crew as they passed a village on the way to Chungthang. They were all fired up with the impending Demo in Delhi. A few tactical maneouvres, such as splitting the crew up into many different vehicles and concealing weapons beneath other cargo on light trucks, had ensured that they had escaped the glare of the Army checkpoints in Gangtok.

The Maestro, however, was not complacent. Thanks to the weather, and Sam's desperate gambit getting his driver to speed on the slippery roads en route to Lachung, Sam had more than a three-and-a-half hours headstart over them. The Maestro reckoned they would reach Lachung by 7.30 p.m.

He looked at the forwarded news feed sent on his satellite phone.

China and the US were trading aggressive rhetoric, engaging in a war of nerves. The Middle-Eastern nations, their geopolitical standing rising in direct proportion to the escalation of international tensions, had begun to flex their muscles. Syria and Iran, not exactly US allies in the best of times, 'advised' the US to act with caution and not repeat 'earlier mistakes'. Russia had also stationed nuclear missiles on its borders with European countries.

The Maestro chuckled to himself again. Unleashing KaalKoot today would be, to put it mildly, more interesting than letting a cat among the pigeons.

He was all primed-up, like a hawk, ready to swoop in when the pigeons scattered.

***

Sikkim, Wednesday, 4.30 p.m.

An Army helicopter ferried an uncharacteristically subdued Damini to Gangtok from Bagdogra.

Not one to let her moods get in the way of her work, she had nevertheless radioed Kunal and requested him to keep the ACG agents in Kolkata on stand-by. She knew she would need their help, but Kunal, bound by the ACG protocol, would be unable to formally give clearance for the agents to go from Kolkata to Sikkim until Damini had concrete proof that her hunch was right.

Damini hoped Sam would get to the Prativisha before the Maestro did. If not, she would have to risk a bad gunfight.

She also hoped that once Sam got the Prativisha, he would not do anything stupid like handing it to the Maestro in exchange for Ananya.

If he insisted, she would have to stop him. By whatever means.

The mere thought of that made her stomach churn.

***

International Cricket Stadium, Delhi, Wednesday, 4.30 p.m.

There was a two-kilometre long queue outside the International Cricket Stadium as the momentum was building up leading to the wildly-hyped match of the century.

As the security guards frisked the forty-five thousand spectators entering the stadium, they did not realise that they should have been focusing their attention elsewhere.

***

En route from Lachung to Yumthang, Wednesday, 4.50 p.m.

Sam was a man possessed. He drove the Tata Sumo with a maniacal frenzy through the hilly road from Lachung to Yumthang.

He needed to move fast. The clock was ticking for the folks in Delhi, and possibly also for Ananya.

The drive over the last hour had been helped by the skies having cleared up, but over the last few minutes, it had begun to rain.

He reckoned that he was now very close to Yumthang. If he moved fast enough, he might reach before the rains reduced visibility to zero.

Sam strained his eyes, trying to battle sleep, fatigue and mental fogginess as he focused all his energy on ensuring that the Sumo raced through the remaining distance.

The rainstorm, however, was moving fast, too, like the proverbial snowball, with high-speed winds venting their fury and visibility reducing quickly to near zero.

Sam braked sharply as he realised, too late, that he was nearing a precarious hairpin bend. On one side was the surface of the hill, while on the other side there was a steep drop to the ravine.

The Sumo skid sharply under the impact of the sudden brakes, but was not able to stop fully in time.

Sam let out a yelp as the Sumo slipped and plummeted down towards the ravine.

CHAPTER 41

Sikkim, Wednesday, 4.55 p.m.

Sam let out a loud yowl as a sharp pain rushed through his left shoulder.

For a couple of moments, he remained in shock till he managed to compose himself and open his eyes.

He could still move his shoulder and arms. Probably just bad bruises and not a fracture, he thought to himself.

To his surprise, he realised that the Sumo had not fallen too low, having gotten entangled in a thick bush on a ledge very close to the hairpin bend.

He gingerly hoisted himself up and forced open the door, easing himself out of the vehicle. With visibility close to zero, he reached for his rucksack and put on his night vision goggles.

He was on a precarious ledge on the hill. There was a steep drop on one side, with the hill on the other.

As he got up to move away from the Sumo, being unused to night vision goggles, he misjudged the angle.

Sam's wail was drowned by the sound of the wind as he slipped and plummeted down from the ledge.

***

Delhi, Wednesday, 5 p.m.

Roads in central Delhi were cordoned off as the heads of state were driven to the International Cricket Stadium in separate motorcades.

The international news media—reporters from newspapers, magazines, websites and television crews—had shown up in full strength. Delhi was effectively the centre of the world for those few hours.

***

Sikkim, Wednesday, 5 p.m.

Sam was stuck. Was this how it was all going to end?

Even if there had been no blinding rain and howling wind, there would still have been nobody to see him fall or hear his call for help. There was not a soul around for miles together.

He was swinging precariously from an outcrop of rock jutting out from the hill. His shoulder was badly bruised from the crash, but the biggest problem was that he had no way of getting back to the ledge.

The outcrop of rock would not hold Sam's weight for longer than a few minutes. And while Damini was tracking him on his satellite phone's GPS, he would be long dead before she arrived.

Was he destined for a lonely death, away in the hills where nobody would find him?

But maybe that was fitting. That he had spent his childhood years in the hills, and would die in the hills he so loved.

In that moment, while hanging precariously, Sam decided something quietly.

That if he made it out of here, he would spend his life doing things that he enjoyed the most.

A collage of images flashed rapidly through his mind. Everything else be damned, he would do the things that made life worth living.

Like trekking up the hills.

Drinking cold coffee, topped up with ice cream.

Spending more time with friends.

Listening to more music.

Going out dancing.

Most of all, he would not shy away from his feelings for the woman he loved.

He would do all this, and more, if only he could make it out of here alive.

***

Sam's eyes widened as he caught sight of another narrow ledge just below where he was hanging.

He would have to perform a craftily executed jump to get to the ledge, but it was within the realm of possibility. The weight of the rucksack was proving to be an unbearable burden, but he could not let go of it without himself losing his grip.

Sam muttered a small prayer, held his breath and jumped, rucksack still strung over his shoulders.

As he jumped, the micro-GPS device which had been planted in his rucksack by the craggy, bearded man from the rocket bus fell out and down to the rocks below.

***

The Mansion, Wednesday, 5.05 p.m.

The man sitting in the control room at the Mansion had been continuously staring at the moving blip on his screen for the past few hours. He rubbed his eyes tiredly as the blip came to a stop.

He clicked on the computer's mouse a couple of times as the satellite picture around the blip enlarged. He then picked up the earphones off the brass handle-rail and dialled a number.

'Yes?' the voice on the other line said. It was the Maestro himself.

'The rookie seems to be hovering around the same point, sir. Either he has found the place, or he has dropped the GPS, or he is dead.'

'I can see that on my handheld device,' the voice said curtly. 'And don't call him a rookie. There is a saying in my country: it ain't over till you have your opponent's severed head in front of you.'

***

Yumthang, Wednesday, 5.10 p.m.

Sam muttered a small prayer of thanks as he entered Yumthang valley. It was located roughly a hundred thirty kilometres away from Gangtok, at an altitude of 11,693 feet.

The hairpin bend where the Sumo had crashed had been just off Yumthang. He had to brave the pain in his bruised shoulder and the heavy woolen clothing was wearing him down. But the temperamental weather lent him a helping hand, and the skies had cleared up once again. It had just been a five-minute walk to Yumthang valley.

There was no sign of life anywhere in the valley. A couple of shacks which catered to tourists during the day were tightly shut, the owners probably ensconced in blankets in Lachung.

Sam sighed as he recalled a line from a verse.

Climbing unwaveringly up the path beyond the Garden of Heaven.

He had last come to Yumthang seventeen years ago. The Colonel was young and sprightly then, full of life. They had been awed by the multi-coloured carpet of flowers, with pink, blue, red and yellow competing for attention against the green meadows. Sam, then eleven years old, had simply lain down in the grass, among rhododendrons.

A veritable Garden of Heaven.

Things, however, were different now. It was the monsoon season, and the rhododendrons were replaced by tiny primroses. At this hour of the evening, all that registered in Sam's consciousness was the rumble of the Lachung Chu river and the eerie howl of the bone-chilling winds.

***

Along the Lachung Chu river, off Yumthang, Sikkim, Wednesday, 5.25 p.m.

Sam was hiking along the Lachung Chu river, leaving behind the last bastion of civilisation at Yumthang. He found himself gasping a little as he walked, thanks to the progressively declining oxygen levels in the atmosphere.

Sam remembered that during his childhood, the Colonel and he had trekked further up from Yumthang to a place called Yumesamdong, also called Zero Point. He remembered playing in the snow there, without a care in the world.

The emotion seemed alien to Sam now. With Ananya missing and tens of thousands of lives at stake in Delhi, it seemed like the worries of the whole world rested on his shoulders.

The storm had subsided, the rains and mist had reduced and the moon was reflected in the glistening waters of the river. He was surrounded by tall, imposing peaks on all sides, which were reflecting the moonlight on their snow-clad surfaces.

Sam frowned as he looked at his compass. The westerly direction was diverging from the path of the Lachung Chu. Was he missing something?

He took off his night vision goggles to gauge the landscape properly. The moonlight was giving him a headache, thanks to the night vision goggles that were taking ambient light and amplifying it.

Sam heaved a sigh of relief as he looked to the west and found a smaller tributary of the Lachung Chu in that direction.

The stream seemed to emerge from a winding path through what seemed like a very treacherous slope up a barren, icy hill.

So *that* was the river referred to in the verses.

Walking by the river through blinding mists

Crossing the greatest moat of them all

The lion's mane shall meet the scorpion's claws.

There was a deathly silence, and not a soul around for miles.

Not a *living* soul, Sam corrected himself as the local legends from the inn in Lachung came to his mind.

But somehow, in the silence, as Sam contemplated the lonely uphill path along the stream, the reflected moonlight took on eerie hues; the hills seemed more foreboding, and Sam did not find the legends funny anymore.

***

International Cricket Stadium, Delhi, Wednesday, 5.50 p.m.

Bugles went off as the Indian cricket team and the Dream Combo XI team trooped into the field at the International Cricket Stadium. This had been preceded by a five-minute speech by the chairman of the Board of Control of Cricket in India (BCCI) welcoming the dignitaries, and a five-minute classical dance programme to showcase Indian culture to the guests.

In the VVIP box, the US President, the Prime Minister of the UK, and the Indian hosts were sharing a light joke.

The Indian team won the toss and chose to bat.

***

Along the stream near Yumthang, Wednesday, 6 p.m.

Sam slowly made his way along the small tributary of the Lachung Chu.

The weather had cleared up further, and the moonlight was brightly shining through, providing good visibility of the surrounding hills.

It had only been forty minutes from the time he had left Yumthang when Sam—focused on his quest and looking in the westerly direction—saw the unmistakable rock formation atop the hills.

The final clue to his destination.

The lion's mane meeting the scorpion's claws.

It looked different from the way it appeared in the dream. The dream, after all, was not a supernatural realisation. It was his subconscious mind's way of processing the verses.

The rock formation was distinct and striking. Sam was awestruck for a few moments as he stared at the majestic image.

The Gupt-Kandara ought to be nearby now.

***

Wednesday, 6.15 p.m.

Sam's initial euphoria had given way to frustration as he realised that he was still not quite there.

Walking up to the spot where the lion's mane met the scorpion's claws was easy. It was along the stream which was a tributary of the Lachung Chu. But he could not figure out where the entrance to the Gupt-Kandara was located.

And then luck dealt him a helping hand. With the air and the skies continuing to clear up, and visibility by the moonlight getting progressively better, it was on his fourth circuit of the area that he spotted a ledge, almost like a platform, high up on the hill close to the spot where he was standing. The ledge was on the opposite side of the stream.

It looked strikingly similar to a balcony. It had to be some kind of opening either to or from the Hidden Cave.

But the ledge was located on a naked cliff almost three hundred feet above the valley. And the three hundred feet comprised sheer slippery rock, with no ridges or footholds, dropping right down to the stream below.

There was no way any person—except somebody who could fly—could reach the place.

***

Sam hovered for a couple of minutes, trying to find a way to get up to the ledge.

There were no footholds or ridges to hook a rope. Only slippery, icy rocks.

Sam remembered an incident from his childhood when the Colonel had taken him trekking to the Paro Taktsang, the Tiger's Nest monastery in Bhutan. They had eaten at a cafeteria along the way and had a great time together. This was when the Colonel was still his jovial self; before the incident that had changed their lives.

Sam felt a sharp pang of sadness as he realised that time would never come back again. Neither that mood with all its *joie de vivre*, nor the innocence of childhood.

He remembered looking at the temple and asking, 'Gosh, there is no way to get up there.'

'There's always a way,' the Colonel had told him. 'You just have to find it.'

***

Maybe there was a different opening. Maybe finding that was where Sam ought to focus his effort.

He decided to trace the path of the stream, braving the muscle cramps that seemed to be gnawing at his legs.

A little further up, he came across a place where the narrow stream disappeared into the mountain face. Thankfully, the path that he was on also led into the same place.

He had to crouch as his path, with the stream below, burrowed into the mountain. He was probably getting closer to the source of the stream.

He would have to find a convenient spot to cross the stream and get on the same side as the high ledge that he had spotted.

It was dark inside the burrow in the mountain, and he had to switch on his flashlight. To his surprise, he realised that the stream got so narrow inside that he could actually jump from his side of the steam to the opposite side relatively easily.

Sam took the plunge and jumped.

As he got a hold on the rock opposite, he switched his flashlight on again. The stream seemed to originate from right inside the mountain.

As he crawled forward, he saw something that made his eyes widen.

Right where he was crouched, there was a place where the rock was different from the surroundings. Almost as if it was a gateway, a door, distinct from the background.

An untrained eye would not have spotted it. But Sam, as an experienced trekker and nature lover, was sensitive to geology and natural formations. To him, the difference in colour and texture was unmistakable.

He gingerly reached forward and touched and prodded the rock at that place.

Sure enough, with a clank and a groan, the rock slid sideways to reveal an opening.

It made sense now. The ledge that he saw on the way here was probably just a vantage point, not the entrance. This one was the real entrance to the Gupt-Kandara, the Hidden Cave.

***

Wednesday, 6.28 p.m.

Sam called Damini using his satellite phone and told her that he had found the Cave.

She said, 'I can see the coordinates of the satellite phone GPS.'

'I'm going in,' Sam said.

Damini's mind raced. This was the moment when she would have to talk Sam out of handing the Prativisha to the Maestro, in case he found an opportunity to barter it in exchange for Ananya.

'Hold on,' Damini said. 'I am already on my way to Chungthang by road. I should be able to reach your coordinates by 11 p.m. You should wait till then.'

'No,' Sam replied. 'We don't have the time. People in Delhi are probably already at risk. I'm going in.'

Damini was a trifle relieved to hear that Sam intended averting the Delhi Demo rather than bartering with the Maestro. 'We have to decide how to handle things once you find the Prativisha.'

'Let me find it first,' Sam replied tersely, as he was again hit by the sinking realisation that he might have a tough choice ahead of him.

***

International Cricket Stadium, Delhi, Wednesday, 6.30 p.m.: the moment of release of KaalKoot

Sylvan paused for a moment to catch his breath. What he was doing was monumental.

By pressing the trigger, he would be unleashing KaalKoot, the deadliest biological weapon ever.

Those directly affected, including the dignitaries and the press reporters, would start feeling the symptoms in an hour. Some would drop dead instantly, and all would die within sixty hours. Some of these people would start feeling delusional and fearful, creating pandemonium. Those indirectly affected in the second, third and fourth rounds—through breath and touch from the primary infectees—would die, too.

The heads of state of most of the developed world would die. Entire governments would scurry about trying to control the disease. But they would all be unsuccessful.

Then the blame game would begin—China, Russia, the US, UK, Germany and France—the world's most powerful countries, with nuclear arsenals that could obliterate the planet many times over.

Sylvan swallowed hard as the implication of what he was about to do hit him.

But he paused no more than a moment.

With a controlled motion, he squeezed the trigger as he started walking across the stands, the special backpack with the cylinders slung over his shoulders. With his handheld device, he signalled to Yash and Yuko to do the same.

***

At the entrance to the Hidden Cave, Wednesday, 6.30 p.m.: the same moment as the release of KaalKoot in Delhi

Sam paused for a minute as the opening in the rock came into view. After this point, there would be no turning back; no second chances. This was not his education venture. He could not just bail out when things got rough.

Here, if things didn't work out, it probably meant that he would die—in an underground grave far away from civilisation.

He shuddered as the memory of a verse from the Yogyaveer's scroll came to mind.

Verse 4

The secret shall be revealed only to the Worthy Heir

That person alone, of supreme faith, courage, stillness and compassion

Shall be able to conquer the Agonies

And prevent KaalKoot from striking again.

Sam sighed. He was no Superman.

Then an image came to his mind—of a woman whose dimpled smile reached all the way to her eyes—and he found himself mustering up the courage.

The opening widened as Sam pushed it, leaving enough space for him to climb in.

CHAPTER 42

Inside the Gupt-Kandara, Wednesday, 6.31 p.m.

The first thing Sam noticed, to his surprise, was that the cave was lit, albeit dimly. After taking a couple of seconds to orient himself, he realised that the light was coming from a series of rocks which were scattered throughout the chamber he was in.

'Probably made of some chemiluminescent material,' Sam thought, remembering his chemistry lessons. While fluorescent material emitted light that had been absorbed earlier, chemiluminescence involved light emission as a result of a chemical reaction.

The walls of the cave, too, were made from a material which reflected the light from the luminescent rocks. The Yogyaveer had sure known what he was doing.

The air inside the cave was surprisingly fresh. Probably recycled through plants? Sam remembered reading about a plant called Devil's Ivy which was considered an effective indoor air purifier.

The rock had shut completely behind Sam, leaving no opening whatsoever. In fact, it had closed so smoothly that it was impossible to discern that an opening had been there at all.

Smooth mechanical engineering, Sam thought. Not bad for a recluse from the 1940s.

The Yogyaveer had clearly kept abreast of engineering progress on his occasional trips to civilisation.

Sam could not see any obvious levers through which the entrance could be opened from the inside. He could not go out the way he had come in.

He was now well and truly trapped. His only bet was to clear the Agonies and reach the inner sanctum.

***

It was reasonably warm. Maybe the material of the cave walls reflected heat, Sam surmised.

He was putting on a gas mask from his rucksack, wary of any trapped noxious gases inside the cave.

Unfortunately, he found himself losing his foothold as the ground beneath him began shaking and moving.

Before he could regain his balance, the mask had slipped out of his grasp, along with his rucksack and flashlight.

***

Inside the Hidden Cave, Wednesday, 6.35 p.m., five minutes after the release of KaalKoot

Sam was bang in the middle of the first Agony. And it was getting the better of him.

He was standing inside the Cave, not on smooth ground, but on a maze of moving, stepping stones.

The stepping stones were separated by chasms, underneath which malevolent, sharp-edged rocks waited. If he lost his footing even once, he would fall and be impaled on the rocks.

The stones were quite narrow, providing just enough space for

Sam to get a foothold, and ample opportunity for him to miss and fall.

Moreover, the stones were actually not within stepping distance of one another. Sam would have to carefully execute a light jump to get from one to the other. This made it difficult as it were.

To top it all, the stepping stones were moving reasonably fast, in seemingly random directions.

Sam cursed under his breath. This was no stepping stone trick. This was a bloody suicide spiral. He would die trying to perform a meaningless foot juggle across moving stones.

For a split second, Sam experienced a sense of doubt about the *raison d'etre* for this whole endeavour.

That one split second of doubt was enough to upset his concentration and make him lose his footing.

With a yell, Sam plummeted to the depths below, towards the sharp rocks waiting to impale him.

***

International Cricket Stadium, Delhi, Wednesday, 6.35 p.m., five minutes after the release of KaalKoot

At first, nobody noticed anything amiss amidst the loud cheering and the excitement at the stadium.

Then a few people started feeling somewhat uncomfortable. Some coughed and wheezed a little, and some felt mildly nauseous.

But none of them thought it was necessary to alert anybody else, yet.

The Indians were batting. There was excitement in the air as the spectators chanted 'India! India!' in unison.

***

Inside the Hidden Cave, Wednesday, 6.37 p.m., seven minutes after the release of KaalKoot

As Sam started to fall, he desperately stretched out his hands and grabbed the nearest stepping stone, scratching himself in the process.

He quickly regained his footing, but he realised that the stones were moving faster than before.

Sam now understood the game.

Basically, there was no time to hesitate. He would have to keep moving. If his confidence and faith in his mission wavered even for a second, it showed in his response time and the stones started to move faster.

The sixth verse from the scroll came to mind.

Verse 6

You lose your faith once, it will slow you down a bit

You lose your faith twice, you still have a chance

But if you lose your faith thrice, the doors of heaven

Will be closed to you forever.

He could afford to make only one more mistake. After that, he would be history.

Just that thought—of fear and diffidence—was enough to make him lose his footing a second time.

***

Delhi, Wednesday, 6.37 p.m., seven minutes after the release

of KaalKoot

A college student, who had come to watch the match with his friends, was the first to try to raise an alarm. His vision had turned slightly blurry, but he had kept quiet. But then, when he seemed to lose sensation in his left hand, he felt a sharp pang of fear and tapped his friend's shoulder with his right hand.

His friend, however, was too busy cheering as the Indian opening batsman hit a six. He did not even notice his own arm acquiring purple overtones.

***

Inside the Hidden Cave, Wednesday, 6.38 p.m.

This time, too, Sam just about managed to latch on to a stepping stone and clutch on to it for dear life.

Two mistakes. This was it.

You lose your faith thrice, the doors of heaven

Will be closed to you forever.

There was no room for even a split second of hesitation now.

Sam decided, with the lightning speed that comes only with adversity, that he had not come this far just to give up.

He would fight, right up to the very end.

He would make no room for hesitation. Or fear. Or diffidence. Or dissonance.

With a renewed sense of purpose, he jumped to the next stone, inching ahead.

***

Inside the Hidden Cave, Wednesday, 6.55 p.m.

The game of stepping stones continued for what seemed like an eternity. With each stone that Sam stepped on, he was moving further ahead, albeit slowly, along the chamber of the cave.

As he juggled his steps to time perfectly with the moving stones, he did not let any other thought enter his mind—neither about the futility of his quest, nor the fear of relationships, not any sense of anger against the Colonel.

As he continued the juggle, he became one with the stones, almost the way a master soccer player becomes one with the ball, or a pianist becomes one with his sonata.

That was the point the Agony had been designed for. After about fifteen minutes of Sam being 'in the zone', the stepping stones slowed, and finally came to a halt.

Sam looked back at the field that he had just succeeded in crossing. The stones were held in place by a system of pullies, probably mechanically tuned to move in a combination of sequences. In all likelihood, the stones had sensors and were geared to move faster once the subject lost his footing, measured by the load on a stepping stone lightening without a corresponding load on any other stone.

Sam was overcome with awe. To a layperson, this contraption would have certainly seemed supernatural. The Yogyaveer must have had excellent mechanical engineering skills to have designed and built this contraption single-handedly. It must have taken him many years. Sam wondered how the Yogyaveer had hauled all the material and supplies required to this remote place without attracting attention.

Even in that dark, dreary cave, Sam could not help feeling smug.

So much for those professors from his engineering college who thought he was as fit for engineering as a buffalo for the Maths Olympiad.

But Sam's surge of pride and relief was short-lived as he realised that the next Agony was right in front of him, and was approaching him. Fast.

CHAPTER 43

Delhi, Wednesday, 7.15 p.m.

A lean man who had lost all sensation in his hands hurriedly made his way to the restroom at the stadium. He anxiously scrambled up the stands, violently brushing past those who stood in his way and creating a mild commotion.

A burly man who was at the receiving end of the shoving hit back and punched the lean man who fell to the ground. The vision of the lean man was already blurry, and he seemed to have lost control of his facial muscles. A couple of college boys standing nearby looked murderously at the burly man. Spoiling for a fight and pumped up with adrenaline, they pounced on the burly man and rained punches on him.

That was when the delusionary, paranoid effects of KaalKoot kicked in, and another man pointed at the burly man and shouted, 'Terrorist, terrorist!'

Five others joined the fistfight, which had, by then, turned into a free-for-all.

Many of those who were trying to punch found that they had lost sensation in their hands, and the skin on them had started turning purple.

To the already explosive cocktail of adrenaline and chaos,

the element of fear was added, taking things closer to tipping point.

***

Lachung, Wednesday, 7.15 p.m.

Bikash got up from his bed at the inn in Lachung where Sam had halted en route to Yumthang. He was looking idly outside when a movement in the distance caught his eye.

He looked closely. It seemed like some vehicles had halted in the shadows a slight distance away from the inn, almost as if they did not want to be spotted.

He put on his shirt and hurried out of the room.

***

There were four vehicles—two light trucks and two SUVs—equipped with ladders, ropes and equipment fit for a small Army operation.

'Army?' Bikash wondered, but then noticed that the vehicles had no markings. He leaned closer from his hiding place.

There were twelve men in all, and they were redistributing the equipment amongst the vehicles

A lean man was ordering the others about; he seemed like a supervisor of sorts.

In the corner stood a man with Caucasian features, observing all this keenly while looking at something on his tablet device. The man was stockily-built, and had a sunken face and thick, black hair.

Despite being of shorter height compared to the rest of the pack, the man in the corner had a striking presence. It was obvious that he was the leader of the pack, while the lean man ordering everybody about was just doing his bidding.

Even as he was keenly observing the activity of the hirelings, his face radiated a hermit-like detachment from their harried activity, and his quiet poise reflected a man with a keen sense of a larger purpose.

But the most striking feature was his eyes. Looking at them even from a distance, Bikash felt a shiver run down his spine.

And it was not due to the cold wind.

Bikash rushed back to the inn as fast as he could.

***

The Maestro paused to smoke a cigar as his men readied the equipment. He watched as the cigar lit up slowly in the rarified air.

The Demo was just the beginning; a prelude.

Getting the antidote—the Prativisha—assuming that Sameer led them to it, would be the really big deal. It would make his dream of planting the bio bomb in thirty cities come true.

He could well imagine the scenario if that came to pass.

People dying all over; panic, as governments and doctors realised they could do nothing to control the spread; rioting in cities, deaths in the countryside, food supplies hopelessly disrupted; trains halted, planes grounded, the world's lifelines coming down to a standstill.

World leaders and the rich would retreat to secure locations to protect themselves from the powerful pathogen, leaving their countries in anarchy.

Perfect conditions for a new leader to take charge of the world.

***

Inside the Cave, Wednesday, 7.15 p.m.

A gigantic gong was headed straight in Sam's direction. It looked really heavy, like a gigantic globe made of steel. If it hit him, it would smash his skull and flatten his body against the walls of the cave.

The gong was connected to the ceiling of the cave through an enormous chain, which seemed to be fashioned from some very hard substance. The chain and the gong were moving in progressively lengthening arcs, almost like a pendulum which gains momentum with every move.

The gong's arc was still short of where Sam was standing, but Sam figured that it would be a question of just a couple of minutes, and maybe five arcs, before it would be upon him.

As the enormous gong hurtled towards him, Sam's mind was in a tizzy. Instinctively, he made a motion to step aside to the next stepping stone.

But as soon as he did that, the gong subtly changed direction towards him. And gained speed.

Sam panicked. Was the gong mechanically connected to the stone he stood on? Would it change direction the moment he stepped away and head straight for him again? And, like with the stepping stones, each such 'mistake' would be punished with a higher acceleration?

If so, he did not have a choice but be smashed to pulp by the gong.

Gingerly, Sam tried stepping away again.

This time, it was unmistakable. The gong decisively altered course towards him, and with more speed.

He was trapped. There seemed to be no option but to face certain death.

The last threads of Sam's sanity snapped violently as the menacing gong hurtled decisively towards him.

Smashed to pulp in a godforsaken cave in the middle of nowhere, where his bones would rot slowly, with nothing for company over the millennia except the dreary, dark walls of this dungeon. That would be his fate.

Sam's mind blanked out as a wail escaped his mouth.

***

Delhi, Wednesday, 7.20 p.m.

The Indian batsman hit a six. Television cameras followed the ball as it landed into the crowd.

Normally, a ball landing in the middle of the crowd would be an invitation to a hundred hands to crane towards the point where it would land, in the hope of catching it and going down in TV history.

This time, however, many people were oblivious to TV cameras as they were droopy-eyed and busy in their own private hell, struggling to come to grips with the fear and paranoia at losing their ability to control their facial muscles.

This coincided with the time that a dignitary from the English delegation fainted.

'Perhaps he got too stressed out watching the Indian team hit a six,' the TV commentator cheekily suggested, five minutes before his co-commentator went to the bathroom to throw up.

***

Inside the Cave, Wednesday, 7.20 p.m.

In those few seconds, Sam again made a decision. If he was destined for a cold, lonely death here, he would at least face it with grace and dignity.

No sooner had he made that decision than the seventh verse from the scroll came to his mind.

Verse 7

The human race spends a lifetime running from fear

That is not the way of the Worthy Heir

He who stares fear directly in the face

Shall pass gracefully from one world to the next.

Was it possible—crazy yet possible—that despite the gong heading towards him, he would actually have to do the counter-intuitive and stay still, rather than stepping away? That the gong was wired to accelerate when it sensed motion, and decelerate when it did not? That he would have to *stare fear directly in the face?*

There was no time to ponder. The gong was ready to launch and would hit him, crushing his skull, in a few seconds. Sam closed his eyes and stood still as a veritable mountain of fear hit him.

The gong launched with a loud clanging motion as a mechanical rotor imparted it with momentum. Any moment now.

Sam grimaced but stood firm as he took the chance.

In those few seconds, nothing seemed to matter . . . not his troubles at work, not his issues with the Colonel. . .

He did not fear anyone or anything. Not even death.

The gong whirred and moved forward swiftly, gaining momentum. Yet, somewhere in its path, as Sam stood still, a series of brakes in its control apparatus seemed to jangle and it slowed down, coming to rest merely inches from Sam's face.

He opened his eyes. What he was experiencing was not relief; it was the peace of a person who, by standing still in the face of fear, had transcended it, albeit for a few seconds.

Sam stood there, facing the gong for a few moments, and then calmly stepped forward and bent slightly as he avoided it and moved on to the next stepping stone.

***

The doorway in front of him opened slowly.

'Phew,' Sam sighed. Finally, a possible way out.

He stepped out. It was dark except for the light from the tunnel behind him. But there was a continuous deafening noise from somewhere below which caused him to stop.

It was just as well, he realised to his utter horror, as his eyes gradually adjusted to the somewhat darker chamber he was in now. He was on a narrow ledge that was jutting out from the edge of a rock, and right ahead of him was a precipitous drop to what sounded like several rivers rumbling below.

The monsoons had not yet arrived in Sikkim. 'Probably an underground stream passing through the cave, fed by a spring or glacier,' Sam thought.

His relief lasted only a second. The doorway closed behind him, and a lever from behind pushed him forward.

He teetered for a second, trying to regain his foothold, but failed and plummeted to the depths below.

CHAPTER 44

Delhi, Wednesday, 7.30 p.m., post half-time, sixty minutes after the release of Kalkoot

It was the Dream Combo XI's turn to bat post the interval. The Indian team had notched up 190 runs with the loss of 4 wickets.

But there were other things which were occupying the spectators' minds.

Something strange seemed to be going on. But there was no odour, no smoke, nothing explicit that people could blame the commotion on.

Paramedics had arrived, wearing masks and gear to protect against hazardous materials. There was an announcement asking everybody to stay calm.

Some people speculated that there had been a gas leak from a chemical facility.

A rumour gained currency in a section of the crowd that a ghost of a dead cricketer had come to haunt the stadium. That set off a mini stampede which the police quelled with some difficulty.

That was when the head of state of one of the European countries noticed his hands going limp.

***

Inside the Cave, Wednesday, 7.40 p.m.

Sam was swept away by the torrent.

He had tried to struggle initially but to no avail. It took him a few moments to recover from the shock of being lashed about by the current, and some more time to adjust to the cold water, which felt like a thousand daggers piercing his body.

Before he could even tune in to his instinctual response and put up even an iota of a fight, he realised that he was paralysed by the searing pain and frozen by the sheer rapidity with which everything was happening.

With a mammoth act of will, he summoned up what seemed like his last reserves of courage, and tried to fight against the current. But the effort was draining him, leaving him with lesser and lesser energy to fight back. He was losing stamina by the second, moving closer to giving up and being engulfed.

What he was experiencing now was not a torrent; this was a maelstrom. But there was no mention of a maelstrom in the verses.

He let go, waiting to be lashed against a rock or die of asphyxiation. He hoped the end would be swift.

An Edgar Allan Poe story about a maelstrom came to Sam's mind while he was waiting to die. The protagonist got out of the maelstrom by remaining still and not fighting or flailing his arms about; by resisting the urge to struggle and not tiring himself out.

The eighth verse from the Yogyaveer's scroll now made sense.

Verse 8

He who is still in the face of the most intense motion

He who observes the flow of the universe with equanimity

For him the waters shall not pose a danger

He shall reach his destination without much effort.

***

Delhi, Wednesday, 7.40 p.m.

Something unprecedented was happening in the VVIP stands at the International Cricket Stadium.

There were six heads of state present, including leaders of most of the free world.

Three of the six had started to exhibit symptoms.

Commando agents in hazmat suits, accompanied by the country's best doctors, had swiftly swooped in on the scene and escorted all the cricketers and leaders out of the stadium.

In order to prevent a stampede, the authorities announced that the match was being temporarily paused due to some technical issues with the pitch.

But, by then, almost a third of the forty-five thousand spectators were contending with nausea in some form—some throwing up in their seats, some trying to rush to the toilets and some others nursing it silently as they found themselves paralysed.

The security personnel tried hard to stem the panic, but it was difficult to do that considering that some of their own people were exhibiting symptoms.

***

Inside the Cave, Wednesday, 7.50 p.m.

Verses notwithstanding, this was one tough gig.

For a few minutes, which seemed like hours, Sam was one with the swirling waters. He was tossed, turned, whacked and mauled, but he stayed absolutely still.

And then the waters started slowing down mysteriously. The whirls grew progressively less ferocious, and Sam was able to gather his wits enough to take deep breaths.

As he looked around, he realised that what he had fallen into was not a river, but a kind of a whirlpool within a confined area. He had not actually been moved forward much; instead, he had been spun around viciously and repeatedly like in a high-speed blender.

And now the blender had finally come to a stop.

If he had tried to fight it, he would have lost energy very quickly, and might have dropped dead by now.

Gingerly, his head still spinning, Sam stepped out of the waters.

But such was the impact of the high-speed churning that he had lost all sense of balance, and fell flat on his face onto the hard cave floor.

***

Sam lay still, in that face-down position, for a few minutes. He had neither the mental nor the physical energy to attempt getting up.

Finally, after what seemed like an effort of a lifetime, he picked himself up.

He was bleeding from his nose and lips; he had probably torn a couple of ligaments in his leg, and his left hand felt like it had just been inside a wringer.

But he would live. For now.

***

Delhi, Wednesday, 8 p.m.

Sylvan, Yuko and Yash had left the stadium after unleashing the pathogen, and met up at a café nearby. They were all under the impression that they had been injected with an antidote.

So, it was with some surprise that Sylvan noticed that Yuko's eyelids were drooping, and he seemed to be struggling to talk.

That was when Yash noticed Sylvan's arms dangling lifelessly, almost as if he had lost the ability to control them.

Sylvan, Yash and Yuko had been the closest to the toxin when it was unleashed. They had inhaled the highest concentration of KaalKoot.

Sylvan and Yuko dropped dead within seconds of each other.

Yash screamed with terror, and started dialling the Mansion on his phone just as he ran out of the café.

But the screen of Yash's phone instrument was dead. The memory of all their handheld instruments had been programmed to auto-destruct in order to avoid detection by the authorities.

Yash tried throwing away the phone as he ran, but he had already lost control over his arm movements.

He collapsed to the ground in a heap.

***

Inside the Cave, Wednesday, 8 p.m.

Sam looked around in the dim light and realised that he was in a confined cylindrical atrium-like chamber, with the whirlpool in the centre.

He looked up. The ledge from where he had fallen was not visible. There was nothing he could hold on to, so there was no way that he could climb and locate the ledge.

As his eyes adjusted to the light, he noticed that the cylindrical chamber had a diametre of around twenty metres, but it had perfectly smooth walls, without any exit.

He had gotten out of the water, but that was small consolation. He was trapped.

***

After five minutes of closely combing the walls of the cylindrical chamber, enduring immense pain from the mauling he had just undergone, Sam finally got his break.

There was a section of the wall that looked somewhat different from the rest. It was close to ground level, at a height of only 3 feet.

Sam gingerly pressed that section, and sure enough, the wall opened up to reveal a small tunnel.

Sam hesitated, then crouched and squeezed into the narrow tunnel, cursing all the extra calories he had consumed in the last few months.

It was completely dark inside; no chemiluminescent rocks there. Sam could not see a thing, but he could pick up enough cues to know that the tunnel did not widen or open up into any larger chamber. It was basically a dark, long hole, 3 feet wide and 3 feet high.

Sam panicked slightly as claustrophobia hit him. Entering the tunnel did not seem like a bright idea anymore.

He moved back a bit, intending to get out the way he had come in.

Unfortunately, that was not an option anymore. The exit wall behind him had slid shut.

He was stuck in a crouched position inside this dark, suffocating coffin, the stuff of his worst nightmares.

CHAPTER 45

Delhi, Wednesday, 8.30 p.m.

The organisers had played highlights from past matches on the TV screen at the stadium in order to not cause panic.

But it is difficult to avoid panic when the better part of forty-five thousand spectators are experiencing strange symptoms and turning progressively delusional. Every exit out of the stadium witnessed a stampede.

In an unprecedented occurrence, the Indian Army was called in to maintain order in the stadium.

The Indian government, in turns aided and prodded by international agencies, evacuated the government delegations and then undertook the largest quarantine exercise ever to have been attempted in the world.

The exit gates were closed. All spectators, other than the cricketers and diplomats who had been evacuated, were ordered to stay put in the stadium.

At least twenty different parts of the stadium broke into pandemonium on this announcement, but they were brought under control by the Army.

Not all the Army personnel had masks and protective suits. Some of the jawaans were beginning to show symptoms themselves, but their instructions were clear. Nobody was to move from their posts.

***

Inside the Cave, Wednesday, 8.35 p.m.

Sam had been in that dark tunnel, crouching in the same position, for a while now.

The lack of oxygen was making him feel woozy. Was he probably beginning to asphyxiate?

He had tried to find some room to wriggle, but he could move neither forward nor backward. The wall behind him had slid decisively shut, with no hooks or levers on it. Meanwhile, the passage was narrower ahead, so moving forward was not an option either.

The absence of light made everything worse, including the claustrophobia.

As he tried to move his head upward, he banged against the hard ceiling of the narrow tunnel and let out a scream.

***

Delhi, Wednesday, 9 p.m.

The international media had been fed a story that Delhi was affected by a virus similar to the SARS virus which had affected Asia many years ago.

This message was intended to give the impression that it was a serious outbreak, while also implicitly offering hope that this epidemic could be contained, just like the SARS epidemic.

Inwardly, however, the secret agencies of the most powerful nations of the world convened in war rooms across the globe were shell-shocked. The delegates and heads of state had been injected with cocktails of botulinum antitoxins, but that did not seem to work. Clearly they were dealing with a genetically modified pathogen here, one that produced a toxin that might have no proven antidote.

***

Inside the Cave, Wednesday, 9 p.m.

The darkness and the silence were intimidating, even more than the constraining physical space. Sam yearned for his smartphone to check his email; for the remote control to switch on mindless TV programmes; for all the silly jokes on WhatsApp; for the loud, mind-numbing beats at the lounge bar near his office. . .

But there was no respite. He was a prisoner in what was almost like a coffin, with nobody to hear his cries.

***

Sikkim, Wednesday, 8.55 p.m.

Damini's driver informed her that they had reached the inn at Lachung where Sam had halted.

The inn was deserted, save for the innkeeper and one other man who was hanging out in the lobby.

Damini took a closer look at him. His description matched that of Sam's driver provided by the Army man who had been shadowing him till Lachung.

***

Lachung, Wednesday, 9 p.m.

Damini could not resist a sigh of relief as she heard Bikash's description of the stocky man with a sunken face and cold eyes who had been with the crew of SUVs and light trucks.

Finally, here was proof that the Maestro was indeed on the trail of the Gupt-Kandara.

She immediately called Kunal from her satellite phone and told him that she had the proof needed to dispatch ACG agents from Kolkata to Sikkim. She also gave him the coordinates of the Gupt-Kandara.

She looked at her watch. If all went well, she might be able to get to the Gupt-Kandara by around 11 p.m. Hopefully.

She also needed reinforcements. She had an M240 machine gun with her, but outside of the Rambo movies, one did not take on twelve baddies with a single machine gun.

The weather had improved. She wondered if the Army post at Lachung might lend her a few men, but she could not afford to lose time waiting for them. They would simply have to follow her when they were ready.

She instructed the driver to leave for Yumthang. He would have to wait there while she covered the journey—on foot—after Yumthang to the Gupt-Kandara.

Guilt continued to gnaw away at her.

She let out an uncharacteristic sigh. It was dangerous to enter into a combat situation with so much self-doubt, but she did not have a choice.

***

Inside the Cave, Wednesday, 9.30 p.m.

For no particular reason, Sam remembered a distant afternoon from his early childhood.

They had gone to a beach near Mumbai: Sam, his parents and their friends. The Colonel had picked up a beautiful sea shell and shown it to the kids—elaborate, intricate, nature's best piece of art. For the rest of that afternoon, Sam and the other kids had scanned the beach looking for shells. They had returned home in a cacophony of fun, games and laughter, Sam carrying a bagful of shells.

Later that night, when the lights were off and the world went to sleep, Sam had heard it . . . the light scraping of the floor. Maybe something was moving over it.

He had gotten up from his bed and then seen it by the light of the moon. A snail was crawling out of its shell, taking tentative steps. A living, breathing, beautiful being, whose existence had been obscured by light and noise. It was now audible in the silence, only to those who could respect the stillness of the moment. A stillness and freedom which Sam had felt as he trekked in the Himalayas after graduation, and even as he had worked on his education venture. A stillness which had gotten shrouded by the noises from outside—the failure of his venture, the success of his peers, society's expectations, and the Colonel's disappointment.

Until a beautiful part of him crawled so deeply into its shell that he almost forgot it existed. Overpowered by his MBA, his job, morning meetings, conference calls, promotions, loud beats of the disco and a blur of unfulfilling relationships . . . and underneath it all, cynicism, bitterness and meaninglessness.

Year after year, he had shut out that inner voice until he heard it less and less. A voice which grew ever so faint that it was almost gone.

Almost.

But not entirely.

Because profound urges stem from a spring so deep that no mortal force can extinguish them. They lie dormant, biding their time, until a ray of light begins to draw them out.

Now Sameer fully understood the importance of what had happened over the last few days.

In trying to find the woman that he loved, he had also found somebody he had lost touch with.

Himself.

***

Crouched in the unbearable darkness and silence of the cave, it all came to Sam.

Memories of that cold night, seventeen years ago, when he and the Colonel got the telephone call. About Sam's mother's death in an accident. He had been eleven years old then.

Maybe, despite his pretending otherwise, the Colonel and he were actually quite alike. Not a father and son separated by a chasm of clashing personalities, but two individuals trying to come to terms with the hand that fate had dealt them. The Colonel, by lapsing into coldness and substituting love with rules, expectations and reprimands. And Sam, by escaping into cynicism.

Suddenly, in that crouched position, Sam felt a strong yearning to get up and give his father a hug. For all those lost years.

***

Along the stream near Yumthang, Wednesday, 9.30 p.m.

The Maestro's party made its way on foot, along with a cart carrying their equipment, by the banks of the tributary of the

Lachung Chu. The storm and the mist had abated considerably, helping their progress.

The Maestro could not help but smile as the caravan stopped in front of a rock formation.

The lion's mane meeting the scorpion's claws.

***

The party led by the Maestro had temporarily camped in front of the ledge that Sam had seen four hours ago. This was the ledge up on the hill opposite the stream which had looked strikingly similar to a balcony but was located on a naked cliff almost 300 feet above the valley.

***

Inside the Cave, Wednesday, 10.30 p.m.

The euphoria of Sam's profound realisations was beginning to die out, replaced by a deadened, sickening feeling that none of his resolutions meant anything if he was not going to make it out of the tunnel alive.

***

Along the stream near Yumthang, Wednesday, 10.45 p.m.

The Maestro and his men had tried getting up to the naked ledge, but it seemed impossible, perched as it were atop 300 feet of sheer, slippery rock with no ridges or footholds.

Like Sam, they reasoned that there ought to be another way up.

Like Sam, they had traced the path of the stream further up and come across the spot where the stream disappeared into the mountain face.

But unlike Sam, who had been trekking in the Himalayas since he was a kid, they had been unable to spot the place where the rock looked different from the surroundings. In spite of being assisted by battery-powered, high-intensity floodlights, they missed the entrance.

***

Inside the Cave, Wednesday, 10.55 p.m.

There are laws even the strongest of wills cannot break. The wooziness of the head and the morbid chatter of his subconscious mind seemed to drive a wedge into Sam's brain.

For a brief moment, his despair turned to hope as he sensed some movement at the narrow end of the tunnel ahead of him.

But it turned to panic as he realised what was causing the movement.

Some sort of large insect, possibly the size of a rat?

That did it for Sam. His mind, already teetering on the brink of insanity, snapped.

CHAPTER 46

Along the stream near Yumthang, Wednesday, 10.55 p.m.

The Maestro and his troops retraced their path to the vicinity of the ledge which was located at a height of 300 feet.

It was time to decide.

Their ladders would not reach that high. Some men from their party would have to reach the highest point possible and then drill holes into the hard rock face by firing heavy-duty darts. They could then try to hoist themselves up to the ledge.

It was tricky, but the Maestro had the equipment. And men that he could dispense with, if the need arose.

***

Damini was tracing the path of the river from Yumthang.

Despite the eeriness of being a lone soul walking by the moonlight through icy cold weather and treacherous terrain, Damini could not help but stop to marvel at the rock formation in front of her.

The lion's mane meeting the scorpion's claws.

***

Inside the Cave, Wednesday, 11 p.m.

An unholy collage of images flashed through Sam's mind—a

story he had once read . . . of a man who was confined to a coffin, alive. Unable to stop the rats that were gnawing away at his eyes, ears and nose, powerless as the vital forces of his life were chewed away, one by one.

Sam closed his eyes, desperately trying to stop the deluge of morbid thoughts. But they kept coming. Images of being stuck in a ditch, with only killer snakes for company, and no way to haul himself out.

The mythological figure Trishanku—the most unfortunate man ever, stuck in an endless purgatory—making it neither to heaven's gates nor to the redeeming fury of hell's fires. Waiting endlessly, yearning for release.

Images of Egyptian mummies, men buried alive as punishment in ancient tombs; of ancient texts that said that not only minds and bodies, but even souls, could suffocate; running from chamber to chamber for centuries, stuck in this tunnel; waiting for deliverance, but hearing only echoes from the walls; of having as company only his own voice from centuries past, and his rotting flesh and bones . . .

Was he going mad?

***

Along the stream near Yumthang, Wednesday, 11.15 p.m.

Damini had perched herself at a height on the hill directly abutting the stream, opposite the ledge.

The Maestro and his team were almost directly below her on the bed of the stream. They were trying to anchor a giant ladder on the bed of the stream.

The bright moonlight, coupled with the floodlights from the

Maestro's team, gave Damini a clear view. She counted a total of twelve people, including men armed with machine guns and grenades.

The Maestro's party had started using ugly machines to drill holes into the icy surface of the hill in order to get footholds to ascend to the ledge.

From a distance, Damini could hear the sounds of thunder as the temperamental weather once again started to play its tricks.

Amidst the still mountains, the drilling machines made a deafening noise which fused with the sound of thunder, almost as if signalling the impending arrival of hell's fury.

***

Inside the Cave, Wednesday, 11.25 p.m.

An image flashed through Sameer's mind in a brief moment of lucidity.

When he had joined Bancroft Cohen, they had made him undergo a series of medical tests. One test in particular came to mind now: the hearing test.

'This won't take long,' the stern-looking, middle-aged lady had said. She had reminded him of his school headmistress.

The room was soundproof. Sameer remembered feeling very still that day. His mind was not chattering, and he had been able to concentrate like never before, almost savouring the beauty of the silence. In the hearing test, he had been able to discern the most intricate and nuanced of sound frequencies, prompting the lady to remark that he seemed to have the hearing of a man, a bat and a dog all put together.

For a second, crouched in the cave, Sam thought that he had finally lost it. Why, of all things, would this memory come to his mind as he was struggling to stay alive?

And then it struck him.

He was hearing something.

Maybe he was hallucinating. His knees and hip were hurting badly, the pain seemingly penetrating right through to the core of his brain. There was no way he could hear clearly through all the pain and the wooziness.

All the same, a tiny part of his mind told him that maybe he really was hearing something. Mild, faint, almost inaudible, but real nevertheless.

***

It was such an insignificant sound that he could hear it only if his mind was absolutely quiet. The slightest hint of anxiety or excitement, and the sound got drowned out.

It was almost as if it was designed to be heard only when he had achieved a state of complete stillness of mind, free from chatter and baggage from the past.

The ninth and tenth verses now made sense.

Verse 9

He who survives the torrent of fear and gets past the ocean of despair

Keeping at bay the ever-lingering insanity

He shall find the rhythm of stillness

And finally hear the sound of his heart.

Verse 10

Silence is the language of the gods

Silence is the deliverance of the soul

What is inaudible to a layperson

Is audible to the seeker who is one with the silence.

For a few seconds, Sam remained silent. Absolutely silent. No trace of thought, no trace of emotion.

And he heard it again. The sound was coming from his right.

Gone again.

Again, Sam waited, his mind still, primed to receive.

And he heard it again. It seemed like a tiny drop of water falling, unmistakably to his right.

His mind's ear followed the sound; it was directly next to his right shoulder.

'The rhythm of stillness.' Sam steadied his nerves, and concentrated.

A light 'tttp'. A drop of water hesitatingly dripping.

He gingerly tried to move his right shoulder, keeping the rest of his body still. It was a superhuman effort. The shortage of oxygen, the stiffness from hours of crouching and the weight of his mind's meanderings all seemed to weigh on his shoulder.

All he could manage was to expand his shoulder muscle towards the source of the sound, but that was progress nevertheless.

It took another fifteen minutes, and ten iterations, and the tip of his shoulder was now close to the source of the sound.

Sam's body ached from the effort, but he paid no attention to that, his mind absolutely still.

He inhaled with difficulty, the lack of oxygen constricting the passages of his lungs, and exerted a final push with his shoulder muscle.

His muscle touched what seemed like a hollow stretch of wall directly adjoining the source of the sound.

The wall moved, slowly at first, then progressively faster, parting with a grinding sound, until it revealed a wide passage beyond.

CHAPTER 47

Inside the Cave, Wednesday, 11.40 p.m.

Sam could barely control a gasp of wonder as the passage led into a massive chamber.

The sanctum of the Gupt-Kandara.

As he reflected on how he cracked the last Agony—by hearing the 'inaudible' sound in the dark, claustrophobic tunnel—Sam felt a surge of respect and admiration for the Yogyaveer who had designed and created this impressive series of tests.

This chamber was much cooler than the rest of the Cave. The chemiluminescent rocks, combined with reflected light from the walls, gave off an almost ethereal glow.

The chamber's ornately carved walls, pillars and platforms were adorned with the most intricate of paintings and sculptures.

Sam squinted as he drew closer. There were images of royal courts, kings and battles, but there were also images from the lives of common people—harvests, festivals, travels, markets and the like.

A complete, uninterrupted narrative of the history of India, conveyed through the most beautiful of artefacts dating back to ancient times. The treasure that the Yogyaveer had spent seventy years guarding.

Bani would be thrilled, Sam mused, as he stood there for a second, bowing, thankful for everything.

There were two mini-chambers leading off the main sanctum, one each to the right and the left. Sam stepped into the one on the right.

It had many alcoves set into the wall. Some of the alcoves contained modern books on a wide range of subjects, including mechanical and electrical engineering. Sam had a 'aha' moment; so this was how the Yogyaveer had kept up to speed on latest technical developments and designed the Great Agonies.

As Sam peered into one of the alcoves, he saw that it contained what seemed like series of old books with intricate lettering, written on dried palm leaves.

He stepped closer and looked at one of the books. The lettering was in Sanskrit.

He realised with shock that he was probably looking at one of the oldest books in existence—a manuscript of one of the Upanishads.

***

Sam left the books behind. He knew Bani would be disappointed, but the experts and the archeologists could follow him and do their bit later. Right now, what he needed was the Prativisha.

Now that he had overcome the Agonies, he found himself besieged with a fresh sense of foreboding.

Should he hand over the Prativisha to the Maestro in return for Ananya? Or should he help save the dying tens of thousands in Delhi?

Would he end up helping a monster who wanted to bring the world to his knees? Or would he end up sacrificing the life of the only woman he had truly connected with?

Sam found himself turning his mind away from these thoughts as he stepped into the other mini-chamber, the one on the left.

***

This mini-chamber felt even cooler than the sanctum. There were many alcoves here, but instead of books, each alcove contained a mushroom, encased in a glass container. Was this the mushroom from which the antidote was extracted? Sam did not know, and he did not want to die trying to find out.

Water was steadily dripping into the alcoves from the rocks. An automatic watering system, Sam observed, that might have been designed to keep this mini-chamber cool. He also noted that the chemiluminescent rocks seemed to emit light of a different colour here than from the rest of the cave.

Clearly, the mushroom was grown in this cave under controlled conditions.

In the centre of the mini-chamber were a series of wooden boxes.

Sam gingerly opened one of them, half-expecting to be poisoned by a pathogen.

The boxes contained a fine powder. Probably concentrated extracts from the mushroom.

The Prativisha—the antidote to KaalKoot. The only thing that stood between the world and its destruction through the bio bomb.

Sam sighed. He had finally found what he had come for.

Now there was nothing that remained between him and the toughest decision of his life.

He would have to choose: between the woman whose quest had got him this far, and the lives of tens of thousands of people in Delhi.

***

Sam walked in to a passage leading out of the sanctum.

To his surprise, the passage abruptly led out of the cave and into the open mountainside.

Sam peered out. He realised that he was on a ledge. This was the same ledge that he had seen earlier in the journey; the ledge that appeared like a balcony and was atop 300 feet of smooth, slippery rock.

There was a pillar on the ledge, around which a thick rope was tied. Presumably the rope could be used to rappel down the hill.

He had never been so happy to see a rope before.

He checked his pockets, intending to take out his satellite phone to call Damini.

Unfortunately, he didn't have it with him. Along with his rucksack and flashlight, it must have fallen off when he was dodging the stepping stones.

***

11.50 p.m.

One hundred feet away, Damini was staring at the ledge incredulously.

Aided by the floodlights that the Maestro's team had put up, Damini had a pretty clear view of both the stream and the rock face opposite, notwithstanding the strong winds and sounds of thunder.

Her surprise at seeing Sam emerge onto the ledge was quickly replaced by alarm as she realised that he was directly in the line of sight of the Maestro's party. They had powerful large-caliber machine guns, and Sam would be an easy target for them.

Sam could not see Damini. There was no way she could signal to Sam without catching the attention of the villains.

If the villains shot Sam, they would be able to get up to the ledge and access the Prativisha. And then there would be no hope for Ananya and the thousands dying in Delhi.

Damini was perched on the hill at a height of about 120 feet, directly above where the Maestro's party was standing near the stream bed.

Right below her was a large rock which was poised somewhat precariously on the hill. If she exerted a superhuman effort, aided by her machine gun, she might be able to pry the rock loose and let it fall down to the river bed.

Unfortunately, the only way she would be able to do that would be to use her full body weight on the rock. That would mean that she, too, would accompany the rock on its downward journey.

***

Damini had only a split second to decide, but she knew exactly what she had to do.

The guilt was gone, replaced only by the clarity of purpose.

It was time to put her life on the line. Yet again.

We become what we repeatedly do.

Putting her life on the line. That was what she did. Repeatedly.

Maybe she was not such a monster after all.

Damini did not hesitate even for a second as she did the unthinkable.

***

It all happened pretty dramatically after that.

The large, precariously poised rock got dislodged from the hill, thanks to Damini's efforts, and fell onto another rock below with a deafening crash.

That rock, in turn, got dislodged, and fell further down the hill, crashing into a series of boulder-like rocks that were loosely wedged.

That was when nature intervened.

The sky, already reeling with the deafening roar of thunder, was suddenly overrun by a cloud which burst right above the stream, inundating the hills off Yumthang with rain.

The falling rocks, aided by the torrent of rain hitting the hill, loosened the boulder-like rocks, and like the proverbial snowball gathering momentum, the entire complex hurtled down the hill in a matter of seconds, gaining weight as it moved.

***

Damini heard the thunder sounding more urgent, felt the full impact of the first rock dashing against the second, and knew that she had helped trigger off a mini-landslide.

She registered the stream below coming closer, as if rushing to meet her, before her head dashed against the falling rocks.

***

From atop the 300-foot-high ledge, all Sam could see was a series of rocks hurtling down the hill, accompanied by the deafening sound of thunder. As he craned his neck, he saw the equipment of the Maestro's crew.

He did not know that Damini was in the vicinity.

Sam did not want to be in the firing line of the Maestro's men. He retreated into the Gupt-Kandara. He would wait there for Damini's people to arrive.

***

The last thing the Maestro saw before his skull was crushed was a gigantic rock hurtling towards him at tremendous speed. This brought back to his mind a distant yet distinctive memory from his childhood in his family's mansion in eastern Europe.

The image was of his alcoholic father, whip in hand, murderous rage curling his lips, and his mother, wailing, clinging, pleading, suffering as she had done for years. And he, watching from the cupboard, feeling helpless, really helpless, wishing fervently that he could be the master of the universe so that he did not have to be helpless again.

And then the rock was upon him, and the world went dark.

EPILOGUE

Thursday, 3 a.m.

It had been a busy night for the ACG, the Indian Air Force and the Army.

The rains in the hills off the Kandara had stopped as abruptly as they had begun.

Damini's handiwork had eased matters for the Army team from Lachung. With six people crushed under the landslide and the remaining seriously injured, the Maestro's team was in disarray. It took the Army's team just a few minutes to subdue them.

Unfortunately, they could not find Damini's body. It had most likely been swept downstream by the river.

With the skies having cleared up, helicopters from the Indian Air Force were able to fly right up to the ledge exiting the Gupt-Kandara and air-lift Sam, along with as many boxes of the Prativisha as were available. The Prativisha, as well as samples of the glass-encased mushrooms from the alcoves in the Gupt-Kandara, were flown to Delhi in Indian Air Force jets.

Sam sighed. With the Maestro dead, there was no prospect now of bargaining for Ananya anyway. The burden of having to make a tough choice had been taken away from him by the turn of events. But along with it, any hopes of finding Ananya had also died.

How he wished he could meet Ananya again somehow. Just once. And tell her how he really felt about her.

If only he had done that when she was still around. Maybe none of this would have happened.

For the first time in seventeen years, Sam held his head in his hands and cried.

***

A crack team in Delhi, comprising some of the world's best doctors, microbiologists, bacteriologists and disease-control specialists, quickly analysed the antidote and split the powdered concentrate into the optimum number of doses so that maximum number of people from the stadium could be treated.

Unfortunately, despite being in concentrate form, the dosages would be enough only to treat around a thousand patients. They would have to be reserved for the foreign dignitaries and senior Indian officials.

The Army battalions maintaining peace in the stadium had to manage an uphill task. For the first time, they were dealing with tens of thousands of innocent, sick people who were also getting progressively desperate, paranoid and delusional.

***

Thursday, 3 a.m.

From one of the mobile phones that had been retrieved from the Maestro's crew, Mini was able to trace the GPS location history to a warehouse in an industrial complex near Mumbai.

The Chief, mortified that he had ignored Damini's pleas, ordered a whirlwind raid on the Mansion, from where the rest of the Maestro's crew were rounded up and a visibly relieved Ananya and a dazed Professor Bavdekar were freed. Ji-hoon Kim, unfortunately, had left the country on Monday night after meeting the Maestro, so he could not be apprehended.

The Chief would put in his papers after this whole episode, citing his 'unforgivable error of judgment' and 'letting down the best agent that he had ever worked with' as the reasons for his resignation. This would mark his permanent retirement from active intelligence work of any sort.

***

Thursday, 7 a.m.

Scientists determined that the antidote would be effective only if administered up to forty-eight hours from the time of infection. After 6 p.m. on Friday, anybody who had not been injected with the antidote would die.

The antidote was first administered to members of the government delegations. As the deadline to administer the antidote was closing in fast, it seemed like the rest—the hoi polloi—would have to die.

That was when Professor Bavdekar, who was by now in Delhi, drew upon his encylopaedic knowledge of Himalayan plant life and observed that he had come across a mushroom growing in the Kumaon hills that was strikingly similar to the glass-encased mushroom in the Gupt-Kandara from which the antidote—the Prativisha—had been extracted.

Helicopters were quickly dispatched, and sure enough, large swathes of land were covered by the mushroom. The relevant compounds were extracted and administered to the affected people.

Meanwhile, only the iron will of the Army jawaans saved the situation from descending into complete anarchy.

Around four hundred people still ended up losing their lives, but Prof. Bavdekar's discovery helped save the lives of the remaining eighty thousand.

***

News channels were abuzz with the tragedy in Delhi, but they had been given a different spin on the events. One of the headlines read: 'Outbreak of a new strain of flu in Delhi brought under control, but claims 400 lives'.

No mention of either the KaalKoot or the bio bomb.

To a nosy reporter in Sikkim who had got wind of the helicopters moving to and fro, another cover story had been fed: 'Six American tourists found dead in landslide in Sikkim'.

A fact unknown to the reporter, of course, was that one of the 'tourists' was the man who used to be known as the Maestro. And that he had come perilously close to bringing the world to its knees.

And nobody, except a chosen few in the Indian Army and the Anti-Conspiracy Group, knew that the common thread behind both the 'new strain of flu' coming under control and the death of the 'tourists' was a young man who had followed the trail of his missing girlfriend.

***

Friday

The young man in question was back in Mumbai.

Sam called Bani, who had undergone a successful surgery and was on the road to recovery.

'So you survived,' Sam said.

'I should be saying that to you, buddy,' Bani laughed.

Sam started laughing, too, slowly at first, and then more freely.

'Maybe you and I are not so different after all,' Bani said. 'We are both the kind that would go to the ends of the earth to find what we seek.'

***

As the evening drew to a close, Sam found himself reflecting on the memory of a person whom he had grown to admire in the short time that he had known her in Goa.

'Goodbye, secret agent Damini,' Sam said quietly as he took in the setting sun.

A line from Harivanshrai Bachchan's famous poem, 'Madhushala', celebrating life through the metaphor of the proverbial house of wine, came to his mind:

Ab na rahe woh peene waale,

Ab na rahi woh madhushala.

As always, something which an English translation could never do justice to.

Those that drank deeply of the wine of life are not around today,

The tavern, the milieu, is gone, too.

Sam sighed. *We become what we repeatedly do*, he remembered her telling him.

Maybe he could take a leaf out of Damini's book and live a life of zest and passion. Maybe he could start the trekking school that he had dreamt of. Maybe read more of his favourite poetry. Or maybe he could travel around the country again and rediscover inspiration, just as he had many years ago when he had started his education venture.

Or maybe he could make a start by just shedding the baggage of the past.

***

Sam called the Colonel.

'Hi,' he said tentatively.

'Hi, son, long time. How are the financial markets treating you?'

'Pa, I've quit my job.'

There was silence for a few seconds.

Sam continued: 'I don't expect you to agree with my decision, but I do want you to respect it. Just like Ma would have.'

There was a deep intake of breath at the other end.

'And, Pa…'

'Uh, yes, beta,' the Colonel's voice was somewhat quivering.

'I was wondering whether you might want to go for a trek in the Himalayas. Just you and I. Just like old times.'

There was a pause, and then the Colonel replied with the voice of someone who had a lump in his throat. 'Anytime, beta.'

***

That evening, Sam sent a resignation email to Ayush and the

human resources department at his firm, and walked out of the doors of Bancroft Cohen for the last time.

Later that evening, Sam nervously took a certain Ms Ananya Shah on a date to Café Royal.

It felt just like their first date. Complete with the chocolate brownies and the ice cream.

Except that this time, Sam did not run away from his feelings. 'I love you,' he said. 'Deeply.'

'I know,' she said, looking deep into his eyes as she brought her lips close to his. 'Next time, you don't need to trudge up to a remote Himalayan cave to prove that.'

COMING SOON

AGNIBAAN

GUARDIANS OF THE FIRE CHAMBER

BY S. VENKATESH

ABOUT THE AUTHOR

Venkatesh wears many hats. In his roles as private equity investor, business leader, entrepreneur and Board member, he has helped businesses thrive and grow. He has spent a significant part of his professional life in the stock markets with Credit Suisse, Deutsche Bank and JP Morgan, and continues to be an avid investor.

Venkatesh has been keenly interested in Eastern philosophy and mysticism right from his college days at IIT Delhi and IIM Calcutta. He has found his inspiration to write in rather curious settings - while crawling through war tunnels in Vietnam, coming face-to-face with a bear in the Nilgiris, chancing upon an Indus Valley ruin while on a road trip, listening to 'Madhushala', or just drinking cutting chai by the roadside. He is passionate about self-discovery and the power of stories to inspire and transform.

Website: www.svenkatesh.in

Facebook: facebook.com/AuthorSVenkatesh

Twitter: @AuthorVenkatesh

Instagram: @authorsvenkatesh

Write to Venkatesh at: s.venkatesh@svenkatesh.in